THE IMMORTAL THRONE

BREE DESPAIN

THE IMMORTAL THRONE

INTO THE DARK BOOK 3

carolrhoda LAB
MINNEAPOLIS

Carolrhoda Lab™
An imprint of Carolrhoda Books
A division of Lerner Publishing Group, Inc.
241 First Avenue North
Minneapolis, MN 55401 USA

For reading levels and more information, look up this title at www.lernerbooks.com.

Cover photographs: © iStockphoto.com/Ulisses40 (forest background); © Balkonsky/Shutterstock.com (shadow texture); © Westend61/Getty Images (couple).

Main body text set in Adobe Jenson Pro Regular 11/17.
Typeface provided by Adobe Systems.

Library of Congress Cataloging-in-Publication Data

The Cataloging-in-Publication Data for *The Immortal Throne* is on file at the Library of Congress.
ISBN 978-1-5124-0583-5 (trade hardcover)
ISBN 978-1-5124-0897-3 (eb pdf)

LC record available at https://lccn.loc.gov/2015044030

Manufactured in the United States of America
1-39238-21115-4/18/2016

For my father, Tai, from whom I inherited my love of art, history, and mythology; and my mother, Nancy, who came to every play performance when I was a teen (even when I only had one line) and now displays a copy of every edition of every book I've ever written proudly in their home. The world would be a better place if every girl had parents as supportive and loving as you both.

All my love,

Bree

THE IMMORTAL THRONE

chapter one

HADEN

I claw at the thick, inky, black veins that have spread through my arm and arch over my shoulder. They ache as if the black was tar seeping through my body, tainting my blood. And I do not know what has caused it.

Stones and twigs bite into my bare feet as I run. My vision fades in and out, blurring the trees in front of me. I stumble on a root and hit my shoulder, hard, on a trunk as I pass, sending pulses of agony shuddering down my blackened arm.

Almost there, I tell myself, fighting the impulse to give up. To stop. To simply abandon my search. *Almost there.*

I break through the trees that line this part of the lakeshore, and find myself on the abandoned neighborhood road that circles the lake. It's dark, but not late. Someone should be out. Dog walkers. Joggers. Students traveling home after a school activity. Olympus Hills is usually buzzing with humans headed from one place to another. Alas, this street is as eerily still as the ones surrounding the mansion I've called home for the last six months. I had gone there looking for Dax, and not only was my house empty, as far as I could tell, all other residences in Olympus Hills were as well. Along with the school, the shops on Olympus Row, and every other place I have checked on my way here.

The smell of smoke lingers in the air.

Where is everyone?

I follow the empty road along the lake, my feet growing heavier with every step. My will is pushed on only by the small gray hellcat who nips at my heels. She is as desperate to find the others as I am.

Brim was the one who found me in the grove. She always finds me. We've been bonded ever since I discovered her in the Wastelands of the Underrealm when she was merely a kitten. She had been tossed from the nest by her mother for being too small. Having been rejected by my own father as a boy and deprived of my rightful place as heir to the throne of the underworld, I'd taken pity on the runty hellcat. She and I have been each other's only *real* family ever since.

When I was chosen by the Oracle of Elysium to become the sole Champion, to travel to Olympus Hills to find Daphne Raines—the Cypher who could restore immortality to my people—Brim had stowed away in my pack and traveled into the mortal world with me. Then I started to fall for Daphne, and Brim took it upon herself to try to win Daphne over on my behalf. And when Daphne and I decided to turn our backs on my quest, to find the Key of Hades on our own rather than sacrifice Daphne to my father, Brim had shown her confidence in me. She had stayed by my side throughout the search for the Key. She had insisted on coming along when Daphne and I were supposed to journey into the Underrealm with the Key to try to destroy the

2

Keres—monstrous beings kept in the Pits of the underworld—to keep them from breaking free and devouring the five realms.

Alas, this is where everything had gone wrong. Our plan was to use the high school's rock opera performance as cover for when Daphne would unearth the Key from where it was concealed in the grove. Then she would unlock Persephone's Gate and enter the Underrealm with Dax, my best friend and self-appointed mentor. I was to follow, as soon as I was able, with Daphne's father, Joe, to complete our mission to destroy the Keres before they could break free from the Pits. However, only minutes before our quest was about to begin, Dax received a mysterious phone call. He thought it had come from his long lost love, Abbie. He insisted that he needed to try to find her, promising to return in time to protect Daphne when she went for the Key. I had sent Brim with him, knowing he might need her help. But the two disappeared, leaving Daphne unprotected when she revealed the Key, except for my servant and half-brother Garrick, whom I had sent to try to stop her.

Garrick. Why hadn't he told Daphne to wait as I instructed? Why had he gone with her to the Underrealm after insisting he would never return there?

I still do not remember exactly how I ended up in the underworld myself, but I do remember the sight of Garrick placing the crown of the Underrealm upon his head. A turn of events I would have never predicted. He'd always seemed to be a mere Lesser to me. How had he been deemed worthy of the crown?

My memories of what happened between when Dax disappeared and when Garrick seized the crown are spotty at best. I remember running to the grove to find Daphne. I remember

3

battling Terresa, a Skylord lieutenant who wanted the Key for herself to destroy my people, and Rowan, my twin brother who'd been sent by my father to complete my quest after I fell for Daphne. I had the upper hand against them until a distraction gave Rowan the advantage. He put me in a black sleep, and the next thing I remember, I was a prisoner, along with my brother, on a boat in the Underrealm. Rowan and I had been apprehended by the royal guard under the new command of Lord Lex, who had staged a coup among the Court against my father, Ren. My brother and I were taken to stand trial with Ren for our failure to bring Daphne and the Key to the Underrealm.

My veins had started blackening then. The cause was unknown to me, as it still is now, but the pain had so consumed me, I didn't care about the Court's verdict. I had been ready to lay my head on the altar and take my final punishment, all so the anguish would end.

And then Daphne had come. She had stormed the throne room with Garrick. I remember being angry instead of relieved to see her. As if I had been rendered incapable of feeling anything but pain. The next thing I knew, the crown was on Garrick's head, and Daphne had made a deal with him to secure my banishment instead of execution. Again, I remember not caring. Daphne leaned across the altar and whispered that she loved me—words I had been longing to hear for months—and I felt nothing. Not until she stabbed me in the chest with a small, ruby-red arrow. Rage and fear had gripped me, and when she tried to kiss me, I perceived it as an attack and fought her off—and then I experienced a moment of clarity. Daphne's words echoed in my ears, and

I realized what she had done. That she had given herself to the Underrealm in order to save me.

I remember screaming and wailing and even blasting myself in the chest in order to escape the hands of my captors who dragged me away from her. Alas, I must have been put in a black sleep once more, because I awoke several hours later in the grove. I had been banished to the mortal realm—and Persephone's Gate was closed. I was stuck in Daphne's world and she was trapped in mine, a prisoner of the Court and their new king, Garrick. Had he somehow orchestrated this turn of events? Had my own servant betrayed me?

When I awoke in the mortal world, the ravaged grove of charred trees and scorched earth was deserted except for the prostrate bodies of my father and brother, who had been banished along with me, and Terresa. There was no sign of Dax, Joe, Ethan—the Skylord prince who proposed an alliance with us to destroy the Keres, which I refused—or even Daphne's "uncle" Jonathan, who had revealed himself to be the god Eros right before Rowan had taken me out. The pain of the blackness spreading through my body afflicted me once more. I would have given up right then if it hadn't been for Brim finding me. She was the spark of hope, encouraging me to fight against the darkness that clouded my mind. She's been the one prodding me to take one painful step after another through the abandoned town. Pushing me on to find the others.

What will I do if I can't?

I pass house after house, all dark and empty, until I come to the one I've been seeking. I stumble again. My hands hit the pavement of the driveway. I see it then. The black veins have crossed over my chest and are spindling down my other arm. What will happen when the black overtakes my entire body?

Brim nuzzles her tiny head against my wrist, urging me to get up. I'm only feet away from my goal.

What will I do if the others *are* there? What will I tell Joe? Daphne's mother? Jonathan—Eros? That she's gone? That I lost her?

That it's all my fault.

Brim meows when I don't move. The fur on her neck is matted with dried blood, reminding me that she must have been in some sort of fight before finding me. *If only she could tell me what happened to Dax.* Brim looks pointedly at the front of the house. A blue light flickers from one of the upstairs windows.

I push myself up, half crawling, half walking to the doorway. I try the bell. Then try pounding on the door until the shocks of pain in my black fist grow to be too much. No one answers.

Brim yowls, pacing in front of a tall, narrow window that flanks the door.

"Smart girl."

I press my hand against the glass and send a shock of lightning from my palm to the window. The glass shatters—spindling out from the point of impact like a spider's web, before it falls away. The sound seems so loud compared to the silent town, it makes me jump even though I am the one who caused it. I stick my hand through the opening and feel around until I find the lock. I turn it until it makes a satisfying click.

My arm bleeds as I enter the foyer. Drops splatter on the white marble floor by my feet. I look at the blood that snakes around my wrist. It's black. Not red.

"Joe!" I call into the house. "Jonathan?"

My voice echoes through the grand foyer. A steady, faint, beeping noise sounds from a box on the wall near the staircase. No one responds. I muster up the strength to climb the stairs, but the light I'd seen flickering from the second-floor window was only a false hope. Only a television that had been left on, tuned to a news station.

"The freak lightning storm that wreaked havoc through Olympus Hills over the weekend seems to have passed, but residents are—"

The reporter's voice is drowned out when the faint beeping noise that followed me up the stairs shifts to a loud screeching siren. It reminds me of the horns the sentinels blast when a pack of Shades or another creature wanders too close to the palace grounds in the Underrealm. I must have tripped an alarm.

My impulse is to flee, but my curiosity to see if anyone will respond to the alarm gets the better of me. Brim paces, bristling and growling at the shrill sound. A voice in the back of my head tells me that I should be concerned about calming Brim, as she grows more and more agitated, but the longer no one comes—no police, no Olympus Hills security—I grow more and more overwhelmed with despair at what it must mean. The smell of smoke in the air, the blackened trees I'd seen in the grove, the lightning storm the weather channel mentioned. The abandoned homes. A battle must have taken place here, one involving Skylords. And now everyone I care about, other than Brimstone, is gone.

I've lost them, too. Just as I have lost Daphne.

As my hope slips away, pain seizes me once more. Not just in my arms and my chest but also a deep, stabbing ache inside my gut. I inspect my side and see black lines snaking over my abdomen.

I am dying. I can feel it.

I want it. That thought settles into my brain and I realize that I welcome the idea of nothingness. *I want to feel nothing.*

I find myself in Joe's garage, a pair of keys in my hand. Then I am in one of his cars, shutting the door before Brim can follow me in. I leave her hissing with displeasure in the garage as I drive away. That voice in my head tells me it is dangerous to leave her behind in this state, but she cannot come where I am going.

Brim is hope. Brim is love. Brim is everything I do not want to allow myself to cling to any longer.

The first time I ever drove, it felt like flying. Like freedom. But all I feel now is the weight of my pain, the pull of my despair, the withering ache of being completely alone. I am filled with that terrifying want that has crept inside my brain—the want for it all to go away. That voice in my mind returns, trying to tell me not to give up. I drive faster, trying to outrun it. I hit the gas harder, and feel a shock of pain in my toes. The black veins—poison, whatever it is—are spreading through my feet.

I drive to the edge of Olympus Hills. The security gates have been left open and I see that the guard booth is empty as I pass it. I head down the hill, away from Olympus, with the intention of heading toward the highway.

My reasoning swings wildly from wanting to leave everything behind to desperately wanting to at least see another person before

I die. Part of me is desperate to prove that I am not alone. That the Skylords have not destroyed everyone I know in this world.

My vision blurs again, going black for a second, and then focuses on two bright lights heading toward me before it goes blurry once more. I slam on the brakes, stopping my vehicle. *Someone else is here!*, that voice says inside my head.

The next thing I know, I am out of the car. Whoever is coming this way, I need to get their attention. I need their help. The lights are moving so fast, I fear they might pass right by without seeing me. I try to wave my arms, but as I lift them, I am gripped with so much pain I stumble forward, clasping them to my chest. My body convulses and I take another couple of steps.

Into the middle of the road.

I look up, squinting my blurry eyes, to see the headlights of the speeding car barreling down on me.

And I feel no desire to move.

My eyes are filled with light. My ears are pierced with the sound of screeching brakes that I know will be too late. I accept that burning rubber will be the last thing I smell.

The impact is as forceful as thunder. I feel my feet lift up off the ground. My body flies through the air. I know I should feel pain. I know I should feel the blow of my body cracking against the pavement. But the last thing I know is the sweet relief of nothingness wrapping around me as if it were a warm embrace. *Daphne, I have failed you*, is the last thing I think before it all fades away.

chapter two

DAPHNE

The search party for the lost Key of the Underrealm left at dawn—or at least what I assumed was dawn, considering I'm trapped in a world without a sun. Through a sleepless night, I'd noticed the light in my queenly bedroom (a.k.a. an ornately glorified prison cell) slowly shift from the pitch black of night to a soft ethereal glow that permeated the small windows at the top of the high marble walls of my room. That strange light grew brighter during the day like a simulation of the rising of the sun, but it gave off no heat. No life. No hope. My room has grown dim once more—like dusk—when the trumpets sound, announcing the return of the search party. And I know even before my *betrothed* storms into my room that he has come back empty-handed.

"It wasn't there," Garrick says, slamming the scrolled map onto my bedside table with such force that the small Lesser boy in the corner of the room almost drops his tray. The servant came with my dinner only moments ago, and now he stands like a cornered animal, as if he wants nothing more than to slip away but is afraid to move and risk drawing his new king's wrath upon himself. From the look of him, all skin and bone and bruises, the boy has already suffered a beating today.

"I told you," I say, positioning myself between Garrick and the Lesser boy, "it was dark and I don't exactly know my way around the Underrealm. I must have made a mistake."

"Are you playing us for fools?" Garrick asks as he picks up the map and shakes it in my face. "Tricking me into leading the entire Court out into the Wastelands, only to look like an idiot on a fool's errand?"

Ironic questions for him to ask, considering he'd been the one fooling us all for six months. It has become more and more apparent that he had been the one lying, playing the role of the cowering, simple, Lesser half-brother so we wouldn't notice that he was plotting to betray us. I hadn't realized he was a threat until the crown was on his head and I was locked inside this palace. Not until he brought me an ancient pomegranate necklace and called me his queen.

"Are you lying to us?" he demands.

I blink at the map in his hand. It is a lie. Everything I've told him about the Key's location is a boldfaced lie, to save Haden. To save myself. The key is gone. Lost. I haven't seen it since we crashed on the shores of Elysium and I fought my way back from the brink of death. For all I know, it's at the bottom of the River of Woe with my best friend, Tobin, who also went missing after the crash. Both possibly never to be seen again.

I push away thoughts of Tobin that nearly pull me under with despair, and I shift my gaze to meet Garrick's eyes. His are red and watery. I don't know if it's from the dust of the long journey or from frustration, but I hold his stare, steady and sure. "As I told you before," I say, "if you want me to get you the Key, you're going to have to take me with you. I'll know the area when I see it."

His lip curls. "Not happening."

Taking me with him had been the original plan. I was supposed to lead them to the place where I claimed to have hidden the Key myself, but Garrick had changed his mind at the last minute, opting to leave me behind. I don't know if this was the result of listening to his new Court or because he senses I'll bolt the first chance I get.

When I promised to bind myself to Garrick and the Underrealm in exchange for him sparing Haden's life, I'd thought I was only buying myself time until Garrick and I could find a way to flee the Court and follow Haden to the mortal world. But now that I know Garrick *is* my captor, escaping from him is my number one priority.

Perhaps it's written all over my face.

I can't help it. I feel desperate, trapped here, knowing that Haden is on the other side without me, stuck in the mortal world without the cure—me—for the black poison that courses through his body. If I can't get to him in time, the Haden I know, the Haden I love, will be lost forever. And what about my family? After the Skylord attack, are Joe, Jonathan, and my mother in a safe place— or could the Skylords have taken them prisoner . . . or worse?

I stop myself from following that thought and shake off the despair again. Worrying and wallowing won't help me escape.

"I'm only trying to be as helpful as possible, Garrick." I dip forward and give a little curtsy in my torn dress—a costume from the play I'd been in only moments before entering the Underrealm. I force myself to smile as sweetly as possible and hope it doesn't look like a grimace.

I wish more than anything that my singing voice worked here in the palace—that I still had the power to control objects with it. Ever since I was a little girl I've been able to hear the ethereal tones, sounds, and vibrations that living creatures and organic matter give off. It wasn't until about three months ago that I learned I could tap into the sounds—by imitating them in song—and use them to control organic objects. I could ask raindrops to dance, throw rocks without lifting a finger, and sail a boat down the River of Woe with only the power of my voice. And most importantly, by imitating the screeching vibration of the Keres, I could cause the ferocious shadow creatures to become temporarily solid—just long enough for them to be destroyed. Eventually, I learned my auditory and vocal abilities were inherited from my long-lost ancestor Orpheus (the Great Musician of mythological fame). Even though controlling objects with my voice is a newfound power, I've come to rely on it. But it's failing me now.

Haden had told me once that music was forbidden in the palace, and I had learned the hard way that he had meant *forbidden* in a very literal sense. The palace is somehow magically warded against music of all kinds. This fact was confirmed when I tried to use my vocal powers to unlock the door to my room last night. Not only was the wooden door and its heavy metal lock completely void of any ethereal sound, I couldn't even make a humming noise, let alone sing to try to control them. Absolutely no sound came out when I tried.

I've been buoyed up by music all my life and now I feel like I am drowning in silence in this place. Like it's a special kind of torture designed just for me.

When my musical powers failed on the door, I instead tried to pry the lock with a jeweled comb I'd found in a drawer. My fingers are raw from the effort.

With Garrick still refusing to take me with him out of the palace to search for the Key, I'm going to have to try yet another tactic.

"I never thanked you properly for your present," I say to Garrick, casting my eyes toward the pomegranate necklace on the bedside table.

"You can thank me by wearing it," he says, his voice giving away a mixture of disappointment and desire as he sets down the map and picks up his precious gift.

I knew he had wanted to see me with the necklace around my throat when he'd ushered the servant carrying my breakfast tray into my bedroom this morning before leaving with the search party. He probably expected it as well this evening, but I've left it untouched, along with the food that the servants have brought me. I eventually started to send my breakfast away with the small Lesser boy who brought it, but he gave me a pained look, as if my lack of eating might cause him to be punished. Through a series of gestures, I'd let the boy know he could eat it himself if he wanted. The boy's grimace turned to a look of shock and then to pure joy as he shoved the berries and gristled meat into his mouth. I almost worried he'd make himself sick.

"I'd thought of this necklace the moment we met," Garrick

says, the gold chain dangling from his hand. I think his words are meant to sound romantic, in his twisted little brain, but I have to suppress a shudder. The fact that he had been thinking of me in that way is disturbing, when I had barely noticed him—beyond being a particularly obnoxious accessory in Haden's entourage.

I sit on the edge of the bed. The small boy in the corner, the same one who had enjoyed my breakfast, wavers, my movement having left him exposed once more. His eyes flick toward his new king—a teenaged boy who had been a Lesser like himself only a couple of days ago. The glint of clustered rubies dangling from Garrick's hand catches the young boy's fascination for a moment, but then he looks away as if looking were a crime. Garrick himself stole this necklace once. It had belonged to a former queen—Haden's mother—many years ago. I wonder now just how many dead queens had worn it before her.

How soon will I join their ranks if I don't escape?

I give a little sigh, making sure Garrick's attention stays on me and doesn't shift to the boy. "It is a beautiful necklace," I say, a measured tone of placation blanketing my words. "You should help me put it on."

Garrick's eyes light up. A small smile of satisfaction edges his lips.

I don't want his present. I don't want to wear the necklace. I don't want him to touch me. *But if I can just get him close enough . . .*

I give him an expectant smile, covering the fact that I am sizing him up as he approaches. He's dressed himself in King Ren's golden breastplate along with a tunic and cape made of luxurious black cloth. He intends to look royal, but the effect only makes him appear even smaller. The clothes engulf his thin frame, like he's swimming in gold and velvet and can barely keep his head above water. Garrick can't be more than fifteen. I've got at least two years and forty pounds on him.

I could overpower him easily.

I smooth my hair over one shoulder, exposing my neck as he sits beside me on the bed. I glance at him under my eyelashes, hoping it looks coy and not conniving.

Garrick clenches the chain of the necklace in his fist. And that's when I realize that he may appear thin and frail, but his hands are sinewy and strong from a life of hard labor. And the heat radiating off his body in erratic pulses gives away that he's having difficulty controlling the electric current surging through his muscles.

One false move on my part could send a strike of lightning from those hands straight into my heart.

But this may be my only chance.

If I can overpower Garrick, I doubt the boy in the corner would get in my way. It's the two guards outside the door that will be the challenge, but with their new king as my hostage, I'm hoping they will have to let me pass.

I slip my hand into the secret pocket Dax had sewn into my costume. My fingers wrap around the jeweled comb I have stashed there. Its prongs are particularly sharp after scraping them against the metal lock for half the night. I almost smirk at the idea that I've been a prisoner for less than forty-eight hours and I've already unintentionally made myself a shiv.

Garrick's hot fingertips brush my collarbone as he drapes the thin gold chain around my neck. This time I can't stop myself from shivering. He fastens the clasp but lets his fingers linger longer than necessary. *Now,* I tell myself.

I stretch out my free hand, readying to grab Garrick and push him against the heavy bedposts resembling Corinthian columns, when the boy in the corner startles. He drops his tray. The sound of metal clanging on marble makes both Garrick and me jump, and the comb slips from my pocket and lands on my bedsheets. I hurry to cover it with my skirts as Garrick stands. Did the boy startle because he sensed what I was going to do?

"You clumsy piece of *kopros!*" Garrick shouts at the boy.

"I'm sorry, so sorry, Garrick," the boy says, scurrying to snatch up the tray. A blood-red apple rolls across the floor, but the rest of my dinner looks to have mostly survived the fall. The boy reaches for the apple but then pulls his hand back like he's too afraid to get any closer to Garrick. I follow the stricken look on his face and realize what must've given him such a fright. Garrick has two shadows.

One is shorter and the other far too large to be natural. It quivers slightly, and its movements aren't quite in sync with Garrick's. Before yesterday, I'd seen this phenomenon only once before, when a Keres had attached itself to Joe in an attempt to drain the life from him. Then last night, I noticed it when I watched Garrick walk away through the small window in my chamber's door. I'd almost convinced myself that it was a trick of the light from the flickering torches in the corridor. It hadn't made sense. If Garrick has two shadows, that means a Keres is attached to him—but if that is the case, why isn't he dead yet? The Keres should have sucked his life force dry within minutes.

"You should treat us with more reverence," Garrick says to

the boy, towering over him as the boy kneels on the floor. Garrick reminds me of a kid I knew back in elementary school who would push down the younger kids on the playground in order to make himself feel bigger. "I am not a Lesser anymore. I am your king. You will call us 'your highness' or 'my lord.'"

Us?

This isn't the first time Garrick has referred to himself in the plural today—and I don't think he is just using it in the royal sense. What if Garrick is playing host to a Keres willingly?

To what end, I don't know, but it means Garrick is far more dangerous than his strong hands and a few bolts of lightning. Except when I use my vocal powers, Keres have no physical form. If Garrick set one loose on me or the boy, there would be no way to fight it without my singing voice.

"I am sorry, my lord," the boy says. "And I did not mean to disturb you. It's that I . . ."

"I'm sure he's just faint from hunger," I say, cutting off whatever the boy has to say. "You must remember how it was as a Lesser?"

Garrick's nostrils flare when I mention that word.

"But now as king," I say before he can rebuff, "you can change all that. With me at your side, as your queen, we can make a real difference in this world. And as soon as we have the Key, no one will be able to stop you from being the greatest ruler this realm has ever known."

"We do have changes in mind," Garrick says almost under his breath.

"Then the sooner we get the Key, the better. Let me help you find it, *my king.*"

Garrick stares at me for so long I am afraid he can see right through my intentions. He tilts his head and shakes it a little as if someone were whispering in his ear. "I'll do as I please," he says in a low, grumbling whisper. He clenches his fist and then lunges toward the floor so quickly I think he is about to strike the Lesser boy, but before I can react, he snatches up the red apple. He holds it out to me. "Eat," he says. "The search party leaves again at first light. You will need your strength if you're coming with us."

"Thank you," I say, trying to hide my relief, but my fingers are still tentative as I take the apple from his outstretched hand.

"Don't be afraid to eat here," Garrick says, as if he senses my hesitancy. "You bound yourself to me when you ate the pomegranate seed. Eating again won't affect you more. You are already powerless to leave the Underrealm without my say."

"Yes, of course." I clutch the apple against my white dress. He has pointed out the one thing I had been purposely ignoring with my escape plans. Even if I got away from Garrick and the palace, I am still bound to this world.

But perhaps if I find the Key for myself, that won't matter?

I can only hope . . .

"I'll need new clothes. And shoes." I stick out my foot and show him the tattered ballet flats I made the journey here in. I am going to need something sturdier if I'm going to make a run for it.

"I'll take care of it," Garrick says. "Finish cleaning up this mess," he snaps at the boy, and takes his leave. As he goes, I notice that the number of guards outside my door has been doubled.

chapter three

TOBIN

"57 . . . 58 . . . 59 . . . 60 . . . Ready or not, here I come!" I call
out, my voice echoing through the old mill. I hop down from the
tire swing that is "home base" and dash for the ladder that leads
to the loft. Abbie doesn't know that I peeked. On number 10, I
snuck a look and saw her tiptoeing up the ladder. Abbie always
wins at hide and seek—which isn't all that fair considering she's
thirteen, six years older—but this time I have the advantage.
And if I win, she has to buy me a package of Swedish Fish on the
way home.

I check in the usual corners of the loft and then see an old tarp
that has been thrown over a couple of crates. The fabric shifts ever so
slightly, as if someone were adjusting their position under it. I smile.
"I'm going to find you, Abbie!" I call, already feeling triumph swelling
in my chest. I dash for the tarp and pull it away with a smile, only to
be greeted by the hiss of a mangy stray cat. It swipes at me and I jump
back, almost stumbling to the ground.

A high-pitched giggle echoes from below. I look over the loft rail-
ing to see Abbie sprinting for the tire swing.

"Hey!" I shout.

I jog for the ladder, knowing I'll never catch her in time. She jumps onto the tire with a laugh. "Safe," she calls. "I'm home safe."

"No fair!" I shout as I climb down the ladder. "You doubled back. That's not fair!"

She twirls in the tire swing, leaning back so she's almost upside-down, with her hair draping behind her, touching the ground. She smirks. "You wouldn't have known I doubled back if you weren't peeking, cheater."

"I didn't peek," I say, but my ears burn hot. I've never been a good liar.

Abbie laughs, twirling in the swing. "Cheater, cheater, pumpkin eater," she sings.

I scowl at her.

"Oh come on," she says, waving me over. "I'll give you a push on the swing before we head home. I won't even make you clear the table for me after dinner, even though you lost."

I can't really argue with that. Our brother, Sage, would have never let me out of a chore if he'd been here to win. I jog over to the swing to join her. Only when I get to it, she isn't there. The swing rocks back and forth ever so slightly, but it's empty.

"Abbie," I call, spinning around. "Abbie, where are you?"

She doesn't answer.

A little trill of fear tickles up my spine. "This isn't funny. Where did you go?" I turn back toward the tire swing, but now it's gone as well. As if it vanished into thin air. "What the . . . ?" I try to call out to my sister again, but suddenly I can't remember her name. I frantically whirl around, looking for her. But then I am not sure who it was I was looking for in the first place. And then the walls of the

21

mill start to fade away around me, as if disintegrating. What is hap-
pening? Where am I?

Who am I?

The floor under my feet vanishes and I begin to fall . . .

I startle awake, blinking my eyes and taking in my surroundings: pale stone walls and floor, and a heavy, ancient-looking
wooden door stands closed in front of me. The room is lit only
by a single lit torch beside the door. It almost feels as though I am
inside a castle, or a palace, if that were possible. Is that possible?
Where am I? I was looking for someone . . . Someone I wanted safe
back at home . . .

And then all I can recall is the sensation of falling through
empty space.

There's an itch on my back. Right between my shoulder blades.
The itch moves lower. About an inch. The sensation reminds me
of a spider.

I hate spiders.

I tense at the recollection and try to jump from my chair, but
nothing happens.

I try to raise my hands to scratch at my back. My arms won't
move.

I look down to find that my forearms have been engulfed by
the armrests of my chair. My arms have sunk into them as if the
armrests were made of Jell-O—and then solidified like rubber. I
try to yank free, harder now. I use my feet and try to push myself
out. All I manage is to almost topple myself forward, chair and all.
I steady it before I fall.

I am stuck. I am trapped.

The itch burns now like an insect bite.

I shout for help. Screaming at the top of my lungs, while fighting to free myself from the grip of the chair.

I scream until I can't remember why I was screaming in the first place.

My voice falls away. *This chair is so comfortable, why would I want to get up?*

I close my eyes and slip back into my dream.

I'm falling once more through empty space.

CHAPTER FOUR

HADEN

"Are you insane?" a booming voice says from somewhere above me.

Is that you, my god? is all I can think, even though Hades was lost to my world centuries ago. All I can see are the stars behind my eyelids, the echoes of the headlights that have been my undoing. *I must be dead.*

Rough hands grab me. Shake me.

My instincts kick in and I thrash against the hands that hold me.

"Haden, stop!" the voice booms. It's familiar, but I can't place it.

"Are you crazy, standing in the middle of the road? I almost killed you. You could have died." This second voice is different. Familiar. Frantic. Female.

Not Daphne.

"You should have let me," I growl and try to take a swing at my captor. "I should be dead."

Why am I not dead?

"He is crazy," the female says.

"It's the black arrow's poison," a third, older, male voice says. "It's taking him more quickly than I expected."

"What can we do?" she asks.

"Hold him down."

I feel another, smaller pair of hands grab me. I try to thrash harder as two of them hold me down against the pavement, but I am strangely weak. Whoever these people are, they can't be my friends.

"It'll be over in a minute," the third person says to me, and then a sharp jab hits the inside of my right elbow. A second later, the oddest sensation washes through me, as if minuscule bubbles, like in the soda Daphne once made me try, were flitting through my arm.

My vision clears and I see a small green arrow, about the size of a dart, protruding from my arm. "That tickles," I say. The bubbles dance through my body, and I feel as though I am floating a few inches off the ground. Warmth radiates beneath my skin.

Three familiar faces—Lexie, Jonathan, and Ethan—stare down at me, all with varying expressions of alarm. They look so funny from this angle.

"Thank Prada, you're back!" Lexie says.

"Prada?" I ask groggily, feeling warm and floaty all over. "Who's Prada?"

"Did you come back alone?" Jonathan asks.

I shake my head, liking the way it wobbles as I roll it back and forth. "My father and brother are in the grove. Along with Terresa. I tied them up with my toga." I angle my head so I can peer at my prostrate body and realize I've been running around town in my underclothes. I'd landed back in the mortal world in a shredded toga and a small pair of undershorts. Before leaving the grove, I sacrificed the toga to restrain my foes—not that it would make much difference once they awoke from their black sleep and incinerated their fabric bonds, I realize now.

This folly strikes me as particularly amusing.

I hear a car door open and slam. Then a fourth face is looking down at me. Joe.

"Bloody hell. What happened? Where is she?" Joe says, asking the question I've been dreading since I was thrown back through the gate. "Where's my daughter?"

"Daphne? She traded herself to save me," I say, my voice sounding far too high-pitched. "She's trapped in the Underrealm."

I start to shake uncontrollably as the hilarity of the whole situation grips me. I roll on my side and laugh. No, not laugh. Giggle.

"Has he completely lost it?" Ethan asks.

Why is Ethan even here? I think back to when I was struck by what I had assumed was the car, and realize why the blow had felt like thunder. It was because it *was* thunder that had sent me flying. Not the car. Ethan must have used a thunderclap to blast me out of the way. And the warm embrace I'd felt must have been him swooping in from above—Skylords can walk on clouds, after all—to catch me before I hit the pavement. I can't help it. I shake with laughter at the idea that a Skylord prince saved my life.

I'm laughing so hard my abdominals hurt. However, it's a more pleasant pain than the one that had taken me over before I walked out in front of Lexie's car.

Lexie nudges me with her foot. "What did you do to him?" she asks Jonathan.

"I stuck him with a giddiness dart," Jonathan says, squinting down at me.

"You're not Jonathan!" I say, pointing up at him. The black veins in my hand have faded to a bluish gray. "You're Cupid!"

"Yes, that I am," Jonathan says. "Though I prefer to be called Eros."

I guffaw. "I'm being rescued by Cupid!"

"How long will he be like this?" Ethan asks. "I think I preferred the Haden that threw himself in front of oncoming traffic."

Jonathan gives him a cross, fatherly look.

"You're the son of Cupid!" I shift my pointing finger toward Ethan. "*Son of Cupid*," I say in an addled-sounding voice, thinking it is the funniest notion I've ever heard.

"It's only a temporary salve," Jonathan says. "The dart's spell will wear off soon, so we'd better get him somewhere he can't hurt himself before it does."

Ethan scowls but then leans down and scoops me up in his arms. He lifts me, cradled in his arms as if I were a giant baby—*giant baby!*—and carries me toward Lexie's green BMW.

"Your nose looks so big from this close up," I exclaim, bopping him on the nose with my finger.

"Do that again," Ethan growls, "and I will incinerate your entire hand."

I snatch my finger back and pull a face that mimics his scowl in an exaggerated way. "*I will incinerate your entire hand.*"

"Are you sure that was a giddiness dart and not a full-on lunatic spell?" Ethan asks Jonathan as he restrains me—rather forcibly—with a seatbelt.

Jonathan nods. "It's the best I could do in a pinch. My full-strength arrows are gone. All I have left are emotion darts . . ."

27

Ethan gives Jonathan a weighty look, as if the fact that Cupid is almost out of sharp, pointy projectiles is devastating news. I laugh even harder.

"There's no time to worry about that now," Jonathan says.

Ethan clasps his father's shoulder. "Take the boy to Joe's house. I'll see to the grove."

Jonathan and Joe get in the car. Lexie starts the engine and as the car pulls away, I watch with giddy fascination as Ethan uses a blast of lightning to launch himself into the sky. "Wow," I say, clapping my hands. "Do you think he could teach me how to cloud-walk?"

Joe glares from the seat next to mine.

"What?" I ask, shrugging my shoulders exaggeratedly. "It would almost be like flying."

Joe drops his head. He stares at his folded hands in his lap. It almost looks like he's praying. "Daphne," he whispers. "I just hope you're okay."

chapter five

DAPHNE

I sit on the bed in my prison of a bedroom and feel anxiety flood over me. I need to plan. I need to figure out exactly how I am going to get away from Garrick and the Court once we are far enough away from the palace that my vocal powers will (hopefully) return. I need to figure out where I can hide. How I'm going to find the Key. How I can survive in this strange world on my own . . .

My breaths start coming too fast. I'm afraid I'm going to hyperventilate. Whenever I have a big audition or something really stressful on the horizon, I allow myself exactly three minutes to freak out before getting to work. It's an actor's trick that Abbie taught me. But even that amount of time feels like a luxury now. I close my eyes, deciding to give myself one minute, while willing my breaths to become deep and slow. I can't help recounting the crazy series of events that led me to this place.

Only six months ago, I was a small-town girl with two main goals in life: to get my driver's license and to land a music scholarship to a college so I could get away from Ellis Fields. I'd jumped at the chance to move to Olympus Hills with my then-estranged father, so I could take advantage of the school's prestigious music program. Little did I know at the time, Joe was being forced to put me in position to be taken to the Underrealm.

That betrayal still hurts, but I know Joe is a different man now than the one who made a deal, before I existed, to sell my soul in exchange for his fame and fortune.

I stick my hand in my pocket and brush my fingers over the sobriety coin Joe had given me as proof that he was changing for me. He'd even volunteered to come with me to the Underrealm to try to stop the Keres . . .

Only he hadn't come. Tobin had said it was because he thought Joe was passed out drunk, but I couldn't believe it. I couldn't believe that after all we've been through, Joe would leave me hanging when I needed him the most.

I gulp back a cry that aches in my throat. Instead I think of Haden. He'd been so clumsy in his efforts to get my attention when he first arrived in Olympus Hills, I'd found it almost endearing, and soon I'd started to fall for him.

I'd pulled away and fought my destiny when I learned the truth about Haden—that he was an Underrealm champion tasked with bringing me back to his world. But what had really scared me was when I learned the truth about myself. That I was the fated Cypher, the only one who could find the long-lost Key of Hades, and that both the Skylords and the Underlords wanted me and the Key for their own agendas. The Underlords' plan involved possibly sacrificing me to regain their immortality, and releasing the Keres from the Pits to use as foot soldiers in a war against the Skylords—a plan that would surely lead to the destruction of my world and Haden's.

Ultimately, when Haden and I realized that with my vocal abilities and his lightning power, we could destroy the nearly invincible Keres and stop the Court's foolish plans, I embraced the idea that Haden and I, together, could save both of our realms without letting the Key fall into anyone else's hands.

And eventually—despite my better judgment—I also embraced the realization that I am in love with Haden.

I found the Key, and then when Haden was kidnapped and dragged into the underworld by his brother, I decided to use it to go after him. Tobin and Garrick went with me, but I was separated from both when the boat we were sailing to the palace crashed. I lost the Key, almost died, and found myself in Elysium. A guide—Haden's deceased mother, actually—had taken me to the Adamantine Gate, the back door to the Underrealm's royal grounds.

At one point I found myself in the Pits, where I discovered that there were *thousands* of Keres—not the couple dozen Garrick had reported. Had that lie been part of some nefarious plan as well? Had I played right into Garrick's hand when I let him escort me into the throne room of the palace? Had he known all along that being the one to deliver me to the Court would secure his place as the rightful heir to the crown? Had he orchestrated the situation in which I would ask him to come with me to the Underrealm in the first place? Or had he merely taken advantage of the situation at hand?

Whatever the case may be, Garrick is the king now. He was the only one I could strike a deal with to try to save Haden's life. I promised to bind myself to him by eating a ceremonial pomegranate seed and then pledged to help him find the Key of Hades that I claimed I had hidden.

And that is exactly how I found myself here. But the time for dwelling on the past is over. I take one last deep breath.

When I open my eyes, I find the serving boy standing in front of me with his silver tray. My dinner looks a little worse for wear, but my stomach clenches at the smell. I am not sure when I last ate—other than that one pomegranate seed that sealed my fate. Garrick was right: I've been afraid that eating more will only strengthen the binding spell. But I can't help it anymore. I'm too hungry. I take the tray and set it beside me. The meat is stringy and gamey and I wonder if it came from some sort of reptilian beast, and the juice is so thick it reminds me of blood, but considering how long it has been since I've eaten, it might as well be a bacon cheeseburger and a milkshake.

I catch the boy staring at me as I eat. I'm sure I don't look very queenly at the moment—or perhaps he's been hoping I'd give him my food again.

I tear the piece of dark brown, flat bread in half and use it to scoop up what remains of the meat. "Here," I say, handing it to him.

I think he thanks me as he shoves it into his mouth. After a minute of chewing, he swallows and says, "You're going to run away tomorrow, aren't you?"

I am so surprised that he has actually spoken to me that I nod in response. I immediately hope that wasn't a mistake.

"Good," the boy says, eyeing the apple. "I like you. I do not want you to die like the others. All the women die, did you know that? Mortals cannot survive without the sun."

I nod, indicating that I did know that. Haden had said that his mother lasted the longest—seven years—but that others died much more quickly. Being from southern Utah and more recently from California, I am used to being bathed in sunlight. I can already feel the lack of it weighing on me. Like it's getting harder and harder to find the motivation to move. How long *can* I survive here?

I hand the boy the apple. "I like you too, kid."

"Good." He smiles and holds the fruit like it's more precious than my ruby necklace. "You should know there's a network of caves in some cliffs beyond the pomegranate orchards. It stretches out for miles. Someone could hide in there for a long time."

"Thank you," I say, returning his smile. This bit of information may make all the difference. "You know, you speak pretty good English. Do the Lessers get language lessons like the Lords?"

The boy gives me a curious look, his mouth stuffed with apple. "I'm not speaking English," he says. "You're speaking Greek."

I scoff at him, thinking he's pulling my leg. "Whatever, kid."

"No really. Your Greek is perfect. Lessers don't get lessons in anything."

Me speaking Greek makes absolutely no sense. The only language I've ever studied is Spanish, and I can barely do more than ask for directions to the library. "Then how does Garrick know English so well? I guess he could have just picked it up quickly." The people of the Underrealm were naturally gifted mimics. Perhaps it had only taken him a few days to learn English.

"Garrick has always been especially skilled with languages. Even without lessons. I've heard other Lessers say that he even knows how to talk to—" The boy jumps up as the door opens.

A woman—the first one I've seen since arriving here—enters the room, holding a bundle of what I presume are my new clothes. Her skin is so gray and her body is so gaunt, it takes me a moment to realize the woman is probably only a few years older than I am. She wears a fine-looking dress of baby blue chiffon, but it's torn and dirty, as if she's been wearing it for days inside a dank place. I'm not sure what to make of this because Haden once told me that the women who are brought to the Underrealm—Boons, as they're called—live a life of luxury in the Court's harem. The boy quickly hands me the rest of the apple and backs away from me. "I should go, my lady," he whispers. "Good luck tomorrow."

He scurries from the room with my now-empty dinner tray. The woman leaves her bundle for me and starts to follow the boy out. She stumbles and knocks her frail body against the door frame. A guard shouts at her and roughly shoves her into the corridor. "Move it, *Queen* Moira. You're supposed to serve Lord Lex's dinner next."

The guards break into harsh laughter that is barely muffled when they slam my door shut. So this is what has become of the former king's wife? The Court has turned her into a servant? Or is this a new mandate of King Garrick—that all the women should be treated as slaves?

I wonder if—*when*—I escape, if it would be possible to take the other captive women with me. Perhaps even the boy?

No, not now. I will have to save myself before I can try to save anyone else.

I eat the last of my flatbread and then sift through the clothing. It's not exactly the hiking gear I was hoping for. Instead, I find a white dress. It's similar in design to the Grecian dress Dax made me for the play, with a deep V neckline, thick shoulder straps, and an empire waistline, but the fabric is so luxurious and silky that the only word I can think to describe it is buttery. The skirt is draped perfectly, and in the back the fabric is longer, creating a train that in different circumstances I might find romantic instead of inconvenient. The shoulder straps and the empire waistline are beaded with tiny crystals—or perhaps actual diamonds—with threads of what I assume are pure gold. I remember now that Hades had supposedly also been the god of riches as well as the underworld. A dainty crown of gold laurel leaves encrusted with diamonds sits upon a bundle of golden fabric. It's an ensemble fit for a queen. *Or a bride*, I think with a shudder. *Is that what Garrick expects of me?*

Next I find a pair of gold-leafed leather sandals. They're a far cry from the sturdy boots I would want, but still better than my torn-up ballet flats. The golden bundle of fabric turns out to be a thick velvet cloak with a billowing hood. This item I am most grateful for because I imagine without sunlight, it gets cold out there, especially in caves. Assuming I even make it that far . . .

I shake off the negative thought. Now is the time to plan. Tomorrow, I will escape Garrick and the Court.

After that, I will find a way back to my world. I have to, not only for my sake, but for Haden. I *will* get there in time—to give him true love's kiss in order to stop the spread of the poison and restore him to the person I know him to be. To tell him I love him when he can actually comprehend my words.

Nothing can stop me.

chapter six

TOBIN

"Hello, is anybody here?" I call into the house. My voice echoes through the empty rooms. Boxes sit on the porch and a moving truck idles in the driveway, but no one is here.

This is wrong, I think. I know this memory and it is all wrong.

This memory is from my first week in Olympus Hills, but nothing is as I remember it. We've just moved here from our little three-bedroom house a few towns over. I still can't get over how huge our new home is—like it should be a hotel bustling with people, not just the five of us. Maybe that's why it feels so empty . . .

No, they should be here. My family should be here.

I remember running all the way home from school. I'm excited because I finally made a new friend. A girl named Alexis. She likes Star Wars and singing and even shared her Mountain Dew Code Red with me at lunch. But that's not the only reason I'm excited. I want to tell the others that I got a part in my middle school's play. I get to be John in Peter Pan. I didn't think they were going to let me audition because I'm new, but they did, and I landed exactly the part I wanted.

My mom should be here, in the living room, directing the movers. Dad should be in the kitchen on a conference call, speaking in

Japanese. Abbie and Sage should be on the stairs, fighting once again over who should get the biggest room.

That's how I remember this all happening. But they're not here. I race through the empty rooms looking for them but they're nowhere.

They're gone. All gone.

And I am all alone.

I sit on the stairs and cry until I can't remember why I was crying. I can't remember who I was looking for. The house begins to fade away . . .

I awake with a jolt. My body shakes, quivering with pain. I feel as though I have been struck by lightning. A face peers at me through the darkness. I feel like I should know him, but I've already forgotten his name.

"Awake again?" he asks.

I nod.

"Comfy?"

I shake my head but then nod. I am quite comfortable in this chair.

"Good," he says. "You're going to be there for a long time."

"How long?" I ask. I have a sudden recollection of trying to find something. Someone? A feeling of urgency grips me and then fades away along with the recollection.

"Have you ever heard of Theseus?" the young man standing in front of me asks.

When did he get here? I blink at him, already having forgotten his question.

"Silly question," he says, waving his hand. "I suppose if you have heard of Theseus you wouldn't remember. You probably can't even remember your own name at this point."

"I can," I say, but then I am unable to produce it. Something to do with winter perhaps?

"Anyway," the young man says. "Theseus is best known from the myth of the minotaur. He was thrown into a labyrinth as a sacrifice to the beast, only he bested the monster and found his way out with a spool of golden thread. I am sure you've heard that story. But I wonder if you have ever heard of Peirithous?"

When I don't respond, he goes on. "Peirithous was Theseus's best friend. The two were a couple of cocky, douche-bag princes, and riding high on his minotaur fame, Theseus decided he and his bestie deserved to marry daughters of Zeus. Theseus chose a girl named Helen—you've probably heard of her even though you can't remember. She had a 'face that launched a thousand ships' and all that. She was only thirteen at the time, so Theseus decided to snatch her up and keep her hidden from other suitors until she could reach marrying age. Peirithous, being king of the tools, decided that he wanted to wed none other than Persephone— never mind the fact that she was already married to Hades, the god of the Underrealm.

"The two young *heroes* marched right into the underworld and Peirithous, a jackass to his very core, boasted right to Hades's face that he intended to steal away his bride. He even implied that the goddess would prefer *his* company over Hades's. Much to everyone's surprise, the god invited the two mortals inside the palace. He told them they were welcome to take his wife, but only if they would sit and have a drink with him first. He offered the two dick-heads the most comfortable chairs in the palace, but when they sat they were entwined by the chairs. After a few minutes, they completely forgot why they had even come to the underworld. Actually, they completely forgot *everything*.

"You see, Hades had no intention of giving those two his wife. Instead, he sentenced them to imprisonment for life in the Chairs of Forgetfulness, where he could inflict all kinds of punishment on them for their assholery, and they couldn't even remember enough to try to get up and leave. Hades had a really great sense of humor that way. Of course, as the legend goes, Theseus was eventually rescued by his cousin, Hercules, but Peirithous was never freed . . ."

"Is there a point to this story?" I ask. "I'd really like to get back to my nap."

The boy's voice drops lower, as if he's trying to sound sinister. "The point is that Peirithous, after thousands of years, still sits in a chair just like the one you occupy right now. I believe he's in a storage closet somewhere here in the palace. He's just a shell, all of his memories and identity stripped away, but he's still alive. And just as he does not remember anyone, nobody remembers him."

I blink at the young man, struggling to keep my eyes open. I am so very tired. "So?"

"So?" he echoes angrily. "The point is that you are in the same kind of chair. A Chair of Forgetfulness. It will keep you alive, just barely, as it strips away all of your memories, one by one. You'll never be able to escape—not even through death. I can torture you all I want and there's nothing you can do to stop me. And when I get the Key, I will be immortal, which means you will get to be my plaything for the rest of eternity."

He glares at me as if he wants me to ask him why. Or something. I don't know. What were we talking about again?

"All my life I've been treated like a dog. Kicked and scorned and made to fetch. Now it's someone else's turn to be the dog." He pauses and laughs to himself. "Honestly, I had intended to use this chair for Haden—to keep him as my prisoner and inflict on him every pain I have ever suffered, tenfold. But then Daphne had to go and make her binding to me conditional on Haden's banishment to the mortal world. So you got promoted to the position."

"Lucky me," I say and close my eyes.

"Today, Daphne will take me to the Key, and then I will have what I need to set the Keres free . . ."

He goes on talking, but I can't remember why I should be listening to him anymore. I drift off to sleep . . .

I am jolted awake. My body shakes as if I have just been electrocuted. A face peers at me through the darkness. I feel like I should know him, but I've already forgotten his name.

"If all *doesn't* go according to plan today, you know what I'm going to do to you, right?" he asks.

I don't answer. If he's told me this so-called plan, I don't remember.

"You had better hope she takes me to the Key, or else you're the one who is going to pay." He opens his outstretched hand and threads of crackling, blue lightning bloom up from his palm.

The sight brings on the faintest of recollections.

Memories of pain.

He leaves, sweeping out the door with his black cloak trailing behind him.

I close my eyes, already unable to recall what he said.

chapter seven

HADEN

I awake to the smell of lavender, vanilla, and pomegranate lip gloss. All the scents that remind me of Daphne. I am slow to open my eyes, knowing it's too good to be true, for I had been dreaming of her since I fell asleep. Finally, I open them and find that I am in Daphne's bedroom, lying in her bed, her white bedspread tucked all the way up to my chin. I vaguely recall Joe leading me up here while I laughed hysterically about something that had seemed quite funny at the time.

My mouth is dry. My head throbs. And nothing seems all that funny anymore.

A sudden pressure lands on my chest, making me cough. Brim stands on my sternum glaring at me with her bright green eyes. She growls in displeasure and I wonder what I have done to upset her—and then I remember leaving her behind and driving away. And then getting struck by thunder instead of a car. No wonder I ache all over.

"I'm sorry, Brim," I say. "I don't know why . . . I wasn't in my right mind. I am so sorry for leaving you behind. I promise I won't do it again."

Brim is placated by my apology and her growl turns to a purr.

I lift my hand to scruff her cheeks, and see the blue-gray veins sitting under my skin. At least they aren't inky black.

After I give her a good scratching, Brim allows me to get up. I dress myself in a pair of pants—Joe's, I suppose, from how tight they are—and an old Saturn's Ring T-shirt that have been left on the edge of the bed. With Brim perched on my shoulder, I make my way downstairs. I find the rest of the group sitting around the dining room table. Even Lexie, who I had assumed would have returned to her own home at some point, sits with a bowl of colorful loops in front of her. Brim jumps down from my shoulder and bounds over to the bowl of canned fish someone has left out for her in the corner.

"Morning," I say, tentatively standing in the doorway.

The others glare at me. I'm not sure if it's because I had very callously informed them that I returned to the mortal realm without Daphne and the Key. Or because of the rap song—one I'd learned after buying the entire contents of a music store when I first arrived in Olympus Hills—I had decided to sing at the top of my lungs until one o'clock in the morning.

Now that I think about it, that song is much cruder than I remembered it being.

"Looks like someone is feeling more like himself," Jonathan says. "If not a little worse for wear." I notice that Jonathan is a little worse for wear himself. His left shoulder is bandaged and he wears his arm in a sling. Dark circles under his eyes mar his otherwise jovial features.

"What happened to you?" I ask.

"As I told you last night, your brother happened to me,"

Jonathan says. "I tried to stop him from dragging you, unconscious, into the Underrealm. I shot at him with a black arrow but he got off a good blast. I am afraid I missed my mark for the very first time. I take it from the black poison spreading through your veins and your standing in oncoming traffic that the arrow hit you instead of your brother."

So it *is* poison that was seeping through my veins. I recall the details now, that the poison will eventually cause me to lose the ability to feel anything at all. Just as I recall that Jonathan attempted to explain this all to me last night—while I threw kernels of microwave popcorn at his head, trying to coax him into catching them in his mouth.

I shudder, not merely at my cavalier behavior, but at the recollection of how empty and hollow I had felt in those last minutes before getting struck by Ethan. I had wanted to embrace it at the time, but the idea of slipping back into that nothingness terrifies me now.

"Daphne took the cure with her," Jonathan says, "but from your current state, I assume she was unable to administer it."

I shake my head, now sure what *it* was supposed to be.

"So Daphne's really trapped?" Joe asks. He sits on the edge of his chair, hands shaking.

I blink, remembering now that they had tried to question me about what had happened in the Underrealm, but I hadn't exactly made the best interrogation subject. At one point I had made a hat of one of the platinum records that hang on Joe's living room wall and tried to challenge Ethan to a dance-off. And I don't even know what a dance-off is. I don't feel any mirth about the situation now, which means the effects of Jonathan's dart must be waning.

Whatever it was he dosed me with helped to ease off the black poison and also made me act the fool. I'm chagrined by my behavior from last night, but it was still preferable to the overwhelming despair that haunts the edges of my thoughts. I can feel it trying to creep back in.

"Yes," I say, finally answering Joe's question about Daphne.

"There's no way to get her back? We can't storm the gate or . . . something?"

I swallow hard. Without the Key, Persephone's Gate only opens on its own on the fall and spring equinoxes. Our plan had been to use the Key to open the gate a day early, beating the spring equinox, hoping to give ourselves the element of surprise to go in after the Keres. Nothing had gone according to plan, though, and now the Key was lost once more—somewhere in the Underrealm—and the spring equinox came and went while I was in the black sleep. "Persephone's Gate won't open again for another six months," I say, the idea sounding considerably less amusing than the first time I went over the facts with them. "Daphne claimed to know where the Key was, but I'm pretty sure she was bluffing. Her right nostril crinkles a little bit when she's lying."

Jonathan gives a sad smile. "You're right. But don't ever tell her that."

Joe sighs and runs his hand down the side of his face. "I should know that. And I should have been there. She was expecting me to come."

A flash of anger bursts in my chest. Joe *should* have been there. If he hadn't been incapacitated then I wouldn't have had to send Garrick in his place . . .

"I don't know what happened," Joe says. "I was fine—a little parched from running around backstage. I asked someone to bring me my water bottle and then suddenly everything was spinning. I don't remember much after that until . . ."

"I woke you up in a pool of your own drool," Lexie says, finishing for him. "That happens when you get super drunk . . . Or, um, so I've heard."

Joe buries his face in his hands. "I swear I wasn't drinking again. I don't know what happened. All I know is that if I had been there for her—"

"Don't blame yourself," I say, feeling compassion rather than anger. "It was an ambush on both sides of the gate. First Terresa and then Rowan in the grove, and then the Court's army as soon as I was through the gate." I give the others another brief recounting of what I remember happening in the Underrealm—in case they weren't able to make full sense of what I told them about it last night. What with all the laughing and dancing, and tossing things at people, my previous account may have been less than coherent. After I tell them about Garrick taking the crown and the deal Daphne made with him, I fold my cold arms in front of my chest. "Absolutely nothing went as we expected. I'm the one to blame—I should have been more prepared. I should have considered other options."

"If only you'd taken me up on my offer," Ethan says. He had wanted to join forces and use the Eternity Key to take a group of his own loyal Skylords to storm the Underrealm and kill the Keres. It had seemed too risky at the time. I didn't know if I could trust him not to do more damage to my world than he was claiming. If only I'd listened. Or if only I'd just given Rowan the Key to bring back to my father on his own—even *that* seemed like a better alternative than leaving Daphne behind.

If only she hadn't loved me enough to trade her freedom for mine. There were so many *if onlys*.

Heat pricks at the back of my eyes. I cover my face, feeling as if I am about to cry.

"Seems like the giddiness has worn off," Lexie says.

"Thank Zeus," Ethan mumbles.

"Not good," Jonathan says so gravely that I drop my hands and stare at him. "Based on when you fell asleep last night, the dart started to wear off after only three hours. Your metabolism is too quick. I told Daphne that it would take two weeks for the black arrow's spell to take you over completely, but it's only been a couple of days and we already almost lost you once." He pulls a handful of colorful darts from the quiver that is slung over his dining chair. "These emotion darts will help push it off, but these four are the only ones I have left. At this rate, you'll burn through them in no time."

"How much time exactly?" I ask.

"If I ration one per day, then perhaps five or six days. Maybe less. It means you'll have to deal with the mood swings—sadness, anger, despair—and other negative side effects for as long as possible between injections."

Negative side effects. That is putting it mildly. The sadness and anger I can handle. The despair is worse. But it's the parts where I feel nothing—like the moment before the car was about to hit— that terrify me. The irony that I had spent so much of my life *pretending* to be emotionless and unaffected isn't lost on me. I let the tears come that burn in my eyes now. Because feeling *something* is better than feeling nothing.

"If only Daphne had been able to administer the cure," Jonathan says. "A red arrow wasted . . ."

"Red arrow?" I ask. "That was the cure?" I pull the collar of the shirt down to show the others the fiery red wound just above my heart. "She stabbed me with it. Why isn't it working then?"

Jonathan gasps at the sight. "Did she kiss you?"

"Kiss me?" I think of Daphne trying to kiss me over the altar in the throne room. My mind had been poisoned against her at the moment, and I had been so shocked, felt so betrayed, after she stabbed me with that red arrow, I had actually fought her off. "She tried but didn't get the chance."

It wasn't until moments later, when the black poison that had been clouding my mind receded for a moment, that I even grasped the words she had said before trying to give me the cure—that she loves me. But by then it had been too late. I had been dragged away for execution, and in her desperation to save me, she had pledged herself to Garrick in exchange for my banishment instead of my death.

Jonathan's brow furrows. "The arrow Daphne used to try to cure you contained a true love spell. Meaning that it would only work as a cure for someone who had found their true love. But it must be sealed with true love's kiss."

"And she knew this?" I ask, my mind whirling at the thought.

"Yes," Jonathan says. "I made sure of it. I wouldn't have let her go after you if that had not been the case."

That means Daphne truly loves me. The words she'd said

weren't merely something she felt in the heat of the moment. Daphne is my true love, and I am hers.

"However, I worry the lack of sealing the cure has accelerated the black arrow's poison," Jonathan says gravely.

"Will it still work?" Lexie asks. "If Daphne kisses him before it's too late, will it still seal the cure?"

Jonathan nods, but I can tell from the grim look on his face that he's thinking what we all already know: I have only six days, maximum, before the poison takes me, and there are six *months* until the gate will open again to the Underrealm.

"Getting Daphne out of there as quickly as possible is my number one priority, regardless of what it means to me."

"And Tobin," Lexie says pointedly. "You're not leaving without Tobin again."

"Tobin?" I blink at her. "You mean Tobin isn't here?"

Ethan and Jonathan both shake their heads. "He went with Daphne and Garrick to find you," Jonathan says.

"You never saw him?" Lexie asks. "Daphne didn't say anything?"

I shake my head. "I have no idea what happened to him."

Lexie presses her fingers to her lips and sits on the couch next to Joe. I know exactly how both of them feel, which means I am in a rational state . . . for the moment.

"We need to make a plan while I'm still thinking clearly," I say. "Regardless of what's happening to me, we need to find a way to get Daphne—and Tobin," I say, nodding to Lexie, "out of the Underrealm."

"What about Garrick?" Ethan asks.

"I don't think he'll want to leave now that he has the crown."

Ethan crosses his arms. "Yes, but is he a threat?"

"I'm not sure. There was something off about what happened. As if he knew all along that he was going to come out on top . . . like he orchestrated it." I shake my head, not sure where my brain was going with that.

"Garrick was the one who brought me my water bottle," Joe says as if suddenly remembering. "It tasted funny. Acrid. And then everything is foggy after that. Do you think he drugged me?"

I nod, starting to understand—though it's hard to believe—what role Garrick may have played in our plan falling apart. "So he'd be the one I'd send after Daphne when Dax disappeared," I say. "Alas, how would he know Dax would go missing—unless he somehow orchestrated the call that supposedly came from Abbie, luring him away? With both Dax and Joe out of the way, he had the opportunity he needed to take Daphne into the Underrealm, making himself the default heir."

"We're all talking about the same Garrick, right?" Lexie scoffs. "All that kid cared about was perving on cheerleaders and playing Xbox. I doubt he's some mastermind who could pull off usurping the king on purpose."

"Unless that's the way he *wanted* you see him," Ethan says. "Most of the world knows me as a drawling truck driver, most of this town thinks I'm a schoolteacher, and up until yesterday, most of the Sky Army thought I was on their side. Maybe the boy only plays the part of the simpleton."

Simpleton isn't exactly a word I would use to describe Garrick. However, I understand what he means. I feel anger rolling through me at the idea that Garrick may not be what he seems, but I try to push it away. I need to concentrate on the problem at hand before I lose control again. "Garrick's involvement is beside the point right now."

"Garrick is the only point I care about." Ethan shoves his hand toward the ground, pointing. "A child sits on the throne of the Underrealm now, and I need to know what his intentions are. What will he do if he finds the Key? Will he be able to stop the Court from using it to free the Keres?" He puts his hand on the hilt of his sword. He looks so strange standing in Joe's modern dining room in his full Skylord armor. "While I feel for you and your lost friends, my mission remains the same. The Keres must be destroyed."

"Then we should join forces after all," I say, stepping toward him. "You can't destroy the Keres without Daphne, if you remember that detail. Her voice is the only thing that will make them solid enough to kill. Which means rescuing her should be the top priority for both of us." I don't know how I feel about putting Daphne in harm's way once again, but I do know that I need all the help I can get to bring her home. "Help me find Daphne, and we'll help you destroy the Keres once and for all."

Ethan nods and extends his hand. I clasp it and he gives it a good shake before pulling it away.

"Good," I say. "Now, if only we knew a way to get back through Persephone's Gate without it being an equinox . . ."

A quiet pall falls over the group. Joe covers his face with his hands again. Lexie picks at the colored loops that have grown moisture-logged in her bowl, and Ethan shifts uncomfortably from one foot to the other. Apparently, I am not the only one who is at a loss for an idea.

"Wait," Jonathan says, standing and swinging his nearly empty quiver over his shoulder as if he were ready to run off into battle. "I think I know of someone who might be able to help us."

We all turn toward him. "Who?" I ask.

"Who would know more about coming and going from the underworld than Persephone herself?"

"Persephone?" The goddess of my realm had walked away centuries ago, after Hades was killed. Most Underlords presumed her to be dead. "You know where she is?"

"Not exactly, but I do remember hearing rumors about a century ago—give or take a couple of decades—that she was taken prisoner by the Skyrealm." Jonathan gives Ethan an expectant look.

Ethan nods. "I've heard those rumors as well, though I've never been able to confirm them. I have to admit I always assumed it was part of my grandfather's propaganda campaign against the Underrealm, but I suppose they could be true. However, if that's the case, they'll be holding her in the Black Hole."

"Black hole?" Lexie asks. "Like a literal black hole? Because that's a little intense."

"No, not a literal one, but almost as hard to get to. My grandfather has a secret underground prison where he keeps important political prisoners."

"How can something in the Skyrealm be underground?" Lexie interrupts.

"Ever heard of Mount Olympus?" Ethan asks.

"Only from your, like, five-thousand-page homework assignments," Lexie says. "According to Greek mythology, the important gods live on some floating mountain in the sky . . . Oh," she says, getting it, "the Skyrealm is a floating mountain?"

"Yes. And the Black Hole is a prison inside the mountain. If my grandfather has Persephone, that's where he'd be holding her. However, the prison is a labyrinth, whose entrance magically moves on a regular basis. The schedule of which is only known to a handful of my grandfather's personal lieutenants."

"I gather that you are not one of them," I say.

"Unfortunately, I lost that privilege after my brief sabbatical in the mortal world before returning to the Skylord army. Besides, I showed my hand when I fought against the Skylords in order to safeguard Persephone's Gate. I wouldn't be surprised if my grandfather wants to throw *me* in the Black Hole now. And I would be even more surprised if there isn't a bounty on my head."

I remember now that the thing I had found oh so funny just before being ushered off to another wing of the house had been Jonathan and Ethan's description of a skirmish between them and Terresa's troop of Skylords. Ethan had wanted the Key so he could kill the Keres before they could be unleashed on the five realms, but Terresa had been hell-bent on crashing through the gate in order to exterminate every last member of my Underlord race. If it hadn't been for Jonathan and Ethan's protection, she may very well have succeeded. Ethan had fought valiantly when Terresa and her army wouldn't listen to reason, and Jonathan had lasted for as long as he could with his injured shoulder and depleting supply of arrows. All had almost been lost, until a band of Ethan's own men had arrived and chased the remaining soldiers off. Ethan claimed that the Skylords won't return now that the gate is closed once more.

The battle had been so fierce, with lightning starting fires, that Ethan had brought down a torrent of rain to put them out. To the residents of Olympus Hills, it had looked like the wrath of the heavens had opened up on them. The mayor, most likely knowing that wrath was really the Skylords, issued an immediate, mandatory evacuation.

Which is why the town had seemed abandoned when I returned—and the idea that I had practically thrown myself in front of a moving car because I'd thought everyone I knew had been destroyed, when really they were hanging out in the next town over, had sent me into hysterical laughter last night. It is hardly funny now.

Ethan clears his throat as if he senses my attention has wandered. "However, we do know someone who can lead us to the prison." He points his finger upward. I don't know if he means to indicate the upper floor of the house or the Skyrealm.

"Who?" I ask, following his gesture to the ceiling.

"Terresa," Ethan says. "She became one of my grandfather's lieutenants while I was on my sabbatical. If there's anyone we can get close to who can tell us the location of the Black Hole, it's her. Terresa can take us to Persephone."

"Terresa?" I stare at him, trying not to let my poisoned brain dwell on the fact that the only person who can help us find Persephone is a power-hungry Skylord who would sooner kill me and my entire race than offer any semblance of assistance.

Hades, help us. We're doomed.

chapter eight

DAPHNE

By morning I've come up with what I think is a reasonable escape plan—and one that should take care of two problems at once. I need a distraction, and the fact that Garrick is playing host to a Keres needs to be revealed to the Court. Which means I need to provoke the Keres that is attached to Garrick. I can't risk doing it here in the palace, where I will be powerless to fight it, so my plan is to force it into revealing itself once the search party is far enough away from the palace that my powers will return. My plan is to use my vocal powers to cause it to take solid form, and while the guards fight it off and Garrick is freaking out from having his secret exposed, I will make a break for it and head for the caves that are just beyond the pomegranate orchards that the Lesser boy told me about.

I am so sure of my plan that I do not mind that Garrick has sent four guards at first light to escort me to the stables. I take in my surroundings, appreciating the beauty of the palace for the first time. The walls and floors are smooth, cream-colored marble— alabaster, I think it's called. The walls are adorned with tapestries and relief carvings, all seeming to depict different stories from the Underrealm's history.

I recognize one that tells the story of Persephone accepting Hades's pomegranate and choosing to trade being the goddess of springtime for becoming the queen of the underworld. Another tapestry tells the story of when Hades tried to create a child for barren Persephone and created the Keres by accident. The woven design shows Hades locking the monsters away in the Pits. The tapestry next to it shows Hades's second attempt at creating children—the twins, Life and Death. It depicts the god and goddess's great joy—and then despair when the two children were stolen away by Zeus, who tried to claim them as his own.

The golden doors that lead out to the stable show Hades sending his Keres to steal the children back—and the ensuing battle between the Skylords and Underlords that followed for centuries afterwards.

I wonder if there is another carving or tapestry somewhere else that shows when Orpheus stole Hades's Kronolithe, and then Hades's subsequent death at his godly brother's hands. Haden told me how Zeus had Hades torn into pieces and his body scattered across the five realms so that he would find no honor after his death—so I decide perhaps I don't want to see that story depicted anywhere. Because, you know, gross mental images and all.

I wait with my guards in the stables for Garrick and the Court to arrive. I am shaking with anticipation, revving up to enact my escape plan, when Garrick arrives.

"My queen," he says, taking my hand as if I had offered it to him. He lifts it to his mouth and plants a kiss on my knuckles. It takes all my willpower to smile instead of yank my hand away in revulsion. I need to play the part of the willful queen for another hour or so. "You look as beautiful as I had imagined you would," he says, indicating the white dress, gold cloak, and crown I allowed a couple of the women from the Court's harem to dress me in. "I am very pleased."

That's when I catch it. The use of "my" and "I" rather than "our" and "we."

I squint as Garrick moves past me. The lighting here is dim but I watch for the telltale signs of shadows following him. My heart sinks into my stomach when I realize that today Garrick has only one.

The Keres I had been hoping to use as my distraction is gone.

The search party travels by chariot. The one I share with Garrick is obsidian black, adorned by gold trim. It's pulled by two sleek black stallions the size of Clydesdales. Two chariots are in front of us on the narrow path and two are behind us. I gather from the passengers' clothing that each chariot contains a member of the Court as well as a member of the King's guard for their protection. I am glad that Garrick and I don't have a guard in our chariot, because it will make escaping easier when an opportune moment comes, but it also makes me uneasy as we approach the Wastelands.

I wish now that I had claimed the Key was on the protected Elysium shore rather than in the place where the shades of the dead wander freely, looking for their next meal, but it's too late to change the location from where I'd previously indicated on the map. I have to admit that when Garrick had announced I wasn't permitted on the first search party outing and demanded I show him on a map instead, I had chosen deep in the Wastelands in hopes that perhaps Garrick wouldn't come back.

When the chariots enter the pomegranate orchards, I am taken aback by not only the beauty of the rows and rows of spindling trees dripping with red glistening fruit, but also the smell. It's so fragrant and floral, it reminds me of my mother's greenhouse behind her shop. Tears flood my eyes as I once again wonder what happened to her after the play. She must have been so confused. Panicked. As far as she knew, we were all going to go out for ice cream. If the Skylords did indeed attack, then what happened to her? Jonathan had promised to get her safely out of town, but who knows if he ever made it to her after being injured?

I wipe the tears away, telling myself I need to focus on the task at hand. As we pass from the pomegranate orchards into what I assume, from studying Garrick's map, are the lands that separate the edge of the royal grounds from the desolate wastelands beyond, I test my vocal powers once more. I try to hum a few notes, but no sound comes out. I've been testing my powers every few yards as we travel farther from the palace, but so far I've had no luck.

I had entered the royal grounds through a different way last time, through the Adamantine Gate that separated the grounds from Elysium. And now that I think about it, I hadn't tried to use my powers after passing through the gate until I was in the throne room. I had hoped it was just the palace that was warded against my powers, but my experiments were proving that it was the entire royal grounds. I can only hope that, once we cross into the Wastelands, they will return.

I can see the Wastelands on the horizon now, where the beautiful greenery of the orchards and the royal grounds fades away into a desolate landscape fitting of its name. Before me are rock formations, plateaus, and rocky cliffs made of pale gray earth. It reminds me of my home in southern Utah, but without the beautiful red earth and rocks. Without color the land looks ghostly and foreign, like the terrain of some inhospitable planet.

I search the surface of the cliffs in the distance, hoping to spot an entrance to the caves the boy had told me about. I start to think perhaps he was just toying with me, until I catch a glimpse of a dark hole tucked behind a high, rocky outcropping. I try humming again and gasp when a small, weak, vibration sounds in my throat.

"Are you all right?" Garrick asks.

I nod and give him a sheepish grin. "Just nervous about the Shades, you know. They're kinda freaky."

Although "kinda freaky" feels like an understatement. Other than the Keres in its solid form, I've never seen anything quite as terrifying as the Shades—the souls of the dead who terrorize the Wastelands of the Underrealm, constantly searching for their next meal. They are humanoid in shape but devoid of any defining characteristics. No hair, no eyes, no ears, no noses, their only facial feature being a large gaping mouth, and no way to tell if they're male or female. Their skin is gray, almost the same color as the Wastelands, and leathery, with elongated limbs and fingers, as if they've been pulled and stretched somehow.

"Don't worry," Garrick says, straightening the crown on his head. "We'll be taking a boat once we get to the river. We'll be unreachable then."

The river. I should have realized we would take a boat to avoid the Shades. I bite my lip, knowing that escaping will be nearly impossible once we are on the river, and the odds of surviving on my own will dwindle the deeper we go into the Wastelands. What was it that Garrick had said last time we were here?

On foot . . . you'd never make it. You'd get torn to pieces by the Shades and eaten for breakfast.

I peer into the cliffs, noting the location of the cave entrance, trying to burn it into my mind. I need to escape before we reach the river, and then double back this way. That cave might be my only chance to stay hidden.

A faint noise in the distance catches my attention. I listen closely and realize it's the whisper of dewdrops on the small grasses that speckle the dusty earth of the borderlands. I can hear them singing. I hadn't been able to hear anything like that since entering the palace grounds. The sound is so welcome I almost start to cry again. The silence of the last few days has been one of the most unbearable things about my captivity. Now that I can hear the dew singing, I know my powers are returning.

I listen to the faint little song of the dewdrops and concentrate on humming it back to them. *Come to me,* I think, calling to some droplets that speckle a ghostly grayish flower growing on the edge of the path just ahead. Nothing happens. I hum a little louder, stretching my fingers toward the flower as we pass it. I watch the dewdrops quiver, but they don't follow my command. I'm not strong enough yet—my powers must be like a dead cell phone that needs to recharge before it is useful.

"What are you doing?" Garrick asks.

I drop my hand, and clutch the edge of the chariot as if I need to steady myself. "Sorry, I hum when I'm nervous."

"Well, stop," he growls with a suspicious narrowing of his eyes. "It's irritating."

I turn my head to the side so I can roll my eyes without him seeing. Without the Keres for distraction, I am going to need to improvise my escape plan, and once I am strong enough, I imagine I am going to become far more than irritating.

We ride for what feels like another couple of miles. The rocky cliffs and plateaus melt away into rolling dunes of gray sand the farther we move down the path that leads to the river. The sounds of this strange world grow louder, creating a mixture of foreign melodies. The louder it gets, the more my confidence grows. Then, from over the horizon of the sand dunes, another, eerier sound fills my ears. A terrible, moaning groan I've heard only once before. I know I'm not the only one who can hear it when Garrick stiffens beside me. He grips the reins and whispers, "Shades."

From the sound of them, the Shades are not far off, and the river has just come into sight over the horizon. I see the boat waiting. It's more the size of a yacht than the little skiff I had sailed before using my powers, but I still might be able to handle it.

If only I can get there before the rest of the search party.

"Pick up the pace," Garrick shouts to the front chariot driver. "We need to get to the river!"

The two chariots in front of us speed up, and Garrick commands our horses into a full gallop. The two chariots behind us follow suit. The horses kick up rocks as they run. Each stone gives off a shrill little tone as it flies—which gives me an idea. My escape plan involved finding some sort of weapon, and the flying rocks are exactly what I need. I start humming again, louder this time, knowing Garrick won't hear me over the horses' pounding hooves and the drivers' shouts for them to move faster. I concentrate all my energy as I hum to the rocks, mimicking the tone they put off. If I can only get them to listen . . .

Garrick curses as a rock goes flying past his head.

My aim was a little off.

The next rock I send flying at the driver behind us. This time my aim is true. It hits the guard hard against his knuckles. He drops the reins by reflex, and as he tries to grab hold of them again, I command another rock to pelt him in the head. It clangs hard against metal helmet. He claps his hands to his head and the Heir next to him gives a frantic shout as I send more rocks flying in their direction. One of the horses rears up, stopping their progress. The chariot behind them barely misses colliding into them as their driver veers out of the way.

"What the . . . ?" Garrick glances behind him, and then returns his focus onto our horses. If he hadn't moved so suddenly the next rock would have hit him in the eye. Instead it only grazes his ear. "You're doing this!" he shouts at me. He takes the reins in one hand and tries to grab me with the other. I twist out of his grasp and start singing instead of humming. "Stop!" he commands, but he has no power over me.

I send more rocks flying, pelting him and the other men. A large stone hits one of the horses in the flank—which I feel bad about—but it causes the distraction I need. The horse sets into a frantic run, pulling the reins from Garrick's hand, and as the second horse resists the pull of the first, our chariot loses control. We skid into a spin near the riverbank, and I throw myself from the chariot.

I hit the ground hard on my side and roll, ignoring the flashes of pain in my arm and knee. I hear Garrick shout, and his chariot crashes into the one in front of it. I glance up to see that all five chariots have come to a halt. One of the guards runs to assist Garrick, while another heads in my direction, probably thinking I have merely fallen.

I scramble to my feet, knowing I have to get to the boat before the guard can get to me.

"Stop her!" Garrick shouts.

But I am already on my feet. I gather up the train of my dress and start running, adrenaline pushing me past the ache in my knee, toward the boat.

"My lady," the guard calls. "My lady, let me help you."

"Don't let her get to the boat!" Garrick says. He must have figured out my plan.

The guard doesn't pick up his pace, no doubt thinking there's nowhere I can go. After all, how could one girl sail a boat on her own?

A smirk crosses my lips as I pound down the dock. *I'm almost there.*

I can take the boat. Sail away. Double back to the caves, or go anywhere I want. They'll never be able to catch up to me on foot.

Freedom is less than three yards away.

And then I'm falling. My foot has caught on something and I'm falling forward. My hands and my already injured knee hit the wood planks of the dock. A loud moaning noise fills my ears. I peer down between the slats of the dock and see a featureless face staring back at me. I scream. I can't help it. There's a Shade under the dock, only a few inches from my face. I try to get up but a tight squeezing pain holds my ankle. To my horror, I realize the reason I fell is because the Shade grabbed my foot from between the slats of the dock. "Let go!" I shout at him and try to wrench my foot free, to no avail. The moaning grows louder, and I see that he isn't alone. Two more Shades close in on him, as if coming to inspect his prize.

Were they lying in wait for us? Did they see the boat waiting, and figure dinner must be coming along soon? That seems pretty smart for supposedly mindless predators.

A shout and a crack of lightning from behind draws my attention. I glance back to see another pack of Shades descend on the chariots. Probably the same group we were trying to flee before. I can't help wondering if it was their objective to drive us in this direction.

More cracks of lightning follow as the guards try to scare off the Shades. The one guard who had been following me is distracted by the fight. I turn my attention back to the Shades under the dock, a moment too late. A hand reaches up between the slats and before I can react, it grabs my wrist. With one hard yank, he pulls me flat against the dock. My chin hits the splintery wood and I bite my tongue. Blood fills my mouth. I can feel the Shade's hot breath on my face as he moans in a way that sounds like a victory cheer. Through the opening between the slats, I watch as the two other Shades begin to climb up over the dock. I try to sing, try to hum, but my throbbing, bleeding tongue refuses to cooperate. I've been rendered voiceless.

I tense with fear, as petrified as one of Medusa's victims, and the two Shades close in on me. I am sure that their featureless faces with gaping, hungry mouths are the last thing I will ever see. Their hands claw at me as they pounce.

I hear the sound before I see anything, like a baseball bat swinging through the air and cracking against a ball. With a moaning shriek, one of the Shades goes flying off the dock. The Shade under the dock releases my hand, but then grabs hold of my cloak, holding my head down so I can't see what's happening. I try to claw at the cloak's clasp to free myself, but it's no use. A moment later, another swing and a crack follows, and the second pouncing Shade crumples at my side. A third swing sounds from somewhere over my head and the entire dock quakes, reverberating under me, as if it has been struck by a great force. The Shade holding my hair from under the dock suddenly releases me. It hunches back, cowering, and then breaks away in an apelike run up the riverbank.

I gasp, shocked I'm still alive, and roll onto my back. I look up at my rescuer, expecting to see one of the royal guards—hell, even Garrick—when all I find crouched over me is another Shade. It's at least a foot taller and twice the bulk of the one who had caught me. It holds a large club, or perhaps it's an aged bone, in its gray hands.

"What the . . ."

But I don't get to finish my question. The Shade swings his club at my head. Pain explodes against my temple, and then everything goes black.

chapter nine

HADEN

"You brought Terresa here?" I ask as Ethan gestures at the ceiling of Joe's dining room. I bristle at this idea. Terresa is dangerous and unpredictable.

"Yes," Ethan says. "When we found you in the middle of the road, you told us you'd left her tied up in the grove. I brought her here last night, as well as your father."

"My father?" I take an instinctive step back. King Ren is one of the few people in all the five realms that I have ever been afraid of. I can only imagine his wrath against me now that he has been banished from his own kingdom, his crown stripped from him and given to a boy. "My father is here? In this house? And no one is guarding him?" How could they be so foolish to leave him unwatched? I wouldn't put it past him to burn down this entire house—entire state—to get to me. "Where is he?"

"He's in Marta's wing," Joe says, referring to the part of the house that had once been reserved for his personal assistant. She'd skipped town after it was revealed that she had been the eyes and ears for Simon, one of my father's lackeys, to make sure Joe didn't go back on the deal he'd made to sell Daphne's soul to the Underrealm.

I bolt for the door, preparing myself to face down my father.

"Relax, Haden," Ethan calls after me. "It's safe. They've been taken care of. Neither your father nor Terresa will be causing us trouble for the time being."

"And Rowan?" I ask. "Where is my brother?"

"Rowan wasn't in the grove where you said you'd left him," Ethan says. "I told you all this last night. He must have awoken and hightailed it out of the grove before I got there."

I nod, recalling now we'd had this conversation while I ate cookies Joe had offered me and blew bubbles in my milk with a straw. Who knew you could do that? "Rowan is gone," I say more to myself than to anyone else. I wonder why, upon freeing himself, Rowan had left our father behind. *He* had always been the perfect son.

But Rowan's motives and escape aren't something I can allow myself to dwell on at the moment. Along with Dax's disappearance, those were matters that would have to wait until after Daphne's rescue.

"You said my father and Terresa are taken care of. What do you mean by that?" I ask.

"I'll show you," Ethan says. "Follow me upstairs."

Brimstone stays in the dining room to polish off the rest of everyone's breakfast while the rest of us follow Ethan.

A minute later, I stand with the others outside the window that separates Joe's private recording studio from the recording booth, both located on the second level of his expansive home. Behind the glass, Terresa lies on her side, propped against a few pillows. Her hands are still tied flat against her chest with the strips of my torn toga. I'm surprised Ethan did not replace her bindings with something sturdier when he brought her from the grove, but the positioning of her hands means if she uses her lightning power to burn away the makeshift ties, she will blast herself in the chest. I'd had to do just that in my attempt to stop Daphne from sealing herself to the Underrealm. I find myself wondering if Terresa would be desperate enough to do the same when she awakes.

"How long has she been out?" I ask.

"Since that night in the grove," Jonathan says. "I shot her with a golden arrow and she's been out ever since."

"Is that normal?" I ask. "It's been days."

Jonathan shakes his head.

"I plied her with a sleeping draught," Ethan says, patting a leather satchel he wears slung over his shoulder. "I couldn't risk her waking while my men and I chased off her troops, so I gave her a dose of a sleeping potion. I gave her a second dose before transporting her here. I did the same with your father. He didn't strike me as someone who would make an easy captive otherwise."

"Good thinking," I say. A sleeping potion would be a far better restraint than any chain or rope.

"Frankly, dealing with your father as a prisoner is going to be far more ideal than handling Terresa after she's conscious," Ethan says. "I don't fancy being the man to wake her."

Lexie smirks. "She's that brutal, huh?"

"Quite the opposite. That golden arrow my father shot her with elicits passion. Whoever she sees first upon waking, she will fall in mad, passionate infatuation with. I must admit, I was hoping to keep her asleep until the spell wears off."

"How long will that take?" I ask Jonathan.

"It depends on how greatly she *wants* to fight it off." He clucks his tongue. "I am afraid we don't have time to wait any longer. Perhaps we can use her compromised mental state to our advantage." He shakes his head and pinches his nose between his thumb and forefinger. "I must be out of practice being Cupid, because that sounds so much creepier in the twenty-first century than it did in ancient Greece."

"Nevertheless, you do have a point. So . . . who is going to wake her?" I say, shuddering at the idea.

"I'd volunteer," Joe says, "since I am used to having adoring fans and all, but she looks like she's the same age as my daughter, and she's staying in my home, and that just seems *so wrong*."

"She only *looks* like a teenager, but I respect your reservations," Jonathan says. "I also feel far too old for this job."

"I guess it should be me," Ethan offers. "I am her commanding officer and all. She's my responsibility . . ."

I can see the dread on his face as he hesitates turning the doorknob. I wonder if it's because Terresa is the half-sister of his fiancée. Even if he hasn't seen his betrothed in years, I imagine this whole situation would make for awkward family reunions in the future. Assuming Abbie can even be found. She's been missing for six months and had been in hiding for five years before that. And then there was the issue of her being in love with Dax.

"Oh, just let me do it," Lexie says exasperatedly and pushes her way past Ethan. "It's not like she'll have any chance of seducing me or something. I only play for one team."

"What do teams have to do with anything?" I ask.

She rolls her eyes. "I'll explain it to you later," she says with a smirk. "Along with the birds and the bees, if you need that talk too."

"Birds and bees? What are you talking about?" Am I starting to lose lucidity again? Because Lexie isn't making any sense.

Lexie laughs and doesn't answer my questions. Instead, she pulls open the door and marches into the studio, clapping her hands and shouting, "Rise and shine, sweetie!" When that doesn't work, she grabs one of Joe's electric guitars, plugs it into an amp, and strums against the strings with reckless abandon.

Terresa startles awake, and all four of us men take an instinctive step back from the window as she rolls away from the pillows to look up at Lexie.

Terresa's eyes narrow. "Who are you? Where am I?" she demands. "Why are you holding me here, you filthy mortal?"

I look at Ethan. "Seems as though the spell has worn off."

A panicked look crosses his eyes as the same thought crosses his mind.

"Get back!" he shouts at Lexie as he storms into the room. Terresa has rocked up onto her knees. Ethan grabs Terresa just as she is about to launch herself, headfirst, at Lexie.

Lexie hops backward and Terresa begins to kick and writhe in Ethan's grasp. "What are you doing to me?!" she screams. "Where am I?"

Energy radiates off Terresa, crackling in the air as I run into the room to assist Ethan. Her hands are still bound against her chest.

Maybe she *is* desperate enough to blast herself. Or merely crazy?

Terresa screams at the top of her lungs, "Why are you keeping me from him?" She rams her foot into Ethan's shin. He loses his grip on her. She whirls in the direction of the door. I step in front of her, holding out my arms to block her escape.

Terresa's eyes widen. Undeterred, she flings herself at the obstacle—me—standing in her path. I brace myself for the blow, preparing myself to retaliate, when she suddenly pulls up short. She stops only inches from colliding into my chest. And then she leans her whole body into mine and nuzzles her cheek against my neck. "Oh, Haden, you found me. I knew you would," she whispers, and presses her lips to my throat. For half a second I think she is about to sink her teeth into my jugular, but instead she kisses my neck.

I am too stunned to stop her until she's trailed her lips all the way down to my collarbone. Regaining my senses, I grab her by her bound shoulders and hold her back at an arm's length.

"What's the matter, Hadie," she says, "aren't you happy to see me?"

"Uhhhhh," is the only sound that comes out of my mouth.

"Hadie?" Lexie asks. "So what exactly happened between you two in the grove?" I can hear the smirk in her voice even if I can't see her; all my concentration being focused on keeping Terresa from accosting me again.

I think back on the day before, wishing my memories of the last twenty-four hours weren't so scattered and foggy. "I searched her for her cell phone before I tied her up. She must have woken, if only for second, and looked at me."

"You remember," Terresa says, looking at me as if it were the most romantic thing she'd ever heard.

Kopros. *Terresa is in love with me.*

"Well, on the bright side, getting Terresa to tell us the location of the Black Hole might not be so difficult after all," Lexie says.

"Perhaps," I say tentatively.

We're all outside the window again, watching through the glass as Terresa eats a ham sandwich and a pile of noxious-smelling chips that Joe had referred to as Doritos. I made a deal with her that if she promised not to try to escape or kill any of us, I would untie her and let her have some lunch. I'm not sure how much her cooperation has been determined by her delusions of being in love with me, or the fact that she hasn't eaten in a few days.

Terresa looks up at me mid-chew, and gives a little wave. Her fingers are speckled with orange powder.

It only seemed fair to feed her before we started the interrogation. Perhaps her affinity for me is making me soft. In the Underrealm, I might have starved an adversary for weeks in order to get the information I needed. Then again, that had been the old me. The one that was less human.

I give Terresa a placating wave back. She seems to stay relatively calm and collected as long as I pretend to be receptive to her attention. "Even if we can get the location out of her, how exactly do you propose we storm the Skyrealm's most impenetrable prison?" I ask the group.

The others stay silent for a moment, no doubt ticking off impossible ideas in their heads.

Lexie raises her hand, waving it wildly. "I know. I know. You could pull a Chewbacca."

Joe perks up, nodding. "That could work. But you'd need Terresa's full involvement, not just the location."

"A-chew-what?" I ask.

"Gesundheit," Lexie says, with a quirk of a smile. I can see it in her reflection in the glass. "Sorry, I couldn't resist. Chewbacca. You know, from *Star Wars?*"

I stare blankly at her reflection.

"Seriously, you've been pretending to be a human for six whole months and you haven't heard of the movie *Star Wars?*" She shakes her head in disbelief. "Anyway, so these two dudes and this big furry guy named Chewbacca need to rescue this awesome princess from a prison inside this super badass battle station that's the size of a small moon. Anyway, in order to do it, the two dudes pretend to be Stormtroopers—imperial soldiers—who have taken Chewbacca prisoner. They march him right up to the prison doors and the guards just let them right in." She waves her hand at Ethan. "You said there's probably a bounty on your head, so what if you can get Terresa to march you, Jonathan, and Haden up to the Black Hole as her prisoners?"

"That . . ." Ethan says, sounding a little dumbstruck, ". . . might actually work."

I blink at Lexie. She has never struck me as someone who would watch that sort of thing for entertainment, but I've always suspected there was more to her than her obsession with clothing and manicures. I certainly wasn't giving her enough credit, considering she's the only one who has come up with a somewhat plausible—let alone any—battle strategy. "And this works in the movie?"

"Well, mostly. The princess ends up having to take charge and they all end up in a giant trash compactor . . . But the strategy gets them *into* the prison. Exit strategy is up to you guys."

"I imagine we can handle ourselves once we're in. We've got a god on our side, after all." I nod toward Jonathan. The idea that I was rescued by *Eros* is no longer funny to me.

"Errr, about that," Jonathan says. "You missed the part where I admitted to bluffing about being a god. I am Eros," he says, countering my question before I can ask it, "however, as punishment for my forbidden relationship with the Sky King's daughter, Psyche, my golden bow—my Kronolithe—was taken from me. My arrows and darts were all I have left of my power. After the battle with the Skylords, all I'm left with are four emotion darts. When the last one is gone, my immortality will fade away."

"So then you'll . . ." I begin, realizing what he's saying.

"I'll die," Jonathan continues.

Lexie gasps, and then asks, "Can't you just make more?"

"Not without my Kronolithe."

I swallow hard, realizing that every time Jonathan doses me with one of his emotion darts, he's giving up time from his own life. I am about to protest, but Jonathan holds up his hand and gives me a pointed look, telling me this is not an argument he wants to have right now.

Instead, he goes on, as if he didn't just announce that he was almost out of immortality. "And in the mortal guise I chose for myself, I am not exactly in peak fighting form." He gingerly pats his injured shoulder, but it's obvious from his tone that he is also referring to his rather sizable girth. "I also neglected one other aspect when I suggested this plan to find Persephone: the Black Hole is a labyrinth. In my godly form, I could have searched the prison in a matter of seconds, but as a mortal, it could take years, decades if we get lost. But who's kidding, we'd starve to death first. And if we run into the minotaur, we may never escape. I am afraid I am no good to you as merely Jonathan Lovelace in this fight."

My confidence begins to sink and I can feel despair threading into my thoughts. He is right; without his bow, Eros is no good to us.

"Minotaur?" Lexie asks. "Did anyone else hear him say minotaur? Like a giant half-man, half-bull killing machine?"

I recall one of the late-night stories that Master Crue used to enjoy scaring the young nurslings with back in the Underrealm. It was one of the ancient myths, passed down for centuries, about a king who imprisoned the ferocious, unholy offspring of the queen and a bull in a great, mazelike structure. Master Crue used to tell us that if we weren't good little Underlords, our fathers might toss us in the labyrinth to either get lost and rot or to be sacrificed to the man-eating beast who lived in the center. Perhaps this gruesome tale had been derived from stories about the Skyrealm's prison? If so, the plan to find Persephone is looking bleak at best.

"What if we get it back?" Ethan asks.

"The minotaur?" Lexie asks. "I don't want one of those."

Ethan gives her an impatient look. "I mean Eros's bow. What if we get it back?"

Jonathan shakes his head. "It's been centuries. I wouldn't know where to look—"

"I do," Ethan says. "Grandfather keeps all of his important trophies in his private chambers. There's a golden bow amongst them. It must be yours."

"Are you sure?" Jonathan asks, sounding as though he doesn't want to get his hopes up.

"When I was boy, I remember Grandfather ordering Mother to dust and polish his trophies—he's kept her as a servant since your banishment—and I remember now how she always treated the bow with extra care even though handling it seemed to make her sad. I was decades old before I learned that you, Eros, were my father, so I didn't think of it until now, but I am sure the bow must be yours."

Jonathan lights up, a smile so mischievous and delighted crosses his face, and he really does remind me of a cupid.

"I know the ins and outs of the palace. I could get us to the bow with virtually no trouble, and then with your full power restored, and Terresa's help, we'll infiltrate the prison and rescue Persephone."

"Sounds like a decent plan to me," Terresa's voice echoes through a speaker above my head. I stare at her through the glass. She smiles and points to a line of speakers in the wall. "You know I can hear every word you're saying, right?"

Joe startles as he realizes that his elbow has been resting on the intercom button that connects the studio to the recording booth. "Then you'll help us?" Joe says, speaking into the microphone in the control panel in front of him.

Terresa stands and places her hand on her hip. "Under one condition, and I will not budge on this. I get what I want, or no one is going to the Black Hole."

"Name your demand," Ethan says.

"Haden must kiss me first."

A sinking feeling pulls at my gut. Now I know how Daphne must have felt when Rowan tried to demand a kiss from her in exchange for information.

"What is it with psychopaths and their creepy kissing requests?" Lexie says from beside me.

"I was just thinking the same thing," I say. "I guess it is my turn to 'take one for the team,'" I say, mimicking the words Lexie had used when she had volunteered to kiss Rowan in Daphne's place. Although, she had at least *seemed* to enjoy that encounter with a little too much gusto.

"You can't," Jonathan says. "Daphne . . ."

"I think she'll understand," I say. I don't relish the thought of kissing anyone other than Daphne, but I'm willing to do just about anything if it means bringing her home. That feeling in my gut pulls at me again. I cannot define what the sensation means.

"That's not what I mean," Jonathan says, leaning over to flip the switch that turns off the intercom between both rooms, cutting off Terresa's ability to listen in on our conversation. He turns his back on the window, blocking both of our faces from her view. "Fidelity aside, it is imperative that you do not kiss anyone other than your true love—on the lips, that is—before the cure is sealed. Otherwise, it will fail, and the curse will take you immediately."

I sigh, and that strange sensation moves its way up from my gut into my chest. It feels like creeping, crawling insects spreading through my body.

"Perhaps she can be reasoned with," Lexie says.

"I don't think so," Ethan says. "She's as stubborn as they come. When she wants something, she'll cling to the notion like a wolverine."

I don't care.

Terresa stands on the other side of the glass. She looks expectantly at me, wanting her answer.

"What do you want to do?" Jonathan asks me.

I don't care.

"Haden?" he prompts.

The creeping sensation spreads down my arm. I lift my hand and watch my blue gray veins turn to black. Then the sensation stops. My arm goes numb. It has no feeling at all. "I don't care," I say.

I shake my arm. I can see it there, attached to my body, but I can't feel it. As if it doesn't really exist. I clench my fist, digging my nails into my palm, but I can't feel a thing. I try with my other hand, but it has gone numb as well. I can feel the nothingness spreading through me again.

"Haden?" someone says, but I can't tell who.

I slam my hand against the recording studio's window. But I don't feel the impact. I slam it again, harder, pulsing electricity into my fingers. Cracks in the glass splinter out from under my fist. My blood smears the glass. I should be able to feel the cuts on my knuckles. I long for the pain. I long to feel *something*.

"Haden, what are you doing?" Lexie shrieks.

Terresa drops her lunch and runs to the window. "That's it, Haden. Break the glass and we can be together."

I don't care what Terresa says. I don't care what she thinks. I don't care about Lexie trying to grab my arm. I flick my wrist, flinging her away from me. She stumbles into Joe and the two crash into the chair in front of the mixing board.

"Haden, stop!" Ethan orders. "You're out of your mind again and you're endangering your friends."

"I don't care," I say.

I don't care about anything.

I pull my arm back, preparing to slam it through the glass just in front of Terresa's face. I imagine the flesh being ripped from my fingers. Perhaps I could feel that.

As I am about to swing for the glass, Ethan grabs me from behind. I ram my other arm into his side as he tackles me to the ground. He pins me to the floor and Jonathan scrambles for something in his quiver. I try to push Ethan off me, but Jonathan stabs me with another dart. I can see it protruding from my chest. Otherwise I wouldn't know it was there.

I lose the will to fight back. I lie still as Jonathan grabs one of my numb arms and inspects it. Black, bulging veins pulse under my skin.

I expect to feel that strange bubbling sensation spread through me like the last time Jonathan dosed me, but instead a sick heaviness rolls in my gut. I turn my head as I am gripped by the overwhelming urge to wretch.

"We're losing him," Jonathan says. "Too soon."

chapter ten

DAPHNE

I'm pretty sure I've got a goose egg the size of Maine on the side of my head. I prod at it gently, and a throbbing pain pulses through my skull. I sit up slightly to inspect my surroundings and find that I have been lying on a bed of those ghostly gray flowers I saw growing along the road in the Wastelands. More flowers have been scattered on top of me. At first I think someone has placed me, with great care, in a bed of flowers to rest—but then I remember the Shade and his large bone club, and suddenly realize that perhaps this isn't a bed for sleeping. Perhaps I am the protein portion in a bed of greens—a meal for a hungry Shade.

I sit up quickly. Too quickly. My head swims.

It's dark. The only light source is a flickering torch a few feet away. I try to push myself to my knees, but my left one aches so much I can't support my own weight in a kneeling position. The fall from the chariot must have done some real damage. I hobble to a standing position and put my weight mostly on my right leg. So far, no one has protested my movements, so I pray I am alone.

I hear the drip of water in the distance.

I half hop, half limp toward the torch. I pull it from its perch and use it to inspect my surroundings and discover what I had already suspected. I am in a cave.

Stalactites and stalagmites surround me like great, jagged teeth, and I feel as though I am standing inside the jaws of some great beast. Considering I'm trapped in the underworld, I wouldn't be too surprised if that were the case. Swinging the torch back and forth, I limp away from the sound of dripping water and search for an exit.

It strikes me that in my effort to run away, I had only exchanged my queenly prison cell for a far less comfortable one.

What was it my humanities teacher had said about Greek myths? That they were invented to teach us mere mortals that the more we fight our destiny, the more we bring it upon ourselves. *Perhaps this is the Underrealm's way of telling me it's never going to let me go?*

I shake off the thought. Now is not the time for negative thinking. *There has to be a way out.*

I slide my hand along the cave wall for support and hobble along for another couple of minutes. I am about to turn back and head in the other direction when I see a circular crack of light up ahead. I move closer. Sunlight—or whatever you call the Underrealm equivalent—streams in through a narrow crack around what I realize is the cave entrance. A twelve-foot-tall boulder has been rolled in front to block the opening.

I hear a grunt from somewhere nearby and swing my torch in that direction. The large Shade who took me captive lies curled up and sleeping in a nestlike bed only a few feet away.

I pull the light away, not wanting to wake him, and inspect the boulder. I push at it with my hands, even lean my shoulder into it, but it's too large. There's no way I can move it by hand. But I might be able to move it with my voice . . .

I take a step back and glance at the sleeping Shade. The moment I start singing, he's going to wake, which means I need to be fast. I pat my aching knee and hope adrenaline will be enough to push me through the pain.

Concentrating, I close my eyes and listen for the tone of the boulder. All I hear is the drip, drip, drip, of water and a skittering sound of something like a rat.

How big are rats in the underworld?

I take a deep breath. If the boulder won't sing for me, then I will have to make it listen. I think of the words to the grove's song; that one seemed to have the best effect. I brace myself, readying to run, and open my mouth to sing.

No sound comes out.

Damn it!

I can guess where I am now. I'd bet just about anything we are in the network of caves beyond the pomegranate grove. And I'd double that bet and guess that this particular cave runs through the royal grounds. Which means my powers don't work here.

Perhaps if I turn back and follow the cave, I could find another exit? Perhaps cross into another cave that would lead me off royal land? But that could take days, according to what the boy had told me about this place.

Wishing I'd eaten a bigger breakfast, I turn away from the boulder, and set off in the opposite direction. I only get four gimpy steps when a moaning groan echoes off the cavern walls. I try to run, but the Shade is too quick.

It grabs me by the arms. The torch drops from my hands and nearly starts my skirt on fire. The Shade lifts me away from the licking flame and throws me over his shoulder. The next thing I know, it has thrown me back down on the bed of flowers.

The Shade points a too-long finger at me and lets out a moan that sounds like it is scolding me. Then I notice it, the sound coming out of its gaping mouth isn't just a moan. There are words.

"Yoooou staaaaay!" it orders. "Yoooou staaayyy."

"Okay. I stay," I say, trying to placate him. "I stay."

The Shade cocks its head. If it had eyes, I'd say it was staring at me. It drops down to a squatting position, so it is closer to my level. "Yoooou underrrstand?" it moans.

"Yes." I nod. "I understand. I stay." I pat the flower bed to show him I'm not planning on moving anytime soon.

"Howww?" The Shade moves in closer, for a second I think it's about to climb on top of me. I tense, readying to fight it off, as it reaches its gangly gray hand toward my chest. Its fingers almost brush the pomegranate necklace Garrick had insisted I wear on our journey, but then the Shade snaps its hand away. It scurries back a few feet, and huddles against the cave wall. It reaches a hand out, gesturing in a way that seems to indicate my necklace. "Howww? Howww?"

"My necklace?" I ask.

It nods its head up and down. "Howww?"

"How did I get this?" I ask, hazarding a guess. "My . . . um . . . the King gave it to me."

"Yoouu Kooorrree?" it asks in a way that I might describe as excitedly—but it's hard to tell without facial features. "Beeelong to Kooorree. Youuu Koreeee?"

The Shade sounds as if it's making a better effort to enunciate, but I still don't understand what he's asking.

"Youuu Koooree?" it says, seeming agitated now.

I say the word to myself, trying to figure out what he means. It sounds like it's saying Kory or kohr-ee. "Kore?" I finally ask, remembering where I'd heard that word before. It means "maiden" in Ancient Greek. Another name for the goddess of the underworld. "You mean, Persephone?"

"Yesss." It comes a little closer. "Youu herr?"

"No, I am not Persephone."

It makes an imperceptible grunting noise and rocks back so it's sitting on the ground. "She's gone?"

I nod. "I was told she left a long time ago."

The Shade clasps its hands on top of its head and moans. It's a terrible noise.

"Were you saying this necklace belonged to her?" I say lifting the pendant.

It shakes its head up and down while rocking back and forth. I don't like the idea of making it upset. "How do you know? Did you know her?"

"Yes," the Shade says. "I think I knewww her."

My mouth drops slightly open and it really sinks in that Shades are not just monsters, they're the souls of the dead. The ones who die without so-called honor, and are doomed to haunt the wastelands instead of going to the paradise of Elysium, where dead heroes dwell. "How much do you remember from your former life?" I had been under the impression that the dead had their memories wiped. Haden's mother, who I had met during my very brief stay in Elysium, had no memory of her son or who she was before she died.

"Not much," the Shade says, rocking forward on its knees. "I think . . . I think I was herrrr manservant. She wassss my queen."

"Do you have a name?" I ask him—finding it comforting to think of the Shade as a *him* instead of an it.

"Not that I remember." He seems to look at me. He indicates the diamond laurel leaf crown on my head. If it hadn't been pinned so thoroughly into my hair by the women who dressed me, I am sure I would have lost it by now. "Yoouu new queen?"

"Um, kind of?" I hesitate, realizing this might buy me some leverage with Persephone's servant, then revise my answer. "I mean, yes."

He rocks forward and shoves one fist against the cave floor and bows his head. "New queeen. New goddess. I am yourrr servant."

I almost sputter with surprise, but end up keeping it together. "I don't know about the goddess part," I say under my breath as I stand, but this is definitely a welcome turn of events. For the first time in days, I feel truly hopeful. "Okay, Slim Shady, how about you roll away that boulder over there and help your new queen hightail it out of here?"

"Youu in trouble?" he asks. "Those men chase you? They wwwant to hurt you?"

"Yes," I say, hoping to gain a little sympathy. "That's why I need your help to get out of here."

"No!" he roars and bursts to his feet so suddenly that it leaves me shaking. He grabs my arms. "You stay! You no go. Too dangerous. Your servant protect you. Your servant keep you." He pushes me down until I'm seated once more on the cave floor. "Eat," he says.

"You want to eat me?" I say, my voice shaking.

"I no eat queen," he says. "Youuu eat those!" He points at the flowers. I can tell by the tone of his voice that he won't take no for an answer.

I pick up one of the flowers and raise it to my lips. I tentatively take a bite of one of its gray petals. A taste similar to black licorice stings my swollen tongue. At least it stopped bleeding while I was unconscious.

"Like?" Shady asks.

"Mmmm," I say, making a show of enjoying the bitter flower.

"Good," he says. "I go now. You stay. Be safe."

He heads toward the entrance to the cave.

"Wait," I call, scrambling to follow.

I'm too slow. By the time I make it there on my injured leg, he has already moved away the boulder, exited, and sealed me back inside.

"When are you coming back?" I shout.

No answer comes from the other side.

Crap balls, I think as my leg gives out and I sink to the ground, no longer able to stand. *I could be stuck in here forever.*

chapter eleven

HADEN

I sit at Joe's kitchen counter, holding my hands over my ringing ears. Brim is draped over my shoulder purring, but I don't have the heart to tell her that her usually soothing habit is only making me more nauseous.

Lexie slides a steaming cup of brown liquid in front of me. It at least looks and smells more pleasant than the noxious concoction of tomato juice, raw egg, and hot sauce that Joe tried to ply me with a few minutes ago. "Hot chocolate," she says. "From Olympus Brew. I also brought you a couple of pumpkin chocolate-chip cookies from the bakery. I remember Daphne saying something once about you having a sweet tooth."

"Thank you," I grunt.

"Carbs and chocolate—good for whatever ails ya. Most people might disagree, but hot chocolate is my preferred hangover cure. It will help with the dehydration and hypoglycemia that come from puking so much. Or maybe that's just my excuse, since I don't allow myself sugar on a regular basis."

"Hangover? Is that what this is?" Another wave of nausea hits me and I look away from the cookies even though they're my favorite.

"Plus, you know, chocolate is a mood lifter, so maybe if you eat enough, you'll stop being such a cranky-pants."

"Mmph," is all I can manage.

I have little to no memory of the last few hours. As far as I know, I could have traveled through a time portal from the moment we were standing in front of the window talking about Terresa to when I was huddled over the toilet, losing everything I had managed to eat since returning from the Underrealm.

"How bad was I this time?" I ask.

"Not too bad. You did try to make out with a ficus, but I'm pretty sure that kissing a plant won't invalidate your cure. Mostly, you just barfed. A lot."

"What did Jonathan dose me with this time?" *And why does it feel so much worse than last time?*

"It was a dart that was supposed to make you punch drunk, not much different than the giddiness spell, but it seemed to hit your system pretty hard."

It's probably because I've never been *any kind* of drunk before. I'd never been held in high enough esteem to be offered ale at any of the Underrealm feasts—even the one when I captured and killed the hydra. Rowan had taken the credit and had been allowed to drink from the king's cup, not me. On many occasions, I'd watched other Underlords become intoxicated on rich food and drink, and I never really saw the appeal.

I stifle a foul-tasting burp.

My opinion on the matter still hasn't changed.

I break a piece off a cookie and take a nibble. The sweetness is a preferable substitute for the taste in my mouth. Brim sniffs at the cookie from my shoulder, so I let her have a bite as well. "I thought Jonathan was going to ration the darts one per day," I say after a few bites.

"Well, when you started ranting about not being able to feel anything and then tried to put your hand through the studio window, we didn't really have a choice."

I flex my bandaged hand. It sends sharp twinges of pain up my arm. I never thought I'd be grateful for such a sensation. But at the same time, it makes me worry. The others had meant well by dosing me, and I am sure they did what they thought was best in the moment, but it only makes things more bleak in the long run. Jonathan is now down to only three darts. Only two of which are usable before we reunite him with his bow. There is no way I could ask him to use the last one before then, knowing what will happen if he loses his immortality.

"Plus, none of us were too thrilled with the tantrum you threw," Lexie says with a forced chuckle. "You're pretty strong for a toddler."

"Toddler?" I don't know this word. I look up at Lexie, meeting her eyes for the first time, and my query falls away when I see the purple bruise that sits under her skin, marring her right cheekbone. I avert my eyes, knowing the mark must have been my fault.

"I'm sorry," I say, the words almost sticking in my throat. Apologies are not something Underlords are taught to ever give, but that's not the reason the words are hard to choke out. I don't believe I deserve to be forgiven.

I was raised a warrior, taught to fight from a very young age. I've done far worse, intentionally, to my fellow Underlords, but the idea that the black poison caused me to harm someone while not in my right mind has me reeling with guilt.

I've become a danger to my allies.

What if I'd done worse? What if they can't restrain me next time?

What if it had been Daphne I had harmed?

"Just remind me to give you a ten-foot radius the next you start to lose it. That black poison sure makes you bonkers." She pushes the hot chocolate closer to me. Her words and gesture aren't exactly an acceptance of my apology, but at least she does not seem to hate me.

I pick up the cup of hot chocolate, welcoming the feeling of the heat against my bandaged hand. The steam warms my face and the smell only makes my stomach swish a little. If this is going to help me get back on my feet, then I need to get it over with.

"Tobin always loved Olympus Brew," Lexie says, her voice sounding lower than before.

"I didn't realize you were . . . close." Then again, I had started getting a strange feeling about the two of them after the Valentine's dance.

"We used to be." She sniffs. "A long time ago. And then I messed things up. I wanted to be popular, so I chose different people over him. Now that he's gone . . . I wish I'd made a different choice."

"I know how that feels." There are so many choices I wish I could change right now. I break off half a cookie and push it toward her. I want to say something like "we'll get him back" or "I'm sure he's going to be fine," but I don't want to make a promise I'm not sure I can keep. "The best thing we can do is stick with the plan to find a way back into the Underrealm. On that note, I guess I had better figure out a way to negotiate with Terresa."

"Speaking of which," Lexie says after taking a nibble of the cookie. "I made some headway in that regard while you were busy praying to the porcelain goddess."

"To the what?"

"Toilet, duh. While you were barfing your guts out I had a little chat with our resident lieutenant of crazy town, and I struck a new deal."

I look at her in shock. "What? How? What?"

"Well, first I tried just telling her the truth. That if you kiss her, you'll die. She started crying hysterically."

"Oh, good thinking," I say, lifting the cup of hot chocolate to my mouth. Why hadn't I thought of that right off?

"Yeeeah, turns out not so much. I thought that might have worked since, you know, she's supposedly in love with you, but then being a total psychopath and all, she started blubbering, 'I'd rather have one perfect passionate kiss with Haden and lose him forever, than to have never kissed him at all.'"

I almost choke on a sip of hot chocolate. It burns my throat.

"And that, kids," Joe calls from the pantry where he's been rooting around for something to make for dinner, "is why you should never base a relationship on passion alone. It's never the real thing."

"Says the man who married a woman after only knowing her for thirty minutes," Jonathan says from the kitchen entrance. I wonder how long he's been standing there, listening. It feels awkward talking about matters of the heart with Cupid hanging around.

"Hey, there was more to it than that!" Joe says from the pantry.

Half a second later, Joe's cell phone starts playing a tune from where it lies on the counter next to an open container of tomato juice. I see the name "Demi Raines" pop up on the screen.

Daphne's mother. In all the turmoil, I hadn't thought to ask what had happened to her after the night of the play. I pick up the phone.

"Speak of the devil," Lexie says with a smirk.

"Do not answer that!" Joe says, running out of the pantry with an armload of goods.

He drops a box of waffle cones and a jar of something called caviar on the counter—making me wonder what exactly he's planning on preparing for dinner—and snatches the phone out of my hands. He hits an icon to send it voicemail, and then leans into the counter with a heavy sigh.

"Why aren't you answering her calls?" Jonathan says. "That's the fifth time she's called today. You're going to have to talk to her eventually."

"Nuh uh. Not yet." Joe shakes his head violently. "The longer I can keep the truth from her, the better."

"You mean seventeen years wasn't long enough?" There's a growl to Jonathan's usually jovial voice, and I realize that at some point during the last few days, Joe must have filled Jonathan in on the full story concerning how Daphne had gotten involved with the Underrealm because of his deal with my father. Circumstances considered, I think Jonathan's been holding in his anger—toward Joe and me—extremely well.

I can sympathize with Joe's reluctance to answer Demi's calls. However, if the mother is anything like the daughter, he isn't going to get away with keeping the truth from her much longer.

"Hey, *you're* not answering her calls either," Joe says defensively to Jonathan.

"I promised Daphne I'd make sure her mother got out of town safely. The rest of it is your responsibility."

I vaguely remember now that after Jonathan left the fight between Ethan's men and the Skylords—wounded and nearly out of arrows—he had gone to assure that Joe and Demi had made it safely out during the town's evacuation. Not wanting to show his injury to Demi, Jonathan had instructed Joe to put her on one of the mayor's shuttles to an evacuation center in the next town over and to buy her bus tickets back to Utah for the morning. While I'm relieved that she's on her way back to the safe haven of Ellis Fields, where the Skylords can't touch her, I can see why she'd be frantically calling to see if Daphne is safe.

Not that I want to be the bearer of bad news, either.

Joe's phone starts ringing in his hand. He almost drops it while trying to hit the decline icon. This time, I think I recognize the tune. Perhaps I am mistaken, but I am almost certain the ringtone he's set for Daphne's mother is one of his band's more melancholy love songs.

"*Anyway,* since none of you all are going to woman up and tell the truth to Daphne's mom, I might as well get on with my story," Lexie says. "We are working against a ticking time bomb, so to speak." She hitches her thumb in my direction.

"The floor is yours," Joe says, switching off his phone and tucking it in his back pocket.

"So after I got Terresa to stop crying, I told her that Haden would be so eternally grateful to her for helping us rescue Persephone from the Black Hole that Haden would give her the most passionate kiss any girl has ever been the recipient of . . . So she has to wait until *after* the rescue mission."

"And that helps Haden not die how?" Joe asks. Which was my thought exactly, but somehow it felt selfish to ask.

Lexie leans forward and lowers her voice to whisper as if she is worried that Terresa may overhear her from all the way upstairs. "It helps when you ditch her psycho ass in the Skyrealm and make a break for it."

I blink at her. "You're ruthless, has anyone ever told you that?"

"Only on a bi-weekly basis," she says, inspecting her fingernails. "I didn't get to be the leader of the Sopranos on looks alone, you know."

"She'll take us, then?" I ask. "She agreed?"

"Yes . . . Only there's one more caveat I haven't mentioned . . ." Lexie drops her hand at her side.

I lean toward her on the edge of my barstool. "That being?"

"She wants a bigger fish."

"A bigger fish?" I ask, completely confused. "As in, a salmon?"

Lexie shakes her head. "You really suck with expressions, huh? Anyway, she doesn't want to be implicated in Persephone's escape, and she wants some insurance to cover her butt when the Sky King goes into hysterics over losing his favorite prisoner. Which means she wants a big fish—or a big prize—to be able to offer up to the big honcho in the sky."

"Me?" Jonathan says grimly. "I am on his most hated list, after all."

"I'm not going to let that happen," I say. Daphne would never forgive me if something happened to Jonathan on my watch.

"Good," Lexie says, "because that's not who she wants."

"Who, then?" I ask, "because I'm not willing to trade over Ethan either. We need him to go up against the Keres."

Lexie looks at me. "Your father."

"Ren?" In my ever swinging emotional state, I keep forgetting that my father is here in this very house. Drugged and sleeping in the servant's wing of the mansion. I haven't exactly been in an emotionally stable enough position during the last few hours to want to go in and see him. "She wants to keep my father as a permanent prisoner?"

The plan involves Terresa taking me, Jonathan, and Ethan as fake prisoners into the Black Hole where we can facilitate a breakout—hopefully with Persephone in hand—but we would be leaving my father behind at the mercy of the Sky King? For the last three months—*kopros*, for most of my life—I've seen my father as the enemy, and I also know he's no longer technically the king of my realm, and even though there is no love lost between us, it still feels treasonous to him both as my father and my former ruler to entertain the idea of handing him over to the Skylords.

But Daphne's life is hanging in the balance. And she is in danger not only because of me, but because of the deal my father made to own her soul. He was the one who brought this terrible destiny on her.

"All right," I say. "We give her my father then."

"Are you sure?" Jonathan asks. "The Sky King is known for his talents with torture . . ."

I nod my head before he can go on. "At least Terresa will get one of her demands. I only hope we can trust her."

"We can as long as the passion spell doesn't wear off in the meantime," Jonathan says, "and she still wants that kiss."

"Is that a risk?" I ask. "How soon will it wear off?"

"My arrows are far more potent than my emotion darts, but the subject is the determining factor. It's like the flu. One person may be able to bounce back after a few days, where it takes another person several weeks. Let's just hope she has a poor immune system, so to speak."

"We should get going," I say, lifting my cup of hot chocolate to take it on the road.

"Not so fast," Joe says, mixing what look like minuscule black beads into a bowl of raw chicken eggs. I can't help wondering if he knows any more about cooking than I do. "I'm making dinner here."

Jonathan puts his hand on my arm as if telling me to wait. "Ethan is gathering supplies. The gate to the Skyrealm is at least half a day's journey from here. Based on your last two experiences with the darts, it takes about three hours after an injection before you start to act, um, lucid again. You then seem to have another three to four hour window of rational behavior before the black poison starts to adversely affect you again. We'll leave after dinner and travel as far as the gate. There, we'll make camp, wait for the best time to dose you again, and then wait off the *crazier* effects before crossing into the Skyrealm. This should assure us the most optimal window of performance on your part when we infiltrate the palace. Once I have my bow restored, I will be able to make more. But again, both darts and arrows are only temporary treatments. Nothing I can shoot you up with will be an antidote without Daphne."

I nod. "I understand."

I also understand that if something goes wrong, if Ethan's intel is wrong about the bow's location, or if we can't make it there in time, I may very well not be returning from this trip.

"Oh and BTW," Lexie says, polishing off my last cookie, "Terresa has dibs on carrying you."

"Carrying me?"

"To the Skygate. In the sky, obviously," Jonathan says. "We'll be cloud-walking there. Since my wings were clipped long ago, Ethan will have to carry me—which means Terresa will be your ride."

"Lovely," I say, imagining fending off Terresa's advances while being carried through the air in her arms. If I protest too much, she might decide to drop me.

The front door opens and closes, and I hear footsteps coming toward the kitchen.

"Ethan must be back with the supplies," I say, but when I look up, it's not just Ethan who has entered the kitchen. He's accompanied by a very tall female, with long blond hair, and brilliant blue eyes—Daphne's doppelganger.

"You have a visitor, Joe," Ethan says nonchalantly as he places a duffle bag on the counter.

Joe swings around from the stove with a bowl and a whisk in his hand.

The bowl hits the ground. Yolky black beads splatter across the tile at his feet.

"Demi?" he says.

"Where the hell is my daughter?" she demands.

chapter twelve

DAPHNE

I sit beside the boulder that blocks the cave entrance with a large rock cradled in my hands. Shady has to come back at some point, which means I need to be ready to try to get past him. That's what the rock is for. When he rolls away the boulder to duck back inside, I'll hit him over the head and escape through the opening.

Only, it's been hours—maybe even more than a day—since he left me here, and I'm starting to wonder if he's *ever* coming back. Maybe he's forgotten about me? Maybe he's decided I'm too much of a bother? No, he has to come back. This cave is obviously his home. I'd spent a good long while staring at his well-worn nest before the torch burned out, and there was something in one of the corners that looked (and smelled) like a compost heap filled with rotting vegetation and picked-clean bones—luckily none of which looked large enough to have come from a human. More like from small, birdlike creatures. Once the torch flickered out, the light that peeked from behind the boulder was my only source of illumination. But now even that has faded away. It must be night, because it's as dark as pitch in the cave.

I'm shivering, shaking from the cold, and I shrug deeper into my golden cloak. It's ripped and tattered from my fall from the chariot, but I am grateful for what little protection it offers against the night air. I'd thought about using the torch to start a campfire before it burned out, but then had visions of dying of smoke inhalation. Isn't that what happens if you light a fire in an enclosed space?

I'd never considered myself to be claustrophobic, but the darkness pressing in around me makes me wonder if I am. My stomach clenches with hunger. I finished off the gray flowers hours ago. No wonder Shades are so hungry, if that's their primary food source.

No wonder they came running the second they smelled fresh meat . . .

I shudder and run my hands over the rock I intend to use as a weapon and start to second guess my plan. Shady saved my life after all—twice, actually, if you count not only dragging me away from those Shades at the dock, but also feeding me.

I'll starve if he doesn't come back . . . And hitting him in the head doesn't seem like the best repayment. Maybe I can try reasoning with him?

Can you reason with the dead?

Shady did seem far more cognizant than I had given any of the Shades credit for. I didn't even know they could speak.

My tongue is thick and dry. It has started to throb again. I bit it deep when my head hit the dock. I listen to the drip, drip, drip noise coming from farther back in the cavern. It's enough to drive a person crazy when it's the only sound that seems to exist. Especially for someone who has spent her whole life immersed in music. I listen harder beyond the dripping noise, trying to hear any sound that might indicate that Shady is on his way back. I may not be able to do anything about my hunger on my own, but there is something I can do about my thirst. Only I haven't been able to will myself to do it, for fear of missing my opportunity to escape.

I listen until I can't stand it any longer. There's no way of hearing anything on the other side of the boulder, and my thirst is driving me insane.

I drop the rock, leaving it behind because I need my hands to navigate through the darkness. Near the entrance, the wall of the cave is dry and dusty against my sliding hand, but that eventually gives way to a damp, slick, yet crusty surface that makes me think of a shower that hasn't been cleaned in years. My injured knee aches even more as I walk, stiff from sitting so long. I worry it's more than a bruise or a sprain; perhaps a partially torn ligament. I follow the dripping noise, glad for a keen sense of hearing, until I feel my way to what sounds like a pool. Water drips from a stalactite above, filling it. I sit next the pool, and stick my fingers tentatively in the water—hoping beyond hope there's nothing living in there.

What I find is that the pool is only a few inches deep. A few hours ago, I may have deemed this an unsanitary option, but now I cup some water in my hands and bring it to my mouth. It tastes minerally to say the least, but the cold water is so soothing on my parched tongue and throat that I suck it down and go for another helping.

After I've had my fill, it strikes me that at the rate the water is dripping from above, this pool should be deeper . . . which means it must have an outlet! I stick my hand in the water and feel the slight pull of a current. It flows to the right side of the pool. I hear it then, the slight trickling noise of a small stream of water. It's even darker here than at the entrance of the cave, but I don't let that stop me. If the water is flowing somewhere, that means there is somewhere for it to go. I abandon my plan of waiting for Shady to return and decide to explore the cave instead, like I had wanted to before Shady stopped me the first time.

His words, "Stay here. Too Dangerous," echo in my mind as I follow the trickling stream in the dark. I can't help thinking of that noise I heard earlier that sounded like a rather large rat, or something worse. But I keep going. The cave wall is gradually curving off to the right, as if following the small stream. My already cold feet ache every time a false step lands in the frigid water. The gladiator-style sandals Garrick provided for me are sturdier than my ballet flats had been, but not any warmer. Has no one ever heard of socks and hiking boots in the underworld?

The stream starts to narrow, the water trickling faster, by the sound of it. I pick up my pace, moving as fast as I am physically able in the dark. *This has to be another way out.*

The sound of the trickling changes slightly. More like a gurgle. I get closer to the ground, listening. I hear then what makes the difference. The water has shifted from flowing across the ground and is now flowing down. Like through a drain. I feel the ground with my hands. There's a crack in the cave floor. Not even wide enough to stick my hand in all the way. I slam my fist against the crack, splashing water away from me. The stream is escaping through an outlet—but not one I can follow.

But that doesn't mean there isn't another way out.

I stand once more, using the cave wall for support. I follow its curving path for another few yards. I keep one hand against the wall and the other one stretched out in front of me, feeling for obstacles. When my fingers touch something hard and cold in front of me, I know it's all over. There's a barrier, some sort of wall blocking the path in front of me. This is the end of the line.

But as I start to turn back, I realize—it's not a wall of stone.

I use both hands to feel in front of me. There's a barrier blocking my path. But it's not a vertical wall, and it's not a solid surface. It's . . . It's a pile.

From the feel of it, the pile is made of all sorts of things. Wood, metal, cloth. *Bone?*

I snap my hand back. I reach it out again tentatively and touch the smooth object once more. My fingers wrap around it and I pull. It takes a good yank, but the object comes free from the pile. Smoothing my fingers over it, I realize it's not bone (thank goodness) but a small statue, a figurine of some sort. It's in the shape of a woman but it's missing one of its arms. I feel for another object and find what seems to be some sort of medallion with a broken chain. There are scraps of cloth, and another object turns out to be a cracked wooden wheel. *It's a pile of junk.*

Perhaps Shady is a hoarder?

I start pulling more objects from the pile, hoping for something that might make a more useful weapon than a rock, or perhaps something that will keep me warm. My hand closes on something soft but stiff. I pull it closer to me and find that my fingers have closed around the brim of a hat.

Not just any hat. A short-brimmed fedora.

Like the one Tobin had been wearing the last time I'd seen him. Just before the boat crash.

I clasp the fedora to my chest. "Tobin?" I shout. It's a long shot, I know. But Tobin is never without his hat. "Tobin?" I call again, my voice echoing through the cavern.

I hear movement, the shifting of weight against the cave floor. Someone or something is coming closer in the dark.

"Tobin?" I say, a little more tentatively than before.

A gurgling growl answers me. Two small, glowing circles appear in the darkness. Then another pair. And then a third. Glinting animal eyes. Three pairs of them coming closer, moving as if in unison. I back up instinctively, only to find my way blocked once more by the giant pile of junk.

I'm at a dead end. And that most definitely *isn't* Tobin.

chapter thirteen

TOBIN

"Let's jump in!" *Alexis says with a giggle. She stands at the edge of the swimming pool, wearing jeans and a T-shirt that says* This is not the Princess you are looking for *on the front.*

"We don't have swimsuits," *I whisper to her, because I'm afraid we're going to get caught. This isn't either of our pools. We've just snuck away from what has to be the most boring party in the world. All anyone wanted to talk about was the latest football game.*

"Swimsuits, schwimsuits," *she says.* "Don't be a wuss, Tobin."

"I'm not a wuss, I just don't like getting in trouble."

"I am pretty sure that is the definition of wuss." *Alexis gives me a devious smirk. Then she grabs her nose and jumps into the pool, making a huge splash.*

"Shhh!" *I say, when she comes up to surface giggling.*

"Come in!" *she says, swimming up closer. Water drips from her eyelashes.*

"I don't want to get my clothes wet," *I say. My mom had insisted I wear a suit to the party—which means I showed up looking like the world's biggest dork.*

Alexis laughs and pushes the water in front of her, drenching me with a huge splash. "There," *she says.* "You're already wet, so you don't have any excuse anymore, wussy boy."

I'm standing there in my drenched clothing and for a second my temper flashes hot, but then Alexis leans into a back stroke, still giggling. The fabric of her wet shirt rides up a couple of inches, exposing the skin on her stomach. I feel hot for a very different reason and glance away.

Another splash hits my shoes. "Come in," *she calls.*

The next thing I know, I'm tearing off my shoes and jumping into the pool in my dress-suit, tie and all. I go deep under the water, holding my breath. Alexis swims over to me, smiling. She grabs me by my tie, pulling me closer.

"Kiss me," she says, bubbles floating out of her mouth under the water.

I lean in closer and she grins. I close my eyes, hoping I don't mess up my first kiss . . .

But then nothing happens. I open my eyes and Alexis is gone. I am in an otherwise empty pool. Darkness closes in on me . . .

And I'm drowning.

I wake gasping for air, when a man bursts into the room. No, a boy, I realize as he gets closer. He can't be any older than I am.

Wait, how old am I?

"She got away!" he shouts. "She must have planned this! How could she have planned this?"

Who got away? Alexis . . . Lexie? I blink at him, feeling groggy. His black cloak is torn and there's a smear of what must be dried blood on his cheek. I don't know who this *she* is that he's ranting about.

He advances on me and grabs the top of my chair. "We told you we'd put the punishment on you. We told you we'd make you scream and beg for mercy. We told you you'd pay if she didn't take us to the Key." He shoves his face so close to mine, I can smell his rank breath. "We could blast you until your eyeballs explode. We could fry your skin until it's crispy and falls off your bones. What do you think about that, mortal?"

I blink at him again. What was it he said about crispy skin? Was he talking about KFC?

"We're waiting, Tobin," he snarls. "Start begging for mercy."

"I'm sorry, who are you?" I say through a yawn, wishing he'd let me go back to sleep. "And who's Tobin? Did you say something about chicken?"

The boy roars in frustration, his spittle spraying my face. *What did I say?*

"Dude, you need to brush your teeth, bro," I say. Then wonder why I can't lift my arm to wipe my face.

The boy kicks my chair. "What good is torturing someone who can't remember they're being tortured?"

"Who said anything about torture? I thought we were going to have chicken?"

He stomps away to the door and calls for guards. Two *men* enter the room, both carrying swords.

"Cut him free," the boy orders.

The guards advance on me with their weapons drawn. I wonder why they would listen to the orders of a boy. One stabs his blade into one of the armrests of the chair I sit in. The second guard follows his lead with the other side of the chair. I watch, amused, as they hack at the armrests, and I feel sleepy. I have almost forgotten they were even there until they start yanking on my arms. A strange pain grips my elbows and wrists, as if the chair doesn't want to let me go. *I'm fine with staying*, I think, but then I am free.

They pull me from the chair, and try to place me on my feet. My legs waver as if it has been days since I last stood. One of the men grips me tight, holding me up by the shoulder.

A boy in a torn black cloak and a bloodstained face stands in front of me. *Where did he come from?*

"Where do you want him?" one guard asks.

"On his knees," the boy says. He holds out both of his hands—they're encircled by spheres of what looks like blue lightning. "We want to hear him beg."

The guards push me to my knees. I don't try to fight them because I still don't know what's going on. Is this part of my dream?

"That will be all," the boy says to the guards. Once they're gone, the door closed behind them, the boy steps forward. He clasps his hands into fists and the spheres of blue light disappear as if he extinguished them. I can't help sighing with relief.

"Don't get comfortable yet. We're just going to start slow. Mortals are fragile, after all." He extends his index finger, pointing it at my face. I tense, feeling my eyes widen, as a wisp of blue lighting crackles around his fingertip. He lowers it and jabs his finger into my left shoulder. At first it feels like a little shock, like when you rub your feet on the carpet, and then it grows in intensity. Aching, bursting pain surges down my arm and into my chest. My heart beats so hard it feels like it might break through my ribcage.

Unable to hold it back any longer, I scream.

The boy pulls his finger away. A smirk of delight mars his face.

Sweat puckers up from my pores. I'm panting hard. Just as the pain starts to dissipate, the boy jabs my shoulder again. I don't even try to hold back this time. I scream because it helps ease the pain.

When he pulls back a second time, I fall forward. My left arm is locked up, unable to move, and I barely catch myself with my right hand before my nose slams into the stone floor. "Why are you doing this?" I ask through gritted teeth.

"I'm merely trying to jog your memory." He shocks me again.

I writhe against the ground, my face grinding into the stone. "Who are you?" I ask, bloody saliva dripping from my mouth. He pulls away again. "What do you want from me?"

"You still don't remember?" he says, looming over me. "Do you need another jog?"

"No," I shake my head and roll onto my back. I look up at him from my prone position. I force myself to concentrate through the fog that seems to coat my brain. His face comes into focus. I do know him. We're friends . . . No, allies? There was a gate. A girl. *She* was my friend. I came to help her, and so did . . ."Garrick?"

"Very good," he says. "We knew it would come back to you."

"Why are you doing this? I thought we were on the same team?" I blink rapidly as my mind begins to race. A flood of lost memories hits me like a wrecking ball, and I can barely breathe. I remember Abbie, Sage, my parents, Lexie, Daphne . . . Then the last few days flash through my mind. I remember falling from the boat, almost drowning, being fished from the water by a pack of

Shades and then rescued by a troop of Underlord soldiers. They brought me to their palace. I was brought before their new king . . .

I look at Garrick good and hard, as if really seeing him for the first time. He seems taller all of a sudden, wider. As if I had only ever seen him slouching before. He is dressed like royalty, if not a little worse for wear with the torn cloak and a dented breastplate. A crown of golden laurel leaves sits on his head.

"You're the king now," I say, remembering that first conversation. "You're the one who forced me into that chair. It made me forget . . . forget everything." *But why?* More memories tumble into my brain, and I know the answer. I drop my gaze from his kingly attire to his feet. From underneath his black and gold sandals, two shadows stretch across the marble floor. "You're working for the Keres," I say. "You've been working for them all along. You manipulated everyone, the entire situation, so you would come out on top. You made yourself the king. And now you're trying to get the Key so you can free all the Keres and destroy the Underlords . . . And from there . . ."

"And from there, take over the five realms," he says. "Very good. This will be so much easier now that we're all on the same page."

"What will be easier?"

"Making you pay for Daphne's betrayal." He crouches over me and before I can react, he touches his hands to both of my shoulders. It feels as though his fingers are daggers stabbing into my flesh, but I know it's the electricity. It spreads into my chest, and I can feel my heart rattling in my ribcage . . .

chapter fourteen

HADEN

"Where is she? Where the hell is Daphne?" Demi demands.

"Apt question considering the circumstances," Lexie whispers to me behind her hand. I'm confused for a second before I get that she's making a hell reference.

Daphne's mom places her hands on her hips, and I can see the resemblance to her Amazon warrior ancestors. She glares at Joe.

Joe takes a step back. "I thought you were on your way back to Utah?"

"You think I'd get on some bus to another state when I haven't heard a word from my daughter after a natural disaster? I sat up all night at the shelter trying to call her until my battery ran out. Had to borrow a charger from some kid this morning, and when I saw that I still hadn't gotten a response from Daphne, I started calling *you*," she says the word as if it were a slap in Joe's face. "I would have been here sooner if it weren't for that crazy mayor of yours. She wouldn't let anyone leave the shelter even though the storm has been over for hours. I had to bribe a security guard and spend a week's salary to get something called an Uber to give me a ride back into town now." She narrows her eyes at all of us, taking in the whisk Joe still holds aloft in his hand, dripping egg yolk on his expensive-looking shoes. "And how exactly did you all get back here so quickly?"

Joe stares at her, wild-eyed. He opens and closes his mouth in a way that reminds me of a fish.

"We . . . um . . . never left . . ." Jonathan says.

Demi's eyes widen as if she realizes for the first time that Jonathan is in the room. I imagine that in her rage, she had her sights set specifically on Joe. "And what are *you* doing here?" she asks. "Do you know how many times I've called to see what happened to you when we got split up after the play?"

"Spotty reception . . . at the hospital?" Jonathan offers.

"Hospital? Is Daphne . . ." She takes in his bandaged shoulder and arm sling, and her expression goes from anger to concern. "What happened? Are you okay?"

Jonathan nods. "Just a mild case of . . . getting struck by lightning." He chuckles as if it were no big deal.

Demi's mouth drops open in shock.

Jonathan raises his hand to reassure her he's fine. "I'm okay, really. Just a flesh wound. I went looking for Daphne after the play and had a minor run-in with a small lightning bolt. Daphne and Joe took me to the hospital. They make you turn off your cell phones . . . so that's why you couldn't get a hold of any of us."

"Uh . . . yeah. Hospital. No cell phone," Joe says, and then goes back to looking like a gaping fish.

"I'm glad you're okay, but I wish one of you had thought to pick up a courtesy phone and give me a call. I've been sick with worry," Demi says. "Where is Daphne now? I want to see her."

Joe and Jonathan exchange a look—as if each is silently trying to convince the other to answer the question. Jonathan shakes his head vehemently, letting Joe know it's his responsibility. In turn, Joe looks like he's about to have a panic attack.

Demi's expression starts to narrow again.

"Camping," Ethan says. He steps forward and offers his hand to Demi. "I'm sorry, I didn't introduce myself properly out front. I'm Mr. Bowman, Daphne's humanities teacher." He pulls his hand back when Demi doesn't take it. "We're just headed out on a school camping trip." He points at his duffle bag. "Daphne already left with an earlier group. You probably still can't get her on her cell phone because the reception is lousy in the mountains."

"If Daphne is already in the mountains, then why are you convening in Joe's house?" she asks, her expression becoming skeptical.

"Because . . ." I say. "Because . . . Joe volunteered to provide some snacks for the campers. We just stopped by to pick up the supplies. Isn't that right, Joe?"

"Yesss, that's right." Joe nods. Without taking his eyes off of Demi's glare, he picks up the box of waffle cones and grabs a can labeled "blue cheese stuffed kalamata olives" and hands them to me. "Here you go, kids. Have fun on that camping trip."

"Thanks, Mr. Vince," Lexie says, playing along. We all know that if Joe and Demi get into the truth while we're all still here, we could very well miss our window for heading to the Skyrealm. That's a fight that could last a century.

"Well, we had better get going," Jonathan says, picking up Ethan's duffle with his good arm. "We can get dinner on the road."

He starts backing away to the exit.

Demi whirls on him. "Wait, *you're* going on this camping trip?"

"Uh, yes. Joe wasn't feeling well so I volunteered to take his place as a parent chaperone. That's why I haven't headed back to Ellis yet. I'm sorry, I thought I texted you all of this."

Demi pulls a phone from her pocket. "Oh," she says, looking unsure of herself for the first time as she taps at it. I remember Daphne mentioning that her mom wasn't big on cell phones and technology because everything was within "shouting distance" in Ellis Fields. "I still haven't figured out how to properly use this fancy phone Daphne sent me for Christmas. She said it would cut down on my long-distance bills . . . But I don't know about this thing . . ." She looks up at Jonathan. "Wait, when did you guys have time to coordinate all this? And if you just got struck by lightning, why are you the one going camping?"

"Um, the doctor said that exercise and fresh air are the best medicine," Jonathan offers.

"What?" Demi's tone grows incredulous. "And why is the school going on a camping trip right after a natural disaster? Isn't most of the town still at the evacuation shelter? And . . . And . . ."

We can all see the whole story unraveling, our chance to leave for the Skyrealm about to slip away.

"The trip was prepaid. No refunds. We're bussing kids from the shelter. And now we had better be off," Ethan says in his most authoritative teacher voice before she can ask any more questions. "I would offer to have you along, Ms. Raines, but there's no more room in the car, and I am afraid you don't have the proper footwear for hiking," he says, indicating the thin sandals she wears.

"And Lexie, why don't you go get our *other* camper and help her out to the driveway?" He points up to the second floor.

Lexie nods and looks all too happy to extricate herself from this conversation as she heads off to collect Terresa from upstairs. Demi looks like she's in shock and not quite sure how to respond.

"Sorry to run out on you, hon," Jonathan says. "Joe will explain everything. And Haden, how about you go secure . . . I mean, see if our other parent volunteer is ready to go."

"Other parent volunteer?" I ask.

"Your father. He's coming with us, isn't he?"

"Oh, yes, him." A heaviness settles in my gut, and I worry I am about to get sick again. Or perhaps that feeling is the dread I feel at being in my father's presence once more, even if he is under a sleeping spell. I nod to Daphne's mother. "It was nice to see you again, Ms. Raines. I will tell Daphne you called and make sure she calls you back as soon as she is able," I say, hoping I'm not lying. I want more than anything for Daphne to be able to call her mother.

"But what about . . . What about . . . ?" Joe trails off like he doesn't even know what he was going to say. He looks more than stricken over the idea of being abandoned alone with Daphne's mom.

She, on the other hand, looks completely confused as everyone rushes out of the room.

"Thank you again for the supplies, Mr. Vince," I say, tucking Joe's contributions under my arm. I lean in close and whisper to him, "Give us a head start, and then *tell her*. If she's anything like Daphne, she'll be able to handle it better than you think."

I feel absolutely guilty leaving Joe behind, but also absolutely relieved that I won't have to see Demi's face when she hears the truth about her daughter's whereabouts.

Even running headlong into the Skyrealm, to infiltrate its most safeguarded prison, seems like the highly preferable option.

chapter fifteen

DAPHNE

Three sets of glinting eyes close in on me in the darkness. I try singing to ward them off, but I know it won't work even before it doesn't. I may be deeper in the cave, but I am still somewhere on the royal grounds. The eyes move closer. The sound of growling fills my ears. I grab something from the pile and chuck it as hard as I can at one of the pairs of eyes. I miss, but now the beasts are provoked. With a snarl, they charge. I grab the cracked wagon wheel from the pile and pull it on top of me like a shield. A second later, a great weight lands on the wheel. One of the beasts—no, all of them—are on top of it. I push against the wheel, trying to keep their clawing paws and snapping mouths away from me. One paw rakes my shoulder. Claws tear my flesh and I scream.

It echoes through the cavern, bouncing off the walls. But I know there's no magic to it like when I screamed at the Keres who had attacked my father. I still have no power. The beasts are undeterred. I hear the wagon wheel cracking, giving way under the beasts' weight. I hold it up with one shoulder and grab something else—the statue—from the pile and start frantically trying to beat the beasts back. I get in one good blow. Slamming the base of the figurine between one of the pairs of glowing eyes. I watch as the eyes fade to black. The other beasts screech. A moment later, a paw swipes the figurine from my hand, raking my wrist. I feel blood spurt from the wound, snaking down my arm. I'm bleeding much too quickly.

One of the beasts kicks against the wheel. I feel it finally snap, my only barrier falling away. I hunt for another weapon but only come up with the fedora.

One of the beasts snaps it from my grasp.

"Don't you dare!" I say, and let my hand fly, knocking the hat from its jaws.

The beast snarls at me. It's the noise of an animal that's not just hungry, but angry.

I'm done for.

Then a bright light fills the cavern. I close my eyes against it, raising my arm to fend off another attack, but instead all that follows is a flash of heat and two great squealing screams. Then a fainter pair of whimpers.

I open my eyes and find not three beasts, but one, lying dead or at least dying on the ground in front of me. It's a large animal whose body resembles a rat, except it's as large as wolf—and, you know, has three heads.

A hellrat?

Now I know why Haden's hellcat, Brimstone, can hulk out to the size of a panther on steroids. She'd have to if this is what their average rat looks like. It twitches, prostrate, a flaming torch protruding from its back.

In the light of the flickering deathtorch, I see Shady standing over the three-headed beast.

"Kore!" he moans at me. "I told you to stay. Tooo dangerous!"

"You're the one who left me alone in a cave with that thing," I shout back, even though it's an awfully ungrateful thing to say to someone who has saved my life for a third time now.

"Hellrats will not crossss water," he says. "You would have been ssssafe if yooou stayed."

"Well, you could have mentioned that before."

"That was whaaat 'stay here, toooo dangerous' was supposed to mean!"

I smirk. Maybe it is just my mind playing tricks on me—like that guy in *Castaway* who made friends with a volleyball—but it seems to me that Shady is starting to show a personality.

Shady grabs the beast by the legs and drags it away. He comes back a few moments later with the torch (not seeming to mind the blood dripping from the end of it) in one hand and a bundle of some sort under his other arm. He uses a couple of objects from the junk pile to prop up the torch and then places his bundle on the ground.

"You are bleeding," he says. He kneels next to me and pulls something from the bundle. A red cloak that reminds me of what one of the chariot drivers had been wearing. Shady tears the cloak into strips and wraps one tightly around my bleeding wrist. Then he uses another to bind my shoulder. I notice he turns his face from me as he works, as if either the sight or smell of my blood is bothersome to him.

Please don't mean it makes him hungry.

"You can see?" I ask. "And smell?"

I hope that's not an offensive thing to ask someone without facial features—other than a mouth, that is.

"I see without eyes," he says without giving any other clarification.

He moves to my knee next. After wrapping it in strips of cloth, he takes two thin pieces of wood from his bundle and places them on either side of my leg like splints. The wood is painted black with flecks of gold. Next he grabs a couple of lengths of leather that look like they were cut from a horse's reins. He uses them to strap the splints against my thigh and calf, supporting my injured knee.

"This is all stuff from the chariot crash?" I ask, noticing in his bundle what looks like a breastplate and helmet that must have belonged to one of the guards. "You went back there?"

Shady nods and finishes tying off one of the straps.

"Was he dead?" I ask, pointing at the soldier's helmet.

Shady nods again. "Him and one other. Torn apart by Shades."

"The other, was he a guard or a noble?"

Shady cocks his head to the side as if he doesn't understand the question.

"Was he dressed in black and gold?" I ask, thinking of Garrick. It's a callous thought, but if Garrick didn't survive the attack, then that might mean I was free of the binding spell and could leave the Underrealm without him.

I hold my breath until Shady shakes his head. "No."

"Oh," I say, not sure if I am relieved or not. An ill feeling creeps into my stomach. I can't believe I was hoping for someone else's death in exchange for my freedom. *Is this place changing me?* "You collect things?" I ask, gesturing at the pile.

Shady nods. He almost seems excited that I've asked about his collection.

"This hat," I say, lifting the fedora. There's a tear in the back of the brim from where the hellrat had tried to steal it. "When did you find it?"

"Few days ago."

I gasp. This hat has to be Tobin's. It even has the same periwinkle ribbon around the base. "Where? Was it with someone? Was there a boy . . . ?" I hesitate. "Was there a body?"

Shady is still for a moment. I hold my breath again. Finally he says, "No boy. No body."

I let out my breath, not sure if his words should make me more or less hopeful about Tobin's condition.

"There wasss a boat."

"A boat? You found this at a shipwreck, right?"

He nods.

This time I am hopeful. "Was there anything else there? Like a big golden staff with two prongs?" I say, trying to describe the Key of Hades. Maybe Shady found that too. Maybe the thing I had been looking for was right here in his hoarder's heap! "It's vitally important."

"Did not see staff."

I hang my head.

"Could have been, though. I fished hhhhat from water from my raft. Staff could have been in the boat. I could nnnnot get closer. Shades can nnnnot tread on Elysium shore."

I nod. My guide from Elysium had told me we were safe from Shades on its shores. That was after she had led me back to the shipwreck to look for Tobin and the Key. Both had been missing then, and from the sound of it, they had been gone when Shady happened upon it as well.

"I am sorry I could not assist youuu in this, Kore."

"It's okay. And you can call me Daphne." I pick at the bandage wrapped around my knee, feeling crippled more by doubt than my injuries. Tears start to well in the corners of my eyes. "There's probably nothing you could have done anyway. The Key is probably lost forever. It's probably at the bottom of the River of Woe with my best friend and that old man."

"Old man?"

I wipe at my eyes. "Charon. I think that's his name. The boatman. We found him unconscious at the docks near Persephone's Gate. There was a pack of Shades coming and I didn't want him to get eaten—no offense—so we took him with us. I couldn't find him after the crash. I can only assume he drowned."

"Charon cannot drown," Shady says. He's finished with my bandages and has started adding objects from his bundle to his pile. I can see now in the light of the torch that the heap is at least twelve feet high, and who knows how deep. "He hasss one of those." Shady pats his clavicle. I'm not sure what he's referring to, but before I can ask, he goes on. "It protects him from water. So he can do his job forever."

"Charon can't drown?"

The women of Elysium had told me I was alone when they found me. Tobin had disappeared, and Garrick had survived the crash and wandered off on his own. If the Key had still been there, Garrick would have taken it. I had assumed the old man had drowned—having been unconscious when the boat threw us out—but what if he'd been the first to recover? What if he took the Key? What if all I had to do to find it was find him? "Do you know Charon? Do you know where I can find him?" I try to stand but it's nearly impossible on my own, the way my leg is tied straight with the splint. "Can you take me to him?"

"I can." Shady grabs the torch.

"Good. Let's go."

"Can does nnnnot mean will." Shady crouches down and scoops me up in one arm. "You must recover. You must stay in cave. Too dangerous."

Shady carries me through the cave back to where my bed of flowers had been. I try to tell him why he needs to help me find Charon but it's like he has turned off his nonexistent ears. He deposits me on the ground.

"Food," he says, pointing at a pile of what looks like black turnips. "Blanket." He points at another red cloak he must have brought from the chariot wreckage. "Keep," he says, and points at the fedora I'm still clutching in my hands. "Stay. Be safe."

He leaves the torch propped against the large rock I had been planning on bashing him in the head with. He starts to roll away the boulder that blocks the entrance.

"Where are you going?" There's no point in trying to get up and follow him. It would take me fifteen minutes in my current state.

"Find herbs. I will make salve for your wounds. Hellrat venom issss deadly."

"Venom?" I ask, frantically. "Am I dying?"

Shady makes a strange guttural sound. At first I can't place it. Then I realize that he's laughing. "You're yanking my chain, aren't you?"

He nods, still laughing. "Hellrats do nnnnot have venom. Sorry, I could not helllp it. The look on your ffffaace . . . Mortals are quite expresssssive . . ." He trails off into laughter.

"Great. My Shade thinks he's a comedian," I mumble, and then glare at him. "Aren't I supposed to be your queen or something? Can't I give you orders? Take me to Charon," I say, trying to sound as queenly as possible.

"No," he says adamantly. Some manservant he's turning out to be. "You still need herbs. If infection sets in, that could beee as deadly as venom." He rolls away the boulder and I can see a faint light behind him. It must be morning again. He turns back. "One lassst thing," he says, and gently tosses an object in my direction. "A gifffft for yooou. From my colleccction."

He slips through the opening and then pushes the boulder back in place. The object he tossed has landed a few feet short, so it takes me a couple of minutes to get to it. What I find is a cracked medallion with a broken chain. Possibly the same one from the pile I'd found earlier. However, this time, in the light of the torch, I recognize it. I've seen something like this before. Twice before, actually.

It's a communication talisman.

And if Haden still has his—the one he'd found of Simon's— this means I may have a way of contacting him. That is, if this thing still works.

I run my thumb over the crack in the medallion.

chapter sixteen

TOBIN

I must have passed out. It seems several minutes have passed when my eyes fly open again. I cough and sputter, gasping for air. Every breath burns my lungs. Garrick looks down at me, his eyes almost betraying concern. He has removed his cloak, and his crown sits askew on his head. He lifts his hands from where they were cupped over my chest. Did he just resuscitate me?

"Too much," he says, as if speaking to himself. "I told you it was too much. We need him."

"Need me for what?" I ask between gasps.

"To stop her!" he snarls.

"Daphne?" I ask. "Where is she?"

"We don't know, but you're going to help us find her." He stands, staring down at me from under his crooked crown. "She was supposed to take us to the Key, only she escaped. And now she's out there, probably looking for it on her own so she can keep it for herself. We must stop her."

"How?" I ask, not sure if he means "we" as in he and the Keres, or he and me.

"Bait—the only reason you're still alive."

I try to protest. Try to tell him he might as well kill me because I'd die before letting him get his hands on Daphne and the Key. I try but I can't. I am in so much pain. Breathing aches, and I feel the blisters bubbling up on my burned skin. I can't even move. I want nothing more than to tell him what he can go do to himself, but all that comes out of my mouth is a whimper.

Some hero I am turning out to be.

Garrick grabs his cloak and goes to the door. Opening it, he calls for the guards once more. "Take him to the healing chamber," he commands.

The guards hesitate, standing in the doorway. "My king?" one of them says.

Garrick reels on him. "What?"

"The Court has asked us to summon you. There are other matters that need your majesty's attention . . ."

"What other matters could possibly be more important than finding the Key?"

"Lord Lex has commanded—"

"Lord Lex *commands?*" Garrick seethes and points at the crown that hangs over one ear now. I find myself wondering if he has always been a little unstable, or if having a Keres attached to him is driving him into lunacy. "Does Lex wear the crown? Did the Fates choose him to be your king?"

"No, your highness," the guard says.

"Then what Lord Lex wants is none of your concern. *We* commanded you to take this boy to the healing chambers. Let him stay just long enough so he can walk. He needs to be able to travel by morning."

Garrick sends a swift kick to my ribs. I feel a burst of pain as one of them cracks. I groan from the pain, no longer strong enough to scream.

"My king, if you want the prisoner to be alive in the morning, perhaps that isn't the best—"

"Silence! Would you have dared speak to Ren that way? Do as we command or *you* won't be alive come morning." Garrick storms from the room, pushing his way out between the two guards as he leaves.

A moment later, the guards approach. They grab me by the wrists and drag me toward the doorway. If only I could will myself to pass out again so I don't have to feel the pain of my body sliding against the stone floor.

"Perhaps Lex is right," one guard says to the other.

The other one grunts as if not ready to commit either way to his comment.

"The *king* had better hope he can bring back that Key or he won't be holding on to that crown much longer."

"Or should he be more worried about what the Court will do to him once he does hand over the Key?" the second guard says.

The first guard lets out a small chuckle and then clears his throat as if catching himself.

"Either way, no mere boy is going to hold on to that crown for very long."

Mere boy? I think. *So the guards haven't seen it? They don't know that Garrick has two shadows—they don't know he's working with the Keres? For the Keres. Garrick wants me to think he's some kind of mastermind, but really he's just a pawn. He's being used by the Keres—they're the ones pulling the strings. They're the ones really wearing the crown.*

The guards and the Court are the ones who should be afraid of what will happen when Garrick gets his hands on the Key.

I try to will my mouth to open to say something—to warn them. Of what, I am not exactly sure. But I can't find the strength. My body won't respond to my mind. The two guards drag me up a set of stone stairs, my broken rib slamming against each step. My head feels too heavy to hold up anymore. I let it lull between my arms and pray the pain will stop soon.

chapter seventeen

HADEN

Brim follows me into the servants' wing of the house. I can't tell if she thinks I need protection or moral support. We find my father asleep in the bedroom that had once belonged to Joe's assistant. It strikes me that slumber does not make him appear softer, as it does with some men. He reminds me of a hibernating hydra in its cave—one I do not wish to wake. I approach with caution even though I know he is unconscious. Visions of his wrath—his lightning-laced hands wrapped around my throat—run through my mind. My father tried to electrify my soul once. I would not put murdering me past him now.

I grab a small bottle that sits on the nightstand, assuming it to be the sleeping draught that Ethan dosed him with, and then I heft my father's limp, heavy body over my shoulder. I listen for a moment before entering the foyer, to make sure Daphne's mother is still in the kitchen, and then I carry my father to the driveway where Ethan and Jonathan wait. I buckle my father into the backseat, more with the intention of keeping him upright than with concern for his safety. Brim hops up on Ren's knee and sits like a tiny sentinel, staring at our captive, ready to alert me if he makes the slightest move.

"I guess I should go home," Lexie says after escorting Terresa to the car. "I don't feel like sticking around for the fireworks show," she says, hitching her thumb in the direction of the house. I can faintly hear Demi's voice rising in anger.

"I imagine your own parents are as concerned about your well-being after the storm," I say.

"Ha!" she laughs—but there's a hint of sadness behind it. "My parents probably don't even know about the storm. They didn't even stay for the last act of the play. Their flight to Paris just happened to be at the same time."

"That's . . . awful," I say, even though I cannot imagine my own father ever coming to see me in a musical production. He would have all sorts of choice words if I even suggested it—considering that music is forbidden in my world, and the fact that he hates me with a passion born of fire.

Lexie shrugs as if it's no big deal, but I can see in her eyes that it is. "Eh, it means I get to binge-watch *Real Starlets of LA* and wear my mom's Manolos around the house." She takes off down the driveway and then turns back and calls, "Have fun storming the Skyrealm without me!"

I am surprised at how reluctant I am to see Lexie go, though I know it's neither feasible nor safe to take her into the Skyrealm. Lexie has her various irritating qualities, but she has proven herself to be a true ally in the last three months, and a true friend in the last few days. I know her better than three of my traveling companions, and trust her more than all of them. Except for perhaps Jonathan. Even though I've known him for the least amount of time, he's won me over for the simple fact that he loves Daphne as if she really were his niece. Ethan, on the other hand, I know I can only trust as long as my interests intersect with his goals. My father is a threat—but only if he wakes, and I intend to leave him in the Skyrealm before that happens. *But Teresa is the real wild card*, I think, knowing her allegiance will turn the moment the passion spell has run its course.

Based on the rather filthy suggestion she whispers in my ear once we've all piled into Ethan's car, I gather the spell is still well in effect.

"Excuse me, lieutenant," I say, removing her hand from my thigh, "I am not that kind of Underlord."

"I bet you wouldn't object if Daphne suggested the same," she says, folding her arms in front of her chest. "Daphne, Daphne, Daphne. That's all you care about."

Heat rushes into my face as I let myself imagine for a moment that Daphne would even suggest such a thing, and then push the thought away, letting it be replaced by more disconcerting ones. *Teresa is jealous of Daphne—so what might she do if the spell doesn't wear off anytime soon? What if, when we get Daphne back, Teresa sees her as a threat?*

And more pressingly, what will Teresa do when she doesn't get her promised kiss?

"You're the most beautiful Skylord I've ever met." I give her a small smile that softens her glower, knowing I need to play along with just the right amount of feigned interest. I feel like a piece of *kopros* even though what I said isn't a lie, considering she's the *only* female Skylord I've ever met. Why does this feel so different than when I tried to convince Daphne to fall in love with me?

Duh, you addled idiot, because you were in love with Daphne to begin with.

"I can't wait to walk in the clouds with you," Terresa says, snuggling up against my side and wrapping her hands around one of my biceps. I feel trapped with my too-long legs practically pulled up to my chest in the middle seat between Terresa and my unconscious father.

"Who is carrying Ren?" I ask Ethan, realizing he'll have his hands full with Jonathan. "How are we getting him to the Skyrealm?"

"One of my most trusted comrades will meet us at the rendezvous point," Ethan says, meeting my eyes in the rearview mirror. I must look concerned because he adds, "Don't worry. No one else knows of our plans."

Ethan starts up the car with a jolt of electricity from his hand. It must run on a battery, like mine.

"Hang a right at the roundabout and take us to the other side of the lake," I say, pointing the way for Ethan. "I need to stop at my place first."

I don't realize that I've been holding my breath until I walk into the deserted kitchen of the mansion that I have called home for the last six months. Part of me—all right, most of me—had been hoping to Hades to find Dax here, sitting at the kitchen table, eating tacos for dinner and checking the daily news on his iPad.

I let out a long breath when I realize no one is home, and then regret the deep breath I take afterward. The air in the kitchen is tainted by the smell of sour milk from a crusted-over cereal bowl in the sink. Probably Garrick's. Which means no one has been here for days, besides the cursory search I made when I first returned from the grove.

The others have followed me inside. "I'll be a few minutes," I say as I head upstairs. They wait in the living room.

Brim follows me up to my room. She settles herself in her usual spot at the foot of the bed while I duck into my bathroom. I drop my clothes on the tile floor and take a quick shower, finally getting to wash off the grime that's clung to me since my visit to the Underrealm. I change into a pair of black jeans, a shirt, and a light jacket that are far more comfortable than Joe's too-tight clothes. I grab a backpack and stuff it full of what supplies I think I might need—what does one take to the Skyrealm, anyway? I'm about to leave when Brim stops me with a protesting meow.

"Of course you're coming with me," I say, but then realize what she's trying to alert me to. She prances in front of the air vent next to my bed, giving prodding little yowls.

"It's of no use," I say, patting her on the head.

She nips at my hand, yowling louder.

"Fine," I say. Brim always gets what she wants.

I pull a Leatherman—one of the tools Dax had insisted was essential to my human experience—from my dresser and use it to unscrew the face of the vent. From it, I take the communication talisman and tuck it into my jacket pocket.

"Happy now?"

The talisman is a device the Underlords created for between-realm communication, and normally it might be useful if the group were to get separated unexpectedly, like what happened during my last journey. The only problem is, who would I call for help if I needed it? The only other talisman I know of in the mortal world was destroyed three months ago.

That was the same reason none of us had taken it with us to the Underrealm. Regret grips me, and I wish now that I hadn't destroyed the other one in order to break the connection between myself and my father before he could electrocute my soul. Then again, I would be dead if I hadn't . . .

And maybe Daphne would have been spared all this in the first place if I were . . .

I shake off the dark thought and inspect the veins in my arm. They're a deep navy blue rather than the pale bluish gray they had been when we left Joe's house. My latest dose is wearing off even faster than the last.

Another thought hits me, and I am glad for the distraction. I hadn't taken the time to inspect my father before putting him in the car, so I do not know if he still had his own communication talisman when he was forced through the gate. Or perhaps it had been stripped from him along with his crown?

Did Garrick have it now? Or more likely someone like Lex, who would never take a call a from me . . .

I run down the stairs with Brim close at my heels and find my father propped up on the couch in the living room. I pat down his tunic, hoping to find a talisman in a secret pocket, but it's not there.

"What are you doing?" Ethan asks from the kitchen, where he's rooting through the refrigerator.

"Did my father have anything on him when you brought him from the grove?"

"Not that I noticed," Ethan says. He pulls a carton of orange juice from the fridge and then balks at the smell when he opens the lid.

I contemplate running back to Joe's to search the bed where my father had been sleeping, to see if something may have slipped from his pockets into the sheets. It would be helpful to have two communication devices for our mission, perhaps use them like walkie-talkies in those old spy movies Dax likes. But the ache that pulses through my veins reminds me that time is of the essence. We need to get on the road.

And besides, I *do not* want to walk in on Joe's confession to Demi. If he was following my advice, that is. I would never get out of there again if she knew the truth.

"I wouldn't eat anything in there," I say as Ethan makes to open another carton. "Neither Dax nor I were the best housekeepers over the last few months. That has probably been in there since before Simon died three months ago."

Ethan thrusts the carton back in the fridge and shuts the door. "That explains the smell."

The action reminds me of Daphne. Of when she taught me how to cook French toast so I wouldn't wither away from a steady diet of Dax's fast-food tacos. How she insisted I make the meal myself instead of doing it for me. I remember the way our hands touched and I accidentally dropped an entire bottle of cinnamon on one of the pieces of bread—and how she thought it would be funny to conspire to feed that one to Garrick. But then she still saved him a good piece too.

Electricity pricks at my fingertips from the thought of her. It tingles against the metal of the talisman in my hand. I tuck it into my jacket pocket for safekeeping. Maybe the thing can be used to barter if for nothing else.

Brim gives a satisfied purr and then hops up on to my shoulder. She follows me outside with the others. We all pile back into Ethan's car. I glance back at the house, wishing Dax were one of my traveling companions. I need his help now, as I had needed his help with our mission to the Underrealm. If only I hadn't let him follow that mysterious call that had supposedly come from Abbie. If only he'd been there in the grove to protect Daphne, then maybe none of this would have happened.

If only I had any idea where he is now . . .

chapter eighteen

DAPHNE

I spend the next few hours desperately trying to get the talisman to work. There are no numbers or dials or symbols to give me any indication of how to make it connect to the person I want to call. I try pressing the center stone as if it were a button, I try rubbing it like a genie's lamp, I try holding it up and saying, "Call Haden," as if it operated like Siri on my phone. I try holding it in my hands and thinking of Haden. I try picturing him with my mind's eye until my heart begins to ache with longing.

I contemplate waiting for Shady to return so I can ask him if he knows how to use this thing—but I then I realize that he may have no idea what he's given me. As far as he knows, it's just a medallion on a chain—a pretty gift for his queen—and not a communications device. Since he is trying to keep me captive here, it wouldn't make sense for him to give it to me otherwise. If I dare ask him about it, he might take it away—and then I would have no chance of making contact with the mortal realm.

"Call Haden," I say to the talisman again.

Nothing.

"Call Haden," I say louder and clearer. *Crap, maybe it only understands Greek?* I remember the Lesser boy telling me that I was speaking perfect Greek, but I have no idea how I'd done it . . .

Was it the same with Shady? Was he speaking English or was I speaking . . . um . . . Shadese? And how?

I concentrate on the idea that I can speak Greek and then practically shout, "Call Haden!" at the medallion.

It sits as dark and cold as ever in my open hands.

Tears flood my eyes and I am about to toss it aside in frustration in favor of eating a few turnips for dinner . . . when the idea of turnips makes me remember something. The talisman Haden has doesn't *belong* to him. It had belonged to Simon. Haden found it after Simon's death, hidden in a bag of rotten turnips in Simon's fridge . . .

I clutch my talisman tightly in my hands and try a new tactic.

"Communicate with Simon's talisman," I say to it.

Half a second later the talisman lights up with a faint green glow. It pulses brighter and brighter, as if to indicate that the connection is growing stronger. I laugh with joy, holding the talisman out in front of me. *It's working! I can't believe it's working!*

Now all I need is for someone on the other line to answer . . .

chapter nineteen

HADEN

The rest of the night passes by as an uneventful drive. Ren snores for most of the trip, and I allow Terresa to lay her head on my shoulder to sleep, only having to push her wandering hands away twice. I am grateful for the opportunity to stretch when we finally pull over in a place called Shasta-Trinity National Forest early in the morning.

There's a motorcycle parked near the entrance to the campsite and a woman stands nearby, her arms crossed expectantly.

"Hello," Ethan says, calling to her.

She smiles when she sees him, then smooths her expression into a professional, soldierly look, and nods to him in return. "Captain Bowman."

"This is Lieutenant Jessica Ball," Ethan says, approaching the woman. "The comrade I told you about."

I give her a nod. If Ethan trusts her to help us, then I have to as well. Although, I must admit that when Ethan told me one of his comrades was meeting us, I had pictured a burly warrior, not this petite woman with long, curly, dark hair.

"Ugh, *her*," Terresa says, not quietly, and crosses her arms with a glare.

"Nice to see you, too, Terresa," Jessica says.

"Traitor. Don't you dare make eyes at my man!" Terresa calls to the other woman. "I'm watching you."

"Her man?" Jessica says to Ethan. One of her eyebrows raises in a slightly amused expression.

"Long story," he says. "I'll fill you in later. For now, we should focus on setting up camp. The gate is due north from here." Ethan points straight up at the sky, rather than actual north. The plan is to camp here for the rest of the day, giving us a chance to rest before making the ascent to the gate at nightfall. Skylords do not see well in the dark, so a nighttime infiltration into the palace will improve our odds of going undetected.

Ethan hefts his duffle bag over his shoulder, and Jessica follows him deeper into the clearing. Terresa stomps after them, as if she feels the need to keep a vigilant eye on her supposed rival. However, from the way Ethan and Jessica brush hands as they walk, I get the feeling that Terresa doesn't have to worry about this other woman making eyes at me.

"How are you doing?" Jonathan asks me. His voice sounds especially heavy.

I'm leaning against an old wooden table that sits in the clearing. I stare at my gray-black veins. I've been sucking on bits of a bitter dark chocolate bar that I picked up at a rest stop a few hours ago—testing Lexie's theory that chocolate is a mood enhancer. Its effects are mild, but seem to have staved off the worst mood swings for now. "All right," I say, even if I don't know for how long that answer will be true.

"I can give you a dose now," he says, pulling two small

arrows—one blue, one purple—from his nearly empty quiver. I know a third one is tucked in there, somewhere, not to be used. "But I'd rather save it if you can wait. You never know, something might go wrong up there . . ."

I ache for another dose of emotion. I crave it like a traveler who has been without water for days. Even though I agree with Jonathan's reasoning for waiting, the mere mention of the option to have it now makes it hard to think about anything else.

"I can wait." I tuck my blackening hands into my jacket pockets and walk over to help Ethan set up a small tent. It can't possibly fit more than two people at a time.

When the tent is up, I tell Jonathan and Terresa to take the first shift resting—not wanting to be anywhere near her in confined quarters again—and then I tell Ethan and Jessica I'm going to take a walk. He eyes me for a moment in a way that makes me think he'll protest, but then he nods. I expect Brim to follow me, but she stays and sits at attention, watching Ethan unpack food from a small cooler. She coos when he opens a package of cold cuts. If he's not careful, she might take off his finger in order to get to them.

I walk into the trees, following a narrow, rutted path, until the campsite is well out of sight. I contemplate turning back, but a strange, warm sensation pressing against my side catches my attention. It takes me a minute to realize the source of it is coming from my jacket pocket. I reach in and close my fingers around the chain of the talisman and pull it out. I almost cannot believe my eyes—the medallion pulses with a pale green light.

Someone in the Underrealm is trying to make a connection . . .

chapter twenty

DAPHNE

"Daphne?"

His voice is tinged with shock and disbelief. Still, it's the most wonderful sound in the world. Almost as wonderful as the sight of him. Standing here, in the cave. A pillar of light in the darkness.

"How?" I ask, trying to push myself up to a standing position. "You're here."

"You called me here?" His voice is so filled with astonishment that I can't tell if it's a statement or a question. I don't care. *He's here.* That's all that matters. Haden had once explained that a communication talisman worked like a cell phone, only it didn't just transmit a person's voice to you, it brought their soul. And yet, I still didn't expect to see him here in front of me. His jade-green eyes look tired and his dark brown hair is rumpled, but he's such a sight for sore eyes that just looking at him takes my breath away.

I want to run to him. I *need* to wrap my arms around him. But running is hardly an option with my braced knee.

I take two hobbling steps.

"You're hurt," he says, and then he's the one running to me. He jogs up to me and holds out his arms as if he were trying to steady me as I teeter on my feet. His hands don't make contact, they just pass through me as if I were a ghost. Or if he were a ghost . . .

I gasp, tears filling my eyes once again. "Are you dead?" I whisper.

Part of me worried that Garrick had gone back on his word—that he had sent Haden to an execution rather than banishing him to the mortal world.

"No," Haden says. "Only my soul is here. My body is back in the mortal realm. I forgot in my excitement that I cannot touch you."

"Oh," I say, wiping my tears away with relief.

He lifts his hand to his own eyes. I see it then, the black spindly veins wrapping around his hands and fingers. It has spread so fast.

"That means I can't kiss you?" I want so badly to touch him. To kiss him. To cure him of the poison in his system.

Haden shakes his head. "Only energy can pass between us."

He holds his hand up in front of him, as if he were pressing against an invisible window that separates us. I do the same. Our hands look as though they are touching, but I can't feel anything. A blue spark lights up from the tip of Haden's index finger, giving me a little shock.

"I felt that!" I exclaim with so much excitement that I almost topple over. I steady myself, grabbing my injured knee.

"You're hurt," he says again, dropping his hand away. "What happened? Where are you? This doesn't look like the palace. Did Garrick do this to you?" he says, indicating my bandages. "I'm going to strangle that little rat."

"It wasn't Garrick, but it was a rat," I say. "I escaped Garrick."

"Of course you did," he says, like he wouldn't expect any different.

"Only problem is that I was attacked by some Shades, and now I'm being held hostage by one of them in a cave . . . Well, not exactly hostage . . ."

"You're being held by a Shade?" His beautiful jade eyes are marred with panic. "Daphne, you have to get out of there. It's going to eat you!"

"No, I don't think so. He says he's trying to protect me—"

"Says?" He shakes his head. "Shades do not speak."

I shrug. "This one does. At least to me. And I'm pretty sure I'm safe here for now. A little too safe . . ." I hold my hands up because I can tell he's about to protest. I don't have time for arguing. Who knows when Shady might return—and if he saw me using the talisman, he might take it by force. "Enough about me. I may not have much time. Tell me how you're doing. My mom, Joe, Jonathan? What's happening out there?"

"They're fine," he says. "I'm fine."

He tucks his hands behind his back, and I know he's lying about his condition.

"How long has it been, out there?" I ask, realizing I have no idea if time moves at the same rate in both our worlds.

"A couple of days since I returned."

"Then there's still time. Jonathan said I'd have two weeks."

Haden starts to shake his head, then stops as if he's hiding something.

"What is it?" I ask.

He looks down at the ground.

"Tell. Me."

He pulls his hands out from behind his back. "It's spreading too quickly," he says quietly. "Jonathan doesn't know why—maybe something about my metabolism. He's been giving me something to try to stave off the worst effects, but at this rate, if I'm lucky . . . I maybe have forty-eight hours before it overtakes me completely."

"Forty-eight hours?" I say with disbelief.

Two days? Two days? Here I thought I had a little less than two weeks to find a way out of the Underrealm—a daunting prospect on its own—and now I only have two days?

If he's lucky . . .

"Don't worry," he says. "We have a plan to try to get you out. We're heading into the Skyrealm. We're going to infiltrate a secret prison and try to find Persephone. If there's anyone who knows how to get you out, it's going to be her."

"You're going into the Skyrealm?" Panic rises up my spine. "And you're going to break into a secret prison?"

"Oh, and the Sky King's palace. But that is a bit of a side mission."

"Are you insane?"

"I know it sounds addled, but Daphne, I will do anything to get you out of there . . ."

"I can find my own way out. I have a lead on where I might find the Key—if I can only persuade Shady to take me there."

"Finding the Key would be the best option, but you still won't be able to leave without my help. You're bound to Garrick, which means I'll have to come into the Underrealm and . . ."

"And what, kill him?"

"If I have to." Haden doesn't meet my eyes. "Or drag him out kicking and screaming. Whichever is easiest."

I wonder if it's the black poison talking, or if Haden is really willing to kill his younger half-brother. I wonder if I will be willing to let him . . .

"In the meantime, I'm not waiting for the Key to turn up in the Underrealm. I'm going to do whatever it takes to figure out how to save you, from my end."

I want to protest but I know it won't do any good—just like there's nothing he can say that will stop me from trying to figure my own way out over here. And I don't want to argue, not when our time could be over any second. I lift my hand toward Haden. If he was really heading into the Skyrealm, this may be my last chance to see him. Ever. "Do that again," I say, indicating his hand. I want to feel his energy again.

Haden lifts his hand, but instead of bringing it to mine, he raises it to my face. A small shock of energy lights against my cheek. I lean into it as if it were a caress. He touches his fingers to my shoulder next. It's a small shock. It makes me shudder, and not with pain.

He touches my side.

The shock makes me sigh.

He leans forward and I know what he wants. *Maybe it will even work . . .*

His face is there in front of mine. I know we can't really touch, but I bring my lips to where his are. A spark of energy lights between them. I can feel his energy burst against my lips and it ripples through me. The spark was only a flicker, but it feels like a flame.

A soul kiss.

A noise catches my attention. The sound of stone sliding against stone—the boulder at the entrance of the cave is being moved. Shady is coming back.

I pull away from Haden. "I have to go."

"No," he says, reaching out like he can stop me. "Don't go."

Light from outside edges into the cave.

"I have to."

I drop the talisman, breaking the connection, and Haden disappears.

chapter twenty-one

HADEN

"Daphne!" I shout as she fades away. "Daphne, don't go!"

It's too late. The cave is gone. I am standing in the forest. Completely alone.

"Daphne, no!" I scream.

I collapse to my knees, gripping the talisman in my black-veined hand. I have to get her back. "Call Daphne!" I shout at the medallion. "Bring Daphne back!"

The talisman doesn't listen. It sits lifeless and uncaring in my grasp.

"Bring her back!"

I throw the talisman against the ground. "You worthless piece of *kopros* . . ." Then I snatch it back up again, afraid I've broken it. I slide my fingers over its surface, inspecting it for damage. "Call Daphne," I insist.

Electricity builds under my skin. I can feel it crackling around me. I fight the impulse to fry the talisman for its insolence. The problem isn't the talisman, it's me. I don't know how to make it work.

I'm the worthless one.

Daphne is on her own because of me. She's injured. She's been captured by a Shade. "It's going to kill her. She's going to die!" I'm rocking on my knees, shouting at the talisman. "Bring her back!"

I let a surge of electricity build inside my chest. It surges up my arms. I place my hands over my ribcage. *I'm the one who should suffer. I'm the one who should . . .*

But before I can finish the thought, I am grabbed from behind. It must be Jonathan because Ethan crouches in front of me, looking like he's about to spring.

"Leave me alone!" I shout.

Ethan lunges, wrapping his hands around mine and yanking them away from my chest as a burst of lightning escapes my fingers. The shock flings him away from me. He crashes against the base of a tall, quaking tree. Jessica runs to his side.

I'm rocking again. Ranting something about Daphne. Brim jumps into my lap. She purrs and meows. Normally her presence is calming, but even her soft touch racks me with guilt. I don't deserve to be comforted.

"What in Zeus's name is wrong with him?" Jessica asks.

"There's black poison in his veins. It's making him insane," Ethan sputters. "He'll hurt himself if we don't dose him again."

"I'm on it," Jonathan says, his voice coming from behind me.

"No, I don't want it." I want to be miserable. I deserve to be miserable. Can't they see that? I fling my arm back to knock Jonathan away. Someone else snatches my hand before it makes contact with Jonathan's side. Brim sinks her teeth into my leg.

"It's okay," I hear Terresa say in a crooning whisper. She pets her fingers over my hand. "I'm here, my love."

"Get away from me!" I try to pull away, but her grip is as strong as a griffin's. A sharp pain catches me in the arm and I know it's too late to stop them. Warmth rushes through my veins. After a moment, I feel a strange uplifting sensation. It's not the same as the bubbling giddiness or the drunken heaviness that I experienced before.

A strength pounds in my chest, as if something were trying to break free—but it feels different than an electrical current. More like *power*.

I stand, shaking Terresa's grasp from my arm with ease.

I look down at the others, all sitting on the ground. "Daphne needs our help," I say. "Why are you all lazing about? We shouldn't wait any longer, we should go into the Skyrealm now."

"We agreed to wait until nightfall," Ethan says, as if this were a logical choice.

"I will not wait any longer. Let us do what we came to do." I scoop up Brimstone against my chest and hold my other hand out to Terresa. "You will take me to the Skygate."

"Of course, my love." She hops up and jogs to me. Her arm wraps around mine. "Just say the word."

"Haden, wait," Ethan says.

"Waiting is for cowards." I nod to him and Jonathan. "Are you two coming or not?"

"Haden . . ."

"I don't have patience for protests." I smile at Terresa. "Let's go!"

Terresa wraps her arms around my waist and then pulls me into a crouching position. She's balancing herself on her toes. A burst of lightning explodes from her feet against the forest floor and then she and I are rocketing up into the sky. Wind whips around us, filling my lungs with air.

"*Kalash!*" I exclaim. I've always daydreamed about being able to fly, but this sensation is even more exhilarating than I could have imagined. "I had no idea lightning could be used this way."

Brimstone, on the other hand, is not enthused by flying. She yowls and clings to my chest with her tiny claws.

"It's okay, Brim. I will not drop you."

I hear a second blast and look down to see Ethan, with Jonathan in his grasp, rocketing up after us. A third blast comes a few moments later, with Jessica hefting my unconscious father. The ground shrinks away under them, the forest looking like a scrubby blanket below us. This must be how birds see the world.

It strikes me that the height might normally bother me, but it doesn't now. The higher we get, the closer we are to the Skyrealm. The closer we are to finding Persephone. The closer we are to saving Daphne.

"Can you take us faster?" I ask Terresa.

"Sure thing!" Terresa punches the air and our speed increases so abruptly that I have to cling to her so I don't fall. She gives a laugh that I think is supposed to sound flirtatious, but reminds me more of a cackle. It makes me smile. Perhaps she isn't so terrible after all.

"You must teach me to do this!" I shout over the sound of the wind.

Brim hisses in protest to this idea.

Our upward trajectory only lasts for another minute or so. Terresa slows and we come to a stop. We start to fall, hurtling downward, until she sticks her feet out and we land in a cloud. "Don't let go," she says as I loosen my grip on her arm. I tighten it once more, realizing that even though the cloud seems solid under her feet, it is nothing but water vapor under mine. "I might be able to teach you to rocket, but cloud walking is a Skylords-only trait."

She shifts so she's standing facing me, and places her feet under mine. She takes a step backward while indicating that I should move with her in unison. I probably look like a child walking on an adult's feet, but I could not care less.

Ethan lands with Jonathan in the cloud beside us. "Can we wait for a minute now?" Ethan pants. Jonathan isn't exactly a small man, I note as Ethan struggles to keep his father afloat—who seems a little less enthusiastic than me to be in the clouds. It's probably been centuries since he lost his godly wings.

"I could use a rest also," Jessica says, dragging my father by the wrist behind her through the clouds.

"No," I say. "No more waiting. Take me to the gate."

Terresa complies. As we sail through the clouds, I feel almost as if I were dancing.

From behind us, I hear Ethan ask Jonathan, "What exactly did you give him?"

"A shot of confidence," Jonathan says, his voice wavering. "Only I'm afraid I may have given him too much."

chapter twenty-two

DAPHNE

I grab the talisman and tuck it behind my back as Shady enters the cave. It must be morning, because that strange ethereal light of the Underrealm floods in from behind him. I squint, realizing it's been far too long since I've seen daylight—or even an otherworldly facsimile of it. I think I might go crazy if I have to spend another day inside this cavern.

Shady has some sort of small, scaly animal—of the dead variety—slung over his shoulder. He sets it and a pile of herbs next to the torch. I watch silently as he uses two rocks to grind the herbs into a thick paste, all the while letting my eyes drift occasionally to the cave entrance, which he has left wide open.

Forty-eight hours, my subconscious reminds me. I only have two days to find the Key and reunite with Haden. To kiss him for real and seal his cure.

I glance at the cave opening. *Could I make a break for it?*

I roll my eyes at my own stupid thought. With my injured knee, I'd get about two feet before Shady caught me up. And then what? He might decide I'm too much trouble as a houseguest— caveguest—and decide to eat me for dinner.

No, if I'm going to find Charon, I need Shady to help me.

Shady approaches with the paste he's made. I let him unwrap my bandages, dress them with the soothing paste, and then rewrap them with new strips of cloth. He stops for a moment after finishing my shoulder. His fingers hover over the pomegranate pendant that hangs from my neck.

"Kore," he moans in a whisper as if he were paying the necklace some sort of reverence.

"Do you want it?" I ask, pinching the ruby-encrusted pendant.

"Noooo," he says, snatching his hand away. "Not mine."

I find this weird, considering ownership didn't seem to bother him when it came to the things he added to his hoarder's heap.

"I'll make you a trade," I say. "Help me find Charon, and I'll give it to you. It would make the perfect addition to your collection."

"I am not worthy of thisss thing. You can hear me. Means you are worthy heir, Kore."

"Daphne," I say. "My name is Daphne, not Kore. Kore is gone."

"No! Don't say that. You must be Kore now."

He shuffles away to the entrance of the cave, grabs the small animal and storms outside. I assume he's going to shut me in again, so I am more than surprised when he leaves it open. I grab the torch that extinguished itself nearly an hour ago, and use it as a makeshift cane to hobble to the front of the cave. It takes me a few minutes to get there, but when I poke my head outside the cave entrance, I find that Shady is building up a small campfire on the ledge that surrounds the entrance of the cave. He's positioned the animal on a roasting spit over the fire.

"I'm coming out," I say, advising him of my movement but not asking him for permission.

He grunt-moans in return.

I step outside the cave, shielding my eyes from what feels like noonday sun but isn't, and inspect my surroundings. Other than this rocky ledge, it looks like a sheer incline both above and below. There's no way I could climb down with my injured knee, and Shady must be very strong to have climbed up the cliff face with me over his shoulder.

I step carefully, hugging the wall, as I follow Shady over to the fire, its warmth beckoning me. "I'm sorry, I didn't mean to offend you," I say as I settle myself next to him.

He grunts again. Has he decided to stop speaking to me?

"You must have been a very loyal servant to Kore. You really cared for her, didn't you?"

He nods. "Loyal, yes. Kore wasss compassion. Kore wasss springtime. Kore wasss sunlight. Kore was love. I am only servant. That is why I not worthy. It hasss chosen you," he says, patting his collarbone. "You are Kore now. I mussst protect you. I cannot lose Kore again."

"But I'm not Kore. I'm just a girl who's trying to get home. I'm trying to save my friend—the boy I love . . ."

"You are *not* just girl. Only rightful heir can wield herrr Kronolithe. You are Kore."

"Her Kronolithe?" I ask. "What are you talking about?"

"The pommmmegranate."

"The pom . . . You mean the necklace?" I pinch the pomegranate pendant between my fingers. Is he saying what I think he's saying? "This pomegranate necklace is a Kronolithe?"

He nods and turns the roasting spit. I try to ignore the smell of burning reptilian flesh.

"That necklace is pomegranate Hadessss offered Kore," Shady says. "He fashioned it frrrrom piece of his own Kronolithe. When she accepted it, she traded her mantle as goddess of springtime and became goddess of dead. She cared for them—for us—she became our queen because of her compassion. The dead needed her. Things were better for everyone when she was here . . . Her Kronolithe granted her the powers she needed to fulfill her duties. She could travel the Underrealm with ease, she could talk to the dead, among other things."

"But how can this necklace be a Kronolithe? Garrick said it belonged to many other queens since Persephone left," I say. "Don't you think someone would have noticed if this thing had magical powers?"

"Only a worthy heir can taaaake up the mantle of a Kronolithe."

"But I'm not related to Persephone. Orpheus, yes; and the Amazons too. But I'm pretty sure I am not a descendant of Persephone."

"Blllood does not always matter. It's merely who you are. It chose you—I know you're worthy because you cannnn understand me."

I lean backward away from the fire, feeling too hot all of a sudden. "So the necklace is the reason I can talk to you? And I suppose that's why the Lesser boy could understand me as well . . ."

"Yes," he says, poking the fire with a stick. "Kore could talk to anyone in the Underrealm. Things were better before ssshe left . . ."

"Does this mean I'm immortal?"

He nods and then also shakes his head. "Don't know. Still susceptible to injury," he says, pointing to my bandages. "It may keep you from aging as long as youuu wear it, but it may not protect your life beyond that. I will not risssk letting you get hurt again."

"So Persephone, if she left this behind, does that mean she's no longer immortal?" I think of Haden heading into the Skyrealm, looking for Persephone. Was he on some sort of wild goose chase, looking for a woman who died centuries ago?

"She was goddessss in her own right before accepting Hades's gift. If she took up her old mantle once more when she left, she couuuuld still be alive." The end of his stick has caught flame. He seems to watch it burn with his invisible eyes. I wonder if he is thinking of Persephone.

"So when you said Charon had one of these, you meant he has his own Kronolithe? One that protects him from water?"

Shady nods. "He is the boatman."

"And where would I find him?"

"At one of the docks."

"How many docks are there?"

"Many."

"Could you be more specific?"

"Why?"

I decide to be straight with him. "You know Hades's Kronolithe?"

"Eternity Key. Yes, was lost. Hades died and Kore left."

"Well, guess what, I found it. Only it's lost again. But I think this Charon guy might know where it is. I need to get it back. My friend, he's dying, and I'm the only one who can save him. I need to find the Key so I can open Persephone's Gate and get back to him. He needs me . . ."

"No!" Shady says, pointing that flaming stick in my direction. "You cannot leave again, Kore. The Underrealm needs you. Not your friend." Shady makes a move like he's going to grab me and drag me back into the cave.

I pull away from him. "He does need me. I need to save his life. And then we all need him because he's going to help me destroy the Keres."

"Keres?" he says, pulling back and shaking his head.

"They're bad, right? You're afraid of them, aren't you?"

"Locked away," he says, waving his charred stick.

"Not for much longer. They're going to get out."

Shady makes a horrible moan and rocks forward.

"My friend and I, we were going to use the Key to destroy them, only we got separated and everything went wrong. But you can help me make it right again. I need to find the Key before Garrick—the new king, the one you saw me running from—or the Court get their hands on it. You can help me. I just need to get back to save my friend first."

"No. Kore stay!" He grabs my arm and yanks me toward the cave.

"I'm not Kore. As much as you want me to be, I'm not really her . . ." An idea hits me and I don't know why I didn't think of it several minutes ago. "But what if you could get her back? What if I could get the *real* Persephone to return?"

Shady stops in front of the boulder. He seems to stare down at me. "What do you mean?"

"My friend—the one I told you about, the one I need to save—he's on a mission right now to the Skyrealm. He's trying to infiltrate a Skyrealm prison—to rescue Persephone."

"Skylords have Kore?" This idea seems to really piss Shady off. His fingers tremble against my skin. "Is that why she hasn't returned?"

"Possibly," I say. "But if you help me find the Key, and my friend is successful in finding Persephone, then you and I can open the gate and let her back in."

He lets go of my arm. "Bring Kore back?" I can hear the hopefulness behind his moaning voice.

"Yes. *You* can be the one who brings Kore back . . ."

I trail off because the strangest noise catches my attention. It sounds like someone shouting in the distance—someone shouting my name. I spin around, looking out over the cliff. I don't see anything. Perhaps it was just the wind?

I start to turn back toward Shady when I hear it again.

"Daphne?" someone shouts. "Daphne? Are you out there?"

Distant though it may be, I know that voice.

Tobin!

I step forward, ready to shout back, but Shady grabs me from behind. His hand clasps over my mouth and my call of "Tobin!" gets silenced by his grasp.

I start to struggle. *Tobin is out there! Tobin is alive! He's looking for me!*

Shady holds me tighter and whispers in my ear, "It could beeee a ruse, my queen."

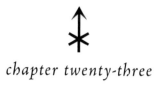

chapter twenty-three

TOBIN

Garrick's guards have dragged me from the wagon once again. I am flanked by four guards. One of them prods me with an electrified staff when I don't move fast enough—which is hard, considering my feet are laden with heavy chains. I swear at him under my breath but pick up my pace before he hurts me again.

They lead me toward gray, rocky cliffs.

Garrick stands in his chariot, only one shadow casting over me. With what little strength I had left, I had contemplated trying to warn the guards again about Garrick's Keres alliance this morning, but the evidence was gone when we left the palace. Garrick's second shadow wasn't with him. I had thought at first that perhaps he had gotten tired of playing host—or more likely the Keres had gotten tired of its host—but I realize now, in the brighter light of the outdoors, that Garrick's secret would have been revealed. Everyone would have been able to see his second shadow.

"What are you staring at?" Garrick snarls, lashing at me with his horse whip. I'd thought he'd be more reasonable without the Keres present, but that assumption had also been wrong. "Do it," he orders.

This is the third time in the last two hours he's forced me to call for Daphne. I don't want to do it. I don't want to help him. I don't want him to find Daphne. But even more than what I want, I *need* the pain to stop.

"Daphne," I shout, hoping she won't hear me.

"Louder," Garrick says.

One of the guards approaches with his crackling staff when I hesitate.

"Daphne!" I shout, raising my volume. "Daphne! Are you out there?"

I stop and listen, hoping a response doesn't follow. Or maybe I do want a response, because then maybe this will be over. Garrick won't make me do this anymore. Perhaps he will let me go back to my chair, where I can forget again.

No, I tell myself. *That's not what I want.*

"Now deliver the message."

"Water first," I say. My lips are cracked and my throat is so parched—I think it may have been days since I've had anything to drink. That was one of the ways Garrick tortured me after removing me from the chair. He would offer me a cup filled to the brim with water but when I would try to drink from it, the water would recede from my lips. Garrick had called it the Water of Tantalus or something like that, and found my desperate attempts to drink it particularly amusing. I had never felt so murderous as when hearing him laugh. If only I had any strength left. "Shouting is difficult. I need *real* water before I can go on."

Garrick looks as if he's about to give me a swift slap instead, but then orders one of the guards to bring me a leather water pouch. He lets me drink just enough to wet my throat.

"Now do it," Garrick says.

"She's not out there," I say.

"I told you to deliver the message." He holds up his hand, showing me the blue lightning that webs between his fingers. Just the sight of it makes the fresh burns in my skin ache anew. I can't take suffering through another.

I face the cliffs again. "Daphne, if you're out there," I shout, "Garrick wants me to tell you that if you don't bring him the Key by first light tomorrow, he'll have me killed."

"Filleted alive, to be more specific," Garrick shouts. "This isn't a joke, Daphne. We know you have it. Bring the Key to the Pits by first light, or you'll never see your best friend again."

Garrick orders the guards to take me back to the wagon. The first few times we had gone through this routine, I had dragged my feet to make it more difficult on the guards, but I don't resist anymore. Not after one of the guards wrenched my arm so hard it dislocated my shoulder.

"Where to next?" one of the guards asks Garrick.

"To the docks," Garrick says. "We'll deliver the message there next. Daphne was injured when the chariot crashed. She can't have made it far on foot. She'll hear us eventually." He glares at me and then says, "For both our sakes, you had better pray she listens."

chapter twenty-four

HADEN

The Skyrealm really is a floating mountain in the sky. A mountain sitting in the middle of a floating island, that is. Grecian-style buildings surround the base of the mountain. I assume this is where the general population lives. Other, grander buildings look as though they have been carved into the side of the mountain. The higher the building, the more grand it appears. A great, shimmering palace sits in the basin of the mountain's tallest peak. The building is so reflective in the sun, it looks almost like a pillar of light, burning on top of the mountain. I have to shield my eyes from it.

I could not see any of this until we passed through the pearlescent gate, hidden inside a cumulous cloud, that guards this realm. I expected the gate to be locked, but Terresa explained that since the gate can only be accessed via cloudwalking, a lock would be redundant. "We are free to come and go as we please," she says. "Though I do not know why any Skylord would leave our paradise of his own free will." She gives Ethan a sidelong glance, and he follows behind us through the gate with Jonathan. When Jessica joins us with my unconscious father, we continue our journey. I am grateful to find that the Skyrealm has solid ground and I can walk on with my own two feet. Though Terresa still insists on clinging to my arm.

There's a small hut just beyond the gate.

"I left you a surprise here," Jessica says, leading the way into the building. "Disguises."

"Great work," Ethan says when he sees the pile of bronze armor inside the building. From the look of admiration he gives his lieutenant, I sense that he wishes he could say more. I wonder how committed Ethan is to his betrothal to the daughter of a Skylord general, who happened to be Tobin's missing half-sister, Daphne's runaway best friend from Ellis Fields, *and* Dax's long-lost girlfriend, Abbie Winters. I'd gotten the impression that Ethan still intended to marry her, despite her affection for Dax. Perhaps his affinity for Jessica was a new development—or one he had not yet acknowledged to himself. I remember Dax once saying something along the lines of, "Often the only ones who can't see the procession coming are the ones who are in it."

My heart aches at the memory of Dax. Once I free Daphne, my next priority will be to find him. How hard could it be to find one missing former Underlord in all of the five realms?

We all begin to change from our street clothing into the white tunics and bronze armor. Jonathan loans his considerable bulk to block me from Terresa's prying eyes (and hands) as I change. Jonathan removes his arm brace and squeezes himself into a tunic, straining its stitching in all directions. He's able to wedge on the bronze wrist cuffs and breastplate, but leaves the helmet and shin guards behind.

Jessica picks up her own helmet.

"You should stay here with our ... friend," Ethan says to her, indicating Ren.

She starts to protest but he interrupts. "Your cover as a loyal Skylord is still intact. You're more useful to my cause if there isn't any suspicion on your head." Ethan gives her a look that makes it clear that he is more concerned for her safety than her cover.

"King Ren is supposed to be *my* prize," Terresa says.

"And you'll get him *after* you take us to the Black Hole," Ethan says. "But first we must visit the palace."

"I'll get *both* my prizes," she says, looking at me. Her expression is both hopeful and menacing at the same time. She looks particularly fierce in her whole Sky Army regalia.

I nod, confident I'll be able to elude her when the time comes. "Now take us to the palace."

Terresa escorts us through marbled streets of the Skyrealm until we come to the base of the mountain. We march like a small brigade of soldiers on our rounds. Jonathan only gets a few side-long glances. From there, Terresa rockets me to the top of the mountain, and Ethan follows with Jonathan. I am glad we do not make the ascent on foot—I do not want to waste the time.

We land only a short climb's distance to the front gate to the royal grounds. "This is as far as I go," Terresa says.

"You're not coming with us?" Ethan asks. His voice is edged with suspicion.

"I agreed to take you to the Black Hole, but I will not be party to stealing from the king. Not even for love. I'll wait here. Come back and find me once you've secured what you're looking for."

Ethan looks at me. "Should we trust her?"

"I don't see the problem," I say. "We can always leave her with a babysitter. You'll keep an eye on her, right, Brim?"

Brim, who is nestled between my tunic and my breastplate, meows in response. She climbs out over my shoulder and jumps down to the ground. She paces back and forth in front of Terresa, already on guard.

"Whatever you do, *my love*," I say to Terresa, "don't do anything that might make Brimstone mad."

Ethan leads us through the gate. He pulls his helmet over his face and barks something authoritative to the guards as we pass. I wonder if the green plume on his helmet signifies a high rank. I should have taken that one for myself.

Once inside the palace, Ethan leaves Jonathan and me to wait behind a wall of tapestries while he goes to scope out the situation in the throne room. I hate waiting. It makes me feel as if I want to scratch my way out of my own skin. Ethan returns from running recon and crouches beside me and Jonathan. "It looks as though my grandfather is gone for the day, but at least six of his guards remain in his chambers."

"Six?" Jonathan asks. "That feels a bit like overkill."

"My grandfather is paranoid, as you might recall. The other half-dozen of his personal guards must have gone with him."

"So how should we proceed? Any plans for drawing them out?" Jonathan asks. "How do we get past *six* guards? I'm not exactly built for stealth these days."

"Easy," I say, wondering why no one else has seen the obvious answer. "We should just ask."

I hear both Ethan and Jonathan protesting but that doesn't stop me from flinging open the door. I march into the king's private living quarters, my fists on my hips. Bronze, eerily lifelike statues of men and women in various poses of supplication line the outer walls of the room. Six guards stand at attention in front of what looks like a collection of artifacts. The king's trophies, no doubt. One guard startles when he sees me.

"Who goes there?" he asks, raising his spear and alerting the others to my presence.

"Oh good, I have your attention already," I say. "My name is Lord Haden, prince—well, former prince—of the Underrealm, and I am here to collect Cupid's bow. I do not plan on leaving without it, so how about you go ahead and hand it over?"

"Haden, stop!" Ethan hisses from behind the half-open door.

I glance back at him. "Don't worry, I know what I'm doing."

"Do you?" he snaps.

When I look back at the guards, three of them have raised their staffs, crackling with electricity, two have swords at the ready, and the last has drawn a bronze bow, with a rather sharp-looking, electrified arrow pointed at my chest.

"Kill him," says one of the men with a sword.

"What?" I say, holding my arms up in an exaggerated shrug. "Did I forget to say 'please'?"

chapter twenty-five

DAPHNE

Shady shakes his hand. I'd bit him, hard, in order to get him to let me go. I can only hope he doesn't get the inclination to bite me back. But that isn't my biggest concern at the moment.

Tobin is out there, alive—but not for long, according to the message he had shouted in front of the cliffs. Do they know I am here, or had Tobin been forced to deliver that message multiple times throughout the Underrealm?

I consider shouting back, alerting Garrick and his men to my presence right away, but without the Key, what good would turning myself over do?

I need the Key before I can do anything.

"You have to help me," I say, pacing in front of Shady. "I need to save my friend. I need to find the Key, and I need your help in order to do it."

"You said your friend is in the mortal world," Shady says. "You said he was looking for Kore. How is he here now?"

"This is a different friend. Haden is my friend who is headed to the Skyrealm. Tobin is my friend who is being held for ransom by the king."

"How can you save them both?" Shady asks. "If youuu trade Key for the one called Tobin, how will youuu use it to return to the one called Haden? Youuu said he will die if you are not reunited. Youuu said we need him to bring Kore back and dessstroy the Keres."

I stop pacing. For a faceless zombie, Shady is awfully logical, and I can't ignore what he is saying. I need the Key to save Haden. I need the Key to kill the Keres. But I also need to give away the Key to save Tobin.

My best friend versus the boy I love.

"What will this king do if he gets the Key?" Shady asks. "You said you need to find it before he or the Court find it. What will they do with it?"

I think of Garrick and his two shadows. His manipulations to get the crown. "Release the Keres," I say, speculating. Garrick must be working with the Keres. And what would they want more than to be freed from their prison?

And what will they do once they're free? I already know the answer: destroy everything.

I'm not just looking at the question of saving Tobin versus saving Haden—I'm looking at the question of Tobin versus the greater good.

But Tobin is here because of me. He traveled to the Under-realm—risked everything—to help me. How can I just walk away from him? How can I leave him to die?

"I can save both of them," I say, pacing again. "There has to be a way to save both. Garrick said I have until first light to save Tobin. Haden told me he has about forty-eight hours left. What if

I can use the Key to get close enough to free Tobin, and then the two of us get out of there before Garrick actually gets his hands on it? Then we can use the Key to save Haden and stop the Keres."

"Annnd get Kore back?" Shady says, his moaning voice hopeful and leading.

I stop pacing and stand in front of Shady. "Yes," I say. "I promise you this, if you help me find the Key and save my friends, I will help you find Persephone."

Shady drops to one knee, his hand pressed against the ground. "Then I ammm your humble servant, Daphne of the morrrtal realm. I will help youuu save both your friends."

"Thank you," I say, fighting back a wave of emotion.

After a moment, I turn away and gaze out over the cliff. "Now all we need to do is find Charon, hope beyond hope he has the Key and is willing to hand it over, and then make it back to the palace before first light tomorrow. Easy peasy." My stomach clenches. There is nothing easy about any of this—let alone the fact that the dock near the gate, where I had first encountered Charon, was at least a day's journey from the palace. And we don't even know if that's where Charon will be. "How on earth are we going to find Charon and get back in time?" I mutter to myself.

"Use your Kronolithe to send ussss there," Shady says.

"*Send us?*"

"Kore's pomegranate gave her ability to move through Underrealm with ease. She would think of where she wanted to go, and her Kronolithe would send her there."

"You mean like teleportation?" I ask, clasping my hand over the necklace.

"I do not know word, 'teleportation,' but I do know it can take youuu from one place to another in this realm in blink of an eye."

"So you're telling me I could have blinked myself right out of your cave anytime I wanted?"

"Yesss," he says. If it were possible for a faceless man to look sheepish, Shady was pulling it off. "That is whyyy I did not tell you."

"Then what are we waiting for?" I ask. "Show me how to teleport ourselves off this rock."

"It is not as simple as youuu make it sound," Shady says, approaching my side.

"Nothing ever is," I say.

chapter twenty-six

HADEN

The electrified arrow sails toward my chest. I deflect it with a burst of lightning from my hand. *Huh, I didn't know I could do that.* The arrow flies off to the left and embeds in the doorframe just as Ethan and Jonathan come charging into the room behind me.

"A present for you," I say to Jonathan, nodding to the arrow.

He grabs it and knocks it into the maple-wood bow we bought at a sporting goods store on our way to the campground. This arrow looks far superior to the graphite arrows that also came from the shop. "Drop your weapon," he orders the guard, whom he has trained in his sights.

"I would do it," Ethan says. "Eros never misses his mark."

"Eros?" the guard lowers his sword slightly.

"It's the fugitive prince," the other sword-bearing soldier says, pointing at Ethan. "There's a price on his head. Kill the others but capture Prince Ethan. We'll eat like the king tonight."

The Skylord archer goes for a second arrow from his quiver, but I am faster than he is. I hit him with a blast of lightning, knocking the bow from his hands. As he scrambles for it, I blast him again. He falls to the ground and I turn in time to block a blow from another guard's spear. In a matter of seconds, I have gained control of his weapon and incapacitated him.

"Good work," Ethan says as I toss him the spear. He lunges into combat with another spear bearer, while Jonathan holds off the swordsman with his raised bow. The man drops his weapon and holds up his hands, no doubt wanting to avoid an arrow slung by Eros himself. It's a good thing he cannot see the wince of pain Jonathan is fighting to hide, from the strain of holding the position with his injured shoulder.

The other swordsman, who must be their commanding officer, barks at the last standing spearman, and the two lunge for me. I have always been a gifted fighter, but today I feel as though I am under some sort of charm. I use my mimic powers to study their movements. In a matter of seconds, I am blocking blows before they barely start to fly and dodging out of the way with ease. I catch the spearman by the back of his cape, and in a twisting move, wrap it around him like a cocoon. I kick him away from me and he collides into the guard who had Ethan locked in combat up until this moment.

"I could have handled that myself," Ethan says, kicking one of the men so he stays down, but he smiles at me and I know he's impressed. "I had my doubts, but this might be my favorite version of you."

Out of the corner of my eye, I see the commander charge at me with his sword. I shove my hand out and grab him by the wrist. With a hard twist of his arm, and an elbow to his diaphragm, I get him to surrender his weapon.

I wrench his arm behind his back and hold the sword to his throat. "I told you I wasn't going to leave without Cupid's Bow, so how about you *please* hand it over now?"

"It's not—"

But before the commander can finish, his words are cut off by the shrill shriek of a female voice. I look up as a woman standing in the open doorway drops the bundle of linens she was holding. Her face is ashen, and I see another scream forming on her lips. If she calls for more guards . . .

I contemplate letting go of the commander and making a move to grab her, but Ethan is faster. He stands between me and the woman, outstretching his hand toward her in a gentle beckoning. "It's okay," he says, removing his bronze helmet. "It's me, Ethan."

"Ethan?" she says, her voice giving away that she hasn't seen him in years. "I'd heard you'd returned to your grandfather's ranks a few months ago, but then I heard rumors. Rumors that you had gone rogue . . ." She takes a step forward, and I am not sure if she is going to strike him or embrace him.

"I'm sorry, Mother," Ethan says, closing the distance between them. "I should have told you my plans."

"Mother?" Jonathan's voice is filled with awe. He lowers his bow and turns toward the two. "Psyche? Is it really you?"

"I'm sorry," she says, squinting at him. "Do I know you?" She looks at Ethan. "Who is this man? What are you doing, my son?"

"Mother, this is—"

But another cry interrupts him. This one from Jonathan. He lunges sideways and then falls to the ground—a crackling, electrified sword protrudes from his chest. In the moment of our distraction, the man he was holding at bay must have grabbed his weapon and struck. Ethan is faster than me once again. He lays the man flat with a lightning bolt and then runs to Jonathan.

"Father?" he says. "Father? Can you hear me?"

"Father?" Psyche, Ethan's mother, says, backing away from the two. "No . . ."

A pool of blood creeps out from under Jonathan's prostrate body. Ethan leans down close to him. "Father, hang on. It's going to be all right."

Jonathan sputters, his lips trying to form a word. "My bow," he finally chokes out.

"Find his bow!" Ethan shouts at me.

I still have the commander in my grasp. I wrench him with me as I scan the various artifacts. Some are in glass cases, and others are mounted on plaques, like they belong in some sort of museum. I see all manner of weapons, even a crown, and what looks like a Gorgon's head that has been wrapped in golden cloth, but I don't see anything that resembles a bow. "Where is it?" I demand, shoving the sword against the commander's throat. The smell of blood and fear stings my nostrils. "Where is Cupid's Bow?"

"It's not here," the commander says.

"Do not lie to me!"

"I'm not." He gestures toward an empty case. "It's gone. I don't know where—"

I've lost patience for subduing the man. He's of no use to us. I cuff him hard across the forehead and then lower his limp body to the ground.

"Mother, do you know—" Ethan starts to say, but when he looks up the woman is gone. The door stands wide open.

"She's changed . . ." Jonathan's raspy voice says. "She's worn down by life. Like me. Still as beautiful . . . as ever. At least I got to see her one last time . . ."

"Father, don't speak," Ethan says. "Save your energy. We'll find your bow." He signals to me. "It's got to be here somewhere."

I scan the room again, searching every case. Nothing. Nothing. Nothing. I can feel my confidence from before whooshing out of me like air from a billows.

Why did I ever think this would work?

Why didn't I see the danger I was putting the others in?

I look back at Ethan and shake my head. He has rolled Jonathan on his back and holds his hand now, squeezing and rubbing it like he's trying to keep it warm.

The memory of my own mother's cold hand in mine flashes through my mind. I held her while she died when I was only a boy. And now because of me, because of my foolhardy plan, Ethan—who had never had the chance to know his father when he was a boy—would have to hold him now as he faded away.

This is all my fault.

I start for the door, not sure if I am leaving to give them privacy, or if I think I can find the bow elsewhere in the palace—but I know from the amount of blood and the pallor that has crept over Jonathan's normally rosy countenance, that even if I searched the entire palace and located the bow, it would be too late.

"Wait," Jonathan says. "My last darts."

I realize it now, his quiver is missing. The one that held his last two emotion darts. Would that restore him?

Ethan and I both search the ground. It only takes a moment to find the quiver clutched in the hand of the guard who stabbed him. He must have ripped the quiver from Jonathan's shoulder when he struck him. Ethan desperately rips out the store-bought, graphite arrows that are no good, and then reaches into the bottom of the quiver, searching for the darts. First he finds what looks like a handful of brittle, metallic blue dust. One of the last two darts must have been crushed during the chaos. He groans and lets the useless particles fall through his fingers. He reaches into the quiver again, even more desperate this time, and pulls out a small, glittering purple dart. He places it in his father's hand and tries to close Jonathan's large fingers around it. "Here," he says. "Take it."

"No," Jonathan says, letting it fall from his hand. "It's not enough."

"Just hang on. It could be enough until we find your bow . . ."

"Too late." He blinks his eyes rapidly. "Give it to Haden."

"No," I say, stepping forward. "I don't deserve it."

"You'll need it. You can still find Persephone. You can still save Daphne." He closes his eyes. "Save her for me."

I kneel next to him, his blood soaking the hem of my tunic. This is even more blood than when my mother died. I reach down and wrap my fingers around the small dart-like arrow. Ethan makes a move as if he wants to stop me, but then pulls back, still clasping his father's hand, and allows me to pick it up.

I hold it for a moment, wanting nothing more than to dose myself right now—to experience anything other than the grief that grips me. But I hold back, knowing that feeling sorrow is a privilege at this time. A gift. An emotion that will etch this moment into my memory forever. I will never be able to forget what Jonathan sacrificed in order to help save Daphne.

No matter how black or bleak things will get in the very near future, I won't allow myself to give in to the nothingness. "I won't give up until she is safe," I say, tucking the arrow into the belt of my stolen uniform.

And then, as if his soul recognizes that someone else has taken possession of his last dart—his last thread of immortality—Jonathan's large body goes limp, and a wheezing breath escapes his lips.

Ethan collapses to his knees next to me. "Oh Zeus," he says into his hands as if he were praying, "why have you let his thread be cut?"

"He hasn't," a woman's voice says. I look up just as Psyche scrambles past us—a large golden bow in her hands. She lays it against Jonathan's chest and wraps his large arms around the bow.

"Take it, Eros," she says. "Take your mantle."

She presses his arms tighter around it, but they fall away.

"It's too late, Mother," Ethan says, holding his hand out to clasp her shoulder.

"No." She throws herself on top of the bow, pressing it against Jonathan's chest. "I've waited centuries to see you again, Eros. I will not allow you to leave me now!"

Ethan grabs her and pulls her away. She collapses against his chest, her dress soaked in her husband's blood, crying tears so painful that I turn away.

For the third time this afternoon, we are interrupted by an unexpected cry from the doorway. Though this time, it is less of a cry and more of a command. Two dozen soldiers file into the room, each with an electrified spear in hand and sword at hip. Before I can even think how to react, we have been flanked on all sides.

"Arrest the invaders," the commanding voice barks. "For breaking and entering, armed robbery, and high treason."

Two guards grab me and pull me to my feet. Psyche tries to protest as they wrench her away from Jonathan's body, but it is evident that they think she was in on our heist. Ethan doesn't struggle as another set of guards pulls him away from his father. Perhaps he's in shock?

"Put them in chains," the voice says, coming closer. Terresa steps through the doorway. She stands in front of us with her hands on her hips. "And then I will escort them to the Black Hole from here."

chapter twenty-seven

DAPHNE

It takes about two hours of practicing before I start to get the hang of using the pomegranate necklace to teleport. Shady has me practice moving only a few feet at a time, popping from inside the cave to the outside. Which he quickly reverses from outside the cave to *inside* when I almost teleport myself right off the edge of the cliff.

The tricky part is visualization. I have to close my eyes and think hard, visualizing where it is that I want to go. The problem is that I let my mind wander, and instead of picturing the landing outside the cave entrance, I start to think about when I stood at the edge, listening to Tobin's message. Instead of landing beside the boulder, I land with my toes hanging over the edge of the cliff. Luckily, I re-visualize a spot inside the cave just before teetering over the ledge.

After playing it safe for a while after that, I start feeling antsy. The time is ticking away, and the light in the sky is beginning to wane. It will be late evening soon. But Shady keeps insisting I'm not ready yet.

"Now try taking me with youuu," Shady says, holding his hand out to me. "Visualize both of us moving to water pool." He points to the back of the cave.

I squeeze Shady's hand, trying not to shrink back at his touch. His gangly fingers remind me of withered carrots. I close my eyes, but instead of visualizing the water pool, I picture the gray rocky ground at the bottom of the cliff. I don't want to practice anymore, I want to get moving.

When I open my eyes and see the gray rock earth beneath my feet, Shady moans at me in disapproval. "What?" I say. "We made it, didn't we?" We are standing at the bottom of the cliff, near a sandy footpath that would take us to the road that leads into the Wastelands.

"And what if we'd reappeared midair?" Shady asks. "We would have fallen to our deaths."

"You're already dead," I say. "And besides, we didn't fall. Now can we move on?"

Shady grunts and holds out his hand once again. I nod and give a little smile—I don't know if it's me getting better at listening or if Shady is getting better at speaking—but outside the cave everything is a little clearer. More hopeful. I can even start to hear the ethereal tones of the rocks and ghostly flowers around us. We must have traveled off the royal grounds.

"You think Charon is most likely on one of his docks?" I ask.

"He is always either on his boat on the river or at one of the docks. His job issss never ending. He must collect and escort the freshly arrived souls of the dead through Underrealm. Trying to catch him at one of the many docks is ooour chance of finding him."

"I've only seen three different docks since I've been here. The one where I was attacked by the Shades after the chariot crash, the one I passed while traversing the Elysium shore, and the one on the beach near Persephone's Gate. I guess we need to start with those since they're the only ones I can visualize."

Shady nods. "The first one you mentioned is closest. Let us start there."

I think back to the dock where I was attacked by those Shades, just before Shady saved me. The only thing I had really gotten a good look at were the slats between the boards where I had fallen. I close my eyes and think about those slats as hard as I can. When I open my eyes, I find myself standing on the dock with Shady, my heel wedged into one of the slats.

"Not here," Shady says. It only takes a moment to glance around and find the dock deserted. Even the boat that had been waiting to take Garrick and me up the river is gone. Had that been the boatman's vessel, or had it been a military ship?

I work my foot free from where it's wedged in the slats while Shady scans the river. My foot is good and stuck, and I am feeling more than grateful that horde of Shades is gone also. "Can I ask you something?" I say when I finally wrench my sandal free. "When you rescued me from those Shades, did you do it because you knew I was the queen, or did you do it because you wanted to take me home for your very own meal?"

Shady grunts. He looks down at the dock where he'd clubbed me in the head. He shrugs his big gray shoulders. "If youuu must know, I considered eating you. Then I saw your crown. I assumed you were important." He waves his leathery hand in my general direction. "Besides, youuu are far too scrawny."

"Ha!" I laugh. Scrawny is not a word that I have ever heard to describe me. Curvy is more like it—if the person is being polite.

Though on a diet of flowers and lizards, I can tell from the way my dress fits that I am starting to lose some of those curves. Something I'll have to rectify with a bacon cheeseburger and the world's biggest root-beer float when I get home.

Shady looks at me with his eyeless gaze. "I do nnnot care for eating people. Only if there is nothing else."

"Well, isn't that noble of you and all." Maybe it's because I've never had a conversation with another Shade, but Shady definitely seemed different from all the others. He is a solitary, thoughtful soul, while the other Shades seem to prefer to run in mindless packs and viciously prey on just about anything that moves. "Are you like an anti-people-atarian?" I ask.

Shady shakes his head like he doesn't understand my question, but then he says, "People have bad texture. Too stringy. And all that hair of yours wouuuld get stuck in my teeth."

I raise my eyebrows at him and stifle a gag at the mental image he just conjured. Shady makes that weird noise again, and I realize he's laughing at me again.

"Suuuch expressions!" he moans.

"All right, funny guy, let's go to the beach by the gate next. That's where I met Charon before, so it seems like the most likely place to find him again."

I take Shady's hand again, close my eyes, and try to concentrate on what details I can remember from that location. We'd been running for our lives at the time as well. What is it with Shades attacking near docks? Finally, I picture the sandy bank where we had discovered Charon lying unconscious. Garrick had thought he was dead, but after checking for his pulse I had insisted on taking the old man on the boat with us to keep him safe from the Shades. I picture the prints our feet had made in the sand.

When I feel soft wet sand under my feet, I know we've made it to the right place. Shady answers my unasked question before I even open my eyes. "Not here, either."

I look around, scanning the horizon, hoping he's missed something.

"Perhaps we should wait," Shady says. "Perhaps he's on his boat already? If there were enough souls waiting, he may have made an early start."

"If only I knew what his boat looks like, I could pop us right over." It is starting to get dark. Once Charon is on the river, the likelihood of catching up with him seems nil. And even with Shady by my side, the idea of hanging out where Shades might decide to come looking for dinner seems like a less than appealing plan. "Let's go to Elysium next. Then stop there and wait. He's bound to deliver a soul to Elysium sooner or later."

"Only rare souls gooo to Elysium," Shady says.

"Maybe we'll get lucky." I hold my hand out to him, but he doesn't take it.

"I cannot go to Elysium," he says. "Shades cannot tread on their shores."

"Right," I say, crossing my arms in front of me. It grows colder as the fake sunlight fades away. "Sometimes, I forget you're a Shade."

Shady cocks his head at me. His gaping mouth twists into the strangest grimace. Then I realize that it isn't a grimace. He's smiling.

In this moment, I can't help but think that Shady reminds me a little bit of Haden. The two of them would probably get along.

My heart aches just thinking of Haden. I turn away and close my eyes. If I can't find Charon—if I can't find the Key—I may never see him again. And even if I do find the Key, if I'm too late and the curse takes him before I can cure him, I may get to see him, but he won't be the same. He won't be *my* Haden, just an emotionless husk of his former self. What if I never get to see Haden's smile again? "I'll go to Elysium. You wait here and see if Charon comes. I'll be back as quickly as possible."

I know Shady is about to protest in his overprotective way, so I picture the lonely dock in Elysium as quickly as possible. It had been night when my guide and I had passed it, but I picture the way it had looked illuminated in the light of Kayla's lamp.

Kayla! Why didn't I tell Haden that I had met his mother? He would want to know that she's okay. That she's a handmaiden to the oracle and not a Shade like he had always feared. We'd had so little time together . . .

I catch my mind wandering and try to center it back on the image of the Elysium dock, but I know I'm off course when my feet land in water. I open my eyes just as the current of the river pulls me under. Water fills my mouth and I choke, trying to keep it from rushing down my throat. I claw at the surface of the river, and bob up once before I'm pulled down again. I close my eyes, thinking of somewhere, anywhere but here.

I feel dry land under me. I open my eyes and find that I am lying on my side on the Elysium shore, just where my boat crashed all those days ago. This was the first place Kayla had brought me to search for Tobin and the Key, and the last place Charon had been before disappearing. No wonder my mind had latched on to that.

In the distance, I see the Elysium dock. A great black boat is just pulling away from the shore.

"Stop!" I shout, run-hobbling to the dock. My feet sink into the wet sand on the riverbank. I'll never make it there in time . . .

Unless I use the pomegranate. Duh! I keep running and grab the pendant while imagining the dock in front of me. My feet hit wood and I am running up the dock now, having bypassed the half mile from where I had been to here.

"Wait," I shout toward the boat as a tall oarsman in a black cloak pushes away from the dock into the river. "Stop!" I shout again. I don't know if he can't hear me or if he doesn't care to listen, but the oarsman continues to paddle into the current.

I peer into the crowded boat as it pulls away. Several ghostly-looking people—or souls, I should say—sit huddled together on a long bench. One man cries, moaning into the shoulder of an elderly looking woman at his side. These must be the souls of those not lucky enough to be dropped off in Elysium. Charon must be taking them to wherever souls are turned into Shades. Out of instinct, I scan their faces, hoping not to see anyone I know.

There's a young woman, clutching her jacket close to her chest. A smear of blood paints her face. Next to her is an empty space on the bench. The current catches the boat and pulls it swiftly down the River of Woe. I close my eyes, picturing the girl and the empty space next to her.

I know I've arrived when I feel the press of cold bodies against me. Someone grabs at my tattered skirts as I stand. I try not to look at any of the souls, knowing my dreams will be haunted with them for weeks to come.

"Charon?" I say, calling to the oarsman.

The cloaked man turns toward me. His face is hooded. He points a bony finger in my direction. "You do not belong here."

"Uh, yeah. I know," I say, taking another step closer. I keep my movements slow and measured, trying not to rock the boat. "You're Charon, right?"

The oarsman raises his withered hand and pulls his hood from his head. The skin is so thin on his face that it almost looks like a skull, and his nose is so large and crooked, it reminds me of a beak. The old man stares back at me with black eyes that are sunk deep in their sockets. He hadn't looked so ghastly when he was unconscious. "Who's asking?" he says. "It's a crime to trespass in the world of the dead."

"I'm from the mortal realm, and yeah, I'm not dead. I almost was, but that's a different story. Anyway, I'm not exactly trespassing since I'm technically Queen of the Underrealm and all. Sort of. But we've met before . . ." I trail off as I feel someone yanking on my cloak. I glance back to see the crying man, trying to get my attention.

"I don't know how I got here," he says. "I don't know where I am. There was a train and I . . ." He looks down at his leg—only it isn't there.

I glance away. "I'm sorry," I say to him. I'm about to explain to him where he is but I have no idea how to go about informing someone that he's dead.

"Sit down and remain silent," Charon says, prodding the one-legged man with his oar.

Okay, so Charon might be old, but that doesn't make him the gentle grandfatherly type.

"Do I know you?" he asks, after pushing the crying man back into his seat. It takes me half a second to realize the question was directed at me.

"Yes, we've met," I say, fending off the hands of the young woman. She's crying now, too, asking if I've seen her boyfriend. I can't help but want to hug her, knowing how it feels to find yourself in a strange land, disoriented, and missing someone you love. "Well, we've sort of met. My friends and I found you unconscious on the beach near Persephone's Gate. We were under attack by some Shades, so we put you in our boat and . . ."

"Oh yes," Charon says. "So you're the reason I woke up on the Elysium shore with a mighty fine headache."

"Yes. But I don't think I'm responsible for the headache."

I try to step closer to him, but the girl wraps herself around my legs. "Have you seen David?" she asks. "Do you know where David is?"

"Sorry, the dead can be quite handsy," Charon says, and bats the girl away from me with his oar. "That's why I recognize you," he says and points at me. "You were the girl with the Key."

"The Key? Yes, yes," I say excitedly. "That's why I'm here. Do you know what happened to it?"

"Of course I know what happened to it." Charon sticks his oar into the water and steers the boat away from an outcropping of rocks. "I took it. One shouldn't leave the Key to the Underrealm lying around. I figured you were dead, so I didn't think you would miss it."

Hope swells in my heart. "Where is it?"

"Hidden somewhere safe."

"I need it. Please take me to the Key."

"Nuh uh uh," Charon says, wagging a bony finger at me. "Everything has its price. You must make me a trade."

I remember now that Garrick had said when we first arrived in the Underrealm that the boatman always required payment of some sort. As it stands, I only have four possessions in this world. The communication talisman that is my only connection to Haden, the sobriety coin that symbolizes my father's commitment to me to become a better man, Tobin's hat that is perched on my head, and the pomegranate necklace that makes it so I can travel through the Underrealm with ease—and without which I will never make it to Tobin or Haden in time. Each item is of great importance to me for personal reasons, but I don't suppose all but one will be considered a fair trade for the Key of the Underrealm.

"I don't have much to give you," I say.

"I do not wish for payment," Charon says, pulling down on the great oar in his aged hands. "I want a favor."

"What do you want?" I ask, even though I have no idea what favor I could offer this ancient immortal.

"What do you suppose an old boatman who has been sailing this vessel day in and day out for all eternity may want?"

I shrug because I have no answer.

"Simple, girly. A break."

"A break?"

"Yes, I want to sit in the corner over there," he says, pointing toward a pile of cushions at the aft of the boat, "with a good book and read for a few hours. That's what I want."

"Um . . . okay. Why don't you do that, then?"

"I think I will. Which means you get to be me for the rest of the night," he says, shoving the handle of his great oar in my direction.

"Me?" I try to take a step back. "For the rest of the night? You don't understand, I need the Key before first light. I need to take it to the palace—"

"You'll be finished by first light. As long as I am done with my book by then." He pulls a copy of what looks like an early edition *Pride and Prejudice* from his robe. "A young woman about your age gave me this in exchange for a ride on my boat about a hundred years ago. I don't get much time to myself to read, you see, and I've been waiting a few decades to see if Elizabeth and Darcy ever get together. Which means I need you to act as me for a few hours, picking up the newly arrived dead and escorting them to their final destinations—if you know what I mean." He raises a knowing eyebrow and makes a clicking noise with his mouth.

I blink at him. He wants me to become the boatman of death so he can read Jane Austen? Charon cracks a big old smile and slaps the oar into my hands while I am too dumbfounded to protest. "I'm not sure I'm the right person for the job," I finally say.

"Someone has to do it," he says as he nestles himself into his nest of cushions. "The dead don't wait. They just keep on coming and coming. In fact, it looks like you've got a new arrival over there."

I follow his crooked finger to where a large black gate stands on the shore of the river, just beyond a new set of docks. I didn't realize we had already traveled so far down the river. Charon's boat must move supernaturally fast. My eye catches the slow movement of the gate swinging open and see a rather large man about to enter. I wonder if these are the main gates of the Underrealm—the ones only the souls of the dead can pass through without the Key. I squint, trying to make out the features of the man who stands at the entrance. Something about him seems familiar. My heart plummets into my gut. I almost drop the oar, rocking the boat precariously.

"Jonathan?"

chapter twenty-eight

HADEN

Terresa handles me with such roughness as she marches us to a cluster of chariots behind the palace, I start to worry that the love spell has worn off and that she really has taken us as her prisoners. Luckily, Brim pokes her tiny head out of the satchel that Terresa carries over her shoulder and gives me a reassuring meow. My worry shifts to gratitude for Terresa's quick thinking in facilitating our transfer to the Black Hole. Only, I wasn't planning on Ethan's mother, Psyche, coming along for the ride.

This means one more person I need to protect as we escape from the Black Hole. One more soul in my hands—that are still shaking from losing Jonathan.

I watch Terresa's men struggle to load Jonathan's large, limp body into one of the chariots. He was supposed to be our secret weapon. He was supposed to be the one who could find Persephone in the labyrinth with his godly powers. Now, searching for her will have to be done on foot. A task Jonathan warned us might take decades, when we only have hours. The confidence that propelled me into the throne room is nearly gone now. I try to cling to it. I can't afford for my mood to go black before our mission is through.

If only the bow had restored Jonathan to Eros. Why didn't it work?

Perhaps it wasn't even the right bow? I didn't get a good look at the weapon, and come to think of it, I haven't seen it since Terresa and her men stormed into the throne room. Did it disappear in the confusion, or did one of the guards confiscate it?

"Where do you want us to take the body?" one of the guards asks Terresa.

"We'll dump it with the other prisoners," she says, "Until the Sky King decides what to do with it. He may want to make a new trophy for his collection."

I shudder at the idea of a giant bronze-dipped Jonathan adorning the Sky King's palace. Those bronze statues that lined the throne room had seemed far too lifelike to merely be statues. I shudder once again at the idea of breaking the news about Jonathan's fate to Daphne. If I ever get the chance.

I don't protest as Terresa drops a black hood over my head. She lets her fingers linger a little too long as she pats me down, as if searching me for weapons, caressing the skin on my arms and throat. Apparently the love spell *is* still working.

For how much longer, I don't know.

It's a shorter ride to our destination than I expect it to be. I am glad for this, as I feel the familiar aching of the black poison spreading through my veins.

Terresa leads us blind into what I assume is the prison. I can't see anything through the thick material of the hood that covers my face. The air grows colder, wetter, the longer we walk. My feet scrape against the hard ground, and I stumble more than once.

We must be in the labyrinth. The feel of the air reminds me of the network of caves just beyond the pomegranate orchard in the Underrealm.

Remembering those caves makes me think of Daphne. For all I know, she's still trapped in that dreadful cave with the Shade that has taken her prisoner. If she's even still alive . . .

I can feel the weight of the small dart tucked into my belt that Terresa didn't bother to confiscate, and I remember the vow I made to myself when Jonathan lay dying. My word must be my bond. I will not give in to the nothingness again.

I clench my fists, straining against the heavy shackles at my wrists, and will my dark thoughts to depart. I concentrate on memorizing the paces and turns as we walk. I know I hadn't been paying close enough attention when we first entered, but maybe I can at least get us closer. After six lefts, three rights, and another three lefts—no, maybe it was four more lefts—Terresa pulls me to a halt. I hear the sounds of metal scraping against stone, and then I am thrust forward and to the ground. I hit my elbow hard when I land and find myself grateful for the shock of pain that shudders through my arm. Pain means I am still in control.

Terresa tears the hood from my head. The following brightness makes it feel like I've been jabbed in my eyes. I had expected it to be dark or dim in this cavern-like cell, but a row of blaring lights fills the high ceiling. I realize something I didn't notice before: I haven't seen a single torch since entering the Skyrealm. They have some form of electricity here. Solar power, I assume. Everything in the Skyrealm is overly bright—which makes sense, since the Skylords do not see well in the dark. I wonder if the lights ever go out in the Black Hole, or if the prisoners are expected to sleep in full light.

I watch as Ethan and Psyche are pushed into the cell and four sweating guards drag Jonathan's body in after them. It seems quite the insult to injury to lock his family in a cell with his corpse. Terresa kneels down in front of me. She clasps her hands against my face and stares into my eyes with such intensity that I am afraid she is going to try to claim her prize early. I brace myself, straining against my chains, as she leans in.

One of the guards clears his throat. "Are you ready, Lieutenant Gordon?"

Her lips stop only an inch away from mine. "You have three hours until the entrance to the labyrinth moves," she whispers. Meet me at the hut where your father sleeps. I will collect my reward in full." She drops something in my lap and then pulls away. "I'm ready," she says to the guards.

She backs out of the cell and one of the guards latches the barred gate.

"This prison hasn't seen an Underlord in almost a century and now we have two in only a week. That's quite the prize, Lieutenant."

"Just you wait," Terresa says to her men. "I have a lead on a much bigger bounty. I expect you'll be calling me Captain Gordon soon. I have a feeling the king will be promoting me to Ethan's position shortly." She gives her former commander a smirk.

As she takes her leave with her men, one of the guards calls back, "Someone will come along to feed you . . . eventually. That is, if the minotaur doesn't make a meal of you first."

The moment the guards round the corner back into the maze, Psyche collapses over Jonathan's body.

"Mother, please, come away," Ethan says, reaching for her.

She hisses something at him I don't understand. Perhaps she's been taken by hysteria. I call Ethan away from her, letting her have a moment to mourn uninterrupted. "What do you think this is?" I say, holding up the thing that Terresa dropped into my lap. It appears to be a spool of very thin, very fine, translucent string.

"Arachne's thread," Ethan says, pulling a bit of it from the spool. It looks almost invisible on its own. "Spider's string. Look," he says, pointing to where the light glints against the invisible thread that is strung from the spool out through the gate. "The guards use it so they don't lose their way in the maze, but to anyone not looking for it, it would either go completely unnoticed or only appear to be cobwebs." He gives me a sarcastic smirk that surprises me, considering the pain I see etched on his face. "She must really like you to risk leaving this with you. She's left us a trail to find the exit."

"Thank you, Terresa," I say, then I feel a pang of guilt in my stomach. I feel like a rogue playing on her emotions—however artificially induced—in order to get what I want. Especially when what I want is someone other than her.

Ethan inspects the bars of the cell door. The opening between them is barely big enough to fit his fist. "Now we only need to figure out how to get through this door."

Almost as if waiting for her cue, a tiny cat head appears between the bars of our cell from the outside corridor.

"Brim!" I say, realizing that I'd thought Terresa had taken her with her.

She gives a muffled meow, jumps through the bars with ease, and prances over to me. She spits something out at my feet as if she were bringing me a dead hellmouse as a gift and rubs against my ankles, looking for approval. I inspect her present more closely and realize it's a set of keys.

"Good girl," I say, giving her a good chin scratch before plucking the keys from the ground. The smaller one fits the shackles at my wrists. After using it, I toss the keys to Ethan. I suspect the larger one will open the door.

"Now we only need to find Persephone," I say as Ethan unlocks his own chains. I glance at Jonathan's body, wishing he were here to fulfill his role—he'd said he could search the labyrinth in a matter of seconds, but I don't know exactly how he had planned on doing it. I had been so overcome with confidence, I hadn't bothered going over every detail of the plan before storming into the Skyrealm. "Do you think we could subdue a guard? Coerce him or her into telling us Persephone's location?"

Ethan shakes his head. "My father has bought the loyalty of every guard in the Black Hole. They won't betray him."

"My kingdom is rich. We could promise them more . . ."

Ethan shakes his head again, a grim expression on his face. "The price is their families' lives. If they betray the king, everyone they love will be put to death. That is how he ensures their loyalty, and I could not live with myself if that happened to someone because of me." He glances at his father and his voice dips lower. His mother is still huddled over Jonathan's body. At first I thought that she had fainted, but now it seems as if she is searching his tunic for something.

"No coercion then," I say. "Just a good old-fashioned wild hydra chase."

"The chances of coming upon a guard are slim anyway. Unless they're transporting a prisoner or delivering food a couple of times a week, the guards don't stay in the prison."

"A prison without guards?" I ask. "I thought this place was impenetrably secure?"

"Between the ever-moving exit and the complicated labyrinth, there's no need for guards in residence. They leave that to the minotaur. I only know of one man who has ever escaped . . ." Ethan's eyes grow wide as he watches Psyche riffle through the folds of Jonathan's tunic. Her hands are still shackled and her movements are clumsy and frantic.

"It has to be here," she mumbles to herself. "It wouldn't leave him on its own."

"Mother, let me unlock your chains," Ethan says in a soothing voice. "We need to leave this place."

"No," she says, glaring at him in a way that almost reminds me of a feral animal. "We will not leave Eros behind to become one of your grandfather's trophies. I *will not* leave him."

"Mother . . ." Ethan trails off and glances at me. I know what he needs to say but can't bring himself to do so. He can't carry Jonathan's dead weight. Not on his own. It had taken four exceptionally large guards to haul him in here.

"We'll manage," I say, clenching my fist, trying to will the numb, weakening sensation that tingles into my fingertips. I don't have much time left.

"He'll carry himself," Psyche says, pulling something from

inside Jonathan's tunic. I think perhaps her grief has driven her mad, until she holds the object up in her hand. It looks like a small golden archer's bow, no bigger than her palm. "I knew it wouldn't leave him. Which means there's still a chance."

"Mother, there's no time. We need to go now."

"There's always time for the ones we love." She presses the minuscule bow against Jonathan's hollow chest. Tears stream from her eyes as she leans over him. "Come back to me, Eros," she says and brushes a kiss over his blue lips.

Her words remind me of what Daphne had said to me when she called my soul back from the Underrealm—when I had been trapped by a communication talisman in my father's throne room. If it hadn't been for her words breaking through to me, I would have died at my father's hands. The love in Psyche's actions, her determination not to give up on her husband, makes me feel as though my heart is shattering into pieces. Tears flood my eyes. I don't fight them back because I am grateful for the emotion, but I have to turn away.

That's why I don't see it at first. The golden light that fills the room as if it were sunrise and we were standing on a mountain peak. It's Psyche's shout that grabs my attention. I whirl around and find her leaning over a man who lies on the ground where Jonathan had been. Only it isn't Jonathan. Or is it . . .

The man is much younger than Jonathan and quite a bit more . . . fit, with curling hair and a chiseled face and arms that remind me of a perfect statue. But his eyes are the same, I see it now as he cracks them open. As is the rosiness that fills his face when he smiles. "Psyche," he says, holding his hand out to her.

"Eros," Psyche says, embracing him. Ethan kneels next to the two.

The blood that had soaked his tunic is gone, as if washed away by the golden light that emanates from the large golden bow in Eros's grasp. As he sits up with the help of Ethan and Psyche, I notice the most curious thing about Jonathan's new form. He has wings. Well, he is Cupid after all.

"Welcome back," I say to Jonathan.

"We thought you were dead," Ethan says, and I can hear the emotion and relief flooding into his voice.

"I think I was," Eros says. "I was standing at the gates to the Underworld. I could see a boat on the shore in the distance. The gate was just opening and I felt compelled to enter, but then I heard you calling to me," he says, reaching out to brush the tears from Psyche's face. "And I had to come. You and I are bound by true love after all."

Psyche throws herself into Eros's arms. The two embrace and kiss in such a way that Ethan and I are both compelled to avert our eyes. After a few moments, Ethan clears his throat. "We should get going. Our time is limited before the exit changes locations and Terresa's trail will no longer be good. We must find Persephone."

Eros stands, drawing Psyche up with him. "This sounds like a job for a god," he says, flexing his wings out and giving them a cursory flap. It must feel good to have them back after all this time.

"Will you fly through the prison then?" I ask.

"That will take too long." Eros folds his wings in against his back. "As a god of the metaphysical realm, I can be a concept. The embodiment of love itself. I can exist in more than one place all at once."

"Come again?" I ask.

"I will show you."

Eros lets go of Psyche and takes a step back. He closes his eyes as if concentrating. I wait, holding my breath, for this conceptualization to happen. After more than a minute, I let my breath out in a cough.

"Is something happening yet?" I ask.

"Not yet," Eros says, clenching his eyes tighter shut. "It's been a long time since I've had my powers. It may take a few tries."

We wait another minute. Ethan looks down at his wrist as if he were wearing a timepiece. Psyche clucks her tongue. I begin to wonder if we need to start a search on foot.

With a snapping noise, Eros vanishes into a cloud of golden mist. It swirls about us, ruffling Psyche's hair, and then gusts out of the cell through the bars in the door as if carried by an invisible wind. The mist separates into several wisps and flies off in multiple directions through the corridor.

So *that* is what he meant.

Persephone will be found in no time . . .

chapter twenty-nine

DAPHNE

He wasn't there. When I finally managed to dock the boat—very little thanks to Charon's clipped instructions as he read from his novel—the man I had seen just outside the gate wasn't there. The man who had looked so much like Jonathan. I started to cry when no one was there. I don't know if it was out of relief that he wasn't dead or out of the desperation I had felt to see a familiar face.

"Looks like we had a return to sender," Charon had said with his nose in his book. "No reason to get all blubbery about it. On to the next stop."

It takes most of the night to collect the rest of the dead. While I had understood the Underrealm to have only two entrances, the main gate and Persephone's Gate, I gather that those two entrances must have several outlets into the Underrealm, based on how many docks I must visit during the night. People seem to be grouped by ethnicity and I wonder if which dock they end up on has to do with their country of origin or which country or region they were in when they died.

I try to ask Charon about it. He looks up from his book with tears in his eyes. "Bah," he says. "Can't have 'em all arriving in the same place. It would be far too crowded."

But that's something I notice about the boat: No matter how many people I pick up—hundreds, perhaps even thousands, after only a couple of hours—the boat never seems to get overcrowded. There always seems to be room for the dead. Perhaps it's because they're not corporeal at this point?

My heart aches for every soul who files onto the boat. Most are deathly quiet, while others ask the same questions over and over again. Where am I? How did I get here? What happened to a various loved one. At first I try to answer, but that only seems to bring on hysteria in the asker. They moan and groan and wail and paw at me. After my second embankment, Charon tells me just to ignore the dead. "Bat 'em away if they get too friendly," he says, flicking his hand as if the dead are merely like flies.

At first I think he's unnecessarily being a cranky old coot, but I begin to understand his callousness when a young girl attaches herself to my skirt, crying for her mother. I don't know how Charon can do this job day in and day out, and not go insane. I scoop the girl up into my arms and sing her the lullaby that my mother taught me when I was young. It's the same song I sang to Brim all those months ago when she had gone into beast mode in the middle of a hospital. It had soothed her into submission. The song seems to have the same effect on the dead. The girl stops crying and leans into my shoulder. The other souls fall into a quiet reverie. Everyone seems to be almost asleep when we pull into a dock that looks different from all of the others. There's a large white building with columns resembling the Greek Parthenon sitting on the shore. A second river with milky white water runs behind it.

No one is waiting on the dock here.

"Where are we?" I ask Charon.

"The end of the line." He closes his book and stretches. "Everybody off!" he shouts.

The souls snap to attention and begin to file off the boat and into the building. It's as though some sort of invisible force draws them there. The girl pats my cheek and then hops out of my arms and follows the rest.

"Where are they going? What happens to them now?"

"The souls will be sorted here. After they are judged, they will drink from the River Lethe, erasing their memories of their mortal life. The majority will then be turned into Shades. The few deemed worthy will return to the boat to be delivered to Elysium, and my rounds will begin again."

"Turned into Shades? Even the little girl?"

Charon doesn't answer.

I think about what Ms. Leeds, my original humanities teacher at Olympus Hills High, had said about Persephone during my first day of class. She said the earliest myths about Persephone claimed that she hadn't been kidnapped into the underworld at all. But that she had freely chosen to go with Hades because she had compassion for the dead. She knew they needed a queen. Someone to care for them. At the time, I had thought that was a weird story. Why would someone give up being the goddess of springtime— sunshine, happiness—in order to become the queen of the dead? But I remember how Shady had said things were better here when

Persephone reigned, and I find myself hoping beyond hope that Haden is able to find her. This place needs its Persephone.

Charon stretches and places his book on top of the pile of objects the souls had been compelled to leave for him in exchange for a ride on his boat. I gather that each person brought with them whatever it was they had on them when they died. The little girl had offered up a rather tattered-looking Barbie as her payment. "You don't suppose there's a sequel to *Pride and Prejudice* tucked in here?" Charon says, poking around the pile. "The book was quite good, but I am not completely convinced that Lizzie and Darcy are going to last . . . Ooh, this looks promising," he says, pulling out a thick book with a torn black cover. I catch a glimpse of white hands holding a red apple on the front before Charon tucks it under his arm.

I clear my throat, hoping he isn't planning on starting another book right away.

Charon hobbles over to me and takes the oar from my hands. "You did well tonight, Daphne. Your end of the bargain has been paid. I will take over from here."

It strikes me that I don't recall ever telling Charon my name. "You'll bring me to the Key now?" I look at the shore, where the last of the souls file into the temple-like structure, and then at the horizon behind it. The sky has grown purple. First light is not far off. "How long will it take to wait for the souls who will be returning to Elysium?"

"No need, no need," he says shuffling over to one of the now vacant benches. He sits and pulls a chain out from under the collar of his robe. A small glittering key dangles from the end of it.

"Is that . . . ?"

"The Eternity Key? Yes."

"You had it with you this whole time?"

"As I said, one doesn't leave the key to the Underrealm just lying about. It was safest on my person."

"But it's so small. And key-like." The last time I had seen the Eternity Key, it was a large, two-pronged staff. A bident. The object dangling from Charon's chain was smaller than my pinkie and looked like an ornate antique key, not a staff.

"Gods don't always want to go hefting the tokens of their immortality around in plain sight. All Kronolithes will shrink in size and change in appearance if you know the magic words."

"*Mikro,*" I say, remembering the word Jonathan had used to shrink one of his arrows to fit in my pocket.

He nods. "'*Megalo*' will make it large again."

I nod in return, wishing I would have known I could shrink the key before I'd gone running headlong into the Underrealm with it. Perhaps I wouldn't have lost it in the first place if I had been able to keep it around my neck. But we had been in mortal peril and in quite the hurry at the time, so I can't blame anyone for not telling me.

Charon unhooks the key from his chain. I notice another small charm around his neck. This one looks like a creature that has the front half of a horse and back half of a fish—a hippocampus, I recall from my mythology textbook. I wonder if that is Charon's own Kronolithe. He presses the key into my hand. "This world needs someone like you, Daphne Raines. It is almost first light, go save your friends."

"Thank you," I say, knowing I definitely never told him my full name. Nor exactly what I needed the Key for.

I attach the key to the chain around my neck and then clasp my fingers around my pomegranate pendant. My first thought is to go back to the dock near Persephone's Gate to look for Shady, but I realize that we never established whether he was going to wait for me there. What if I can't find him? What if it takes too much time?

I look up the horizon and watch the first fingers of pinkish light stretching into the purple sky. There isn't time for delays. I say good-bye to Charon, close my eyes, and picture the spiraling stairway that leads into the Pits, where I am supposed to meet Garrick. My feet lift off the wooden deck of the boat.

chapter thirty

HADEN

"She's not here," Jonathan says when he rematerializes outside the prison cell where Ethan, Psyche, Brimstone, and I wait. He had only been gone for a minute at best.

"Are you sure?" I ask. "Search again."

"I've been through the prison three times. Persephone isn't here, and we need to go. Now."

I have no reply. Every last bit of hope I have left in my blackening body was hanging on this plan. How can she not be here? "Search again."

"You're not hearing me. We need to leave. Now. The minotaur is headed this way."

"How close?" Ethan asks, reaching for his mother's hand.

"If we move fast, we may make it to the exit before it sees us. But like I said, we need to go now."

Ethan and Jonathan usher Psyche into the corridor. I don't follow.

"Come, Haden," Ethan says.

"No. I have to stay. I can't leave without Persephone." Maybe Jonathan missed something. Maybe I can find her on foot.

"Trust me, Haden, she isn't here." Jonathan's voice is flooded with urgency. "Either she was moved, escaped, or was never here to begin with. We need to outrun the minotaur, unless you want this place to become your grave."

"Maybe it would be better to stay in our cell, rather than outrun it," Psyche says.

"We'll lose the exit," Ethan says. "If we wait too long, it will shift locations and we may never find it again." He looks at me and holds out his hand. "Either come with us or hand me the Arachne's thread. I will not let my mother get trapped in here."

I look at the spool of translucent thread in my hand. It's my only lifeline out of this place. Brim butts her head against my ankle, trying to prod me forward. A roar echoes through the corridor. The minotaur is coming.

"Now, Haden," Jonathan commands, his voice echoing with godly authority.

I wrap my fingers around the spool and dash out of the cell. Brim bounds over my feet as I run. Her back and tail bristle when another roar from the minotaur fills the corridor. The others are close at hand as we jog through the maze, following the trail of the fragile string. I can tell Jonathan wishes he could fly, but the corridor is too narrow to spread his wings. After several left and right turns that I would not have recalled on my own, I finally see a shimmering rectangle in the wall up ahead. It must be the exit. The rectangle wavers as if it were blinking in and out.

"It's fading," Ethan says, pushing his mother toward the exit. She reaches back for Jonathan's hand and the two cross through the exit together, vanishing from my sight. Ethan goes next, disappearing into the fading light.

I'm only inches from the exit when I realize that Brim is no longer underfoot. I turn back, looking into the bright corridor, and see that she has come to a halt several feet back. She faces away from the exit, her nose in the air as if she's caught the scent of something. Hellcats are the world's most efficient trackers—Brim could find me anywhere, and once she locks onto a scent it's almost impossible to dissuade her. "Not now, Brim," I command. "Come."

The roar of the minotaur grows louder. It's just around the corner. Brim takes off down another corridor, running deeper into the maze. Following whatever scent she picked up. "No, Brim! We need to leave!"

A hulking, dark form careens around the corner. All I can see are its blazing red eyes, glinting horns, and a mouth full of teeth. I drop the spool and lunge to follow Brim—only to be caught from behind. A strong grip closes over the back of my neck and I am yanked backward. I fall back through the exit. The last thing I see is the hulking creature thunder into the corridor where Brimstone had disappeared.

The hand that pulled me through the exit releases me. I try to scramble for the opening, but the shimmering rectangle evaporates right before I touch it. The exit has moved. All that stands in front of me is a stone wall. No, the mountainside. I claw at it with my fingers, as if I can pry the mountain open. "Brim!"

I sink to my knees, clutching my head. Once again, an invisible barrier has cut me off from someone I love. I don't know how to save her, as I don't know how to save Daphne. Not now that the hope of Persephone is gone. "Brim, no."

"I'm sorry, Haden," Ethan says. "We can come back. We can find another way in. Another day."

"Another day?" I say through clenched teeth. "No, we get Terresa and we find Brim now. I promised I would never leave her behind again."

"There's no time. The new entrance could be hundreds of miles from here. It would take too long . . ."

"She's with the minotaur!"

"Your cat will be fine," Jonathan says, stepping forward. I can hear the doubt in his voice.

"She's not merely my cat. She's my friend. She's my family. And now she's gone. Just like Daphne." I stand, feeling the sudden urge to take a swing at Jonathan. "All because of you. This was *your* plan. You're the one who led us here with your false promises of finding Persephone."

"They weren't false promises." He flaps his wings. "It was a hope."

"A false hope. A lie," I say, realizing it. "You tricked us into coming here. You knew Persephone wasn't here. You knew it, but convinced us to come here anyway. To storm the palace and get your bow back. You even finagled it so we'd rescue your wife from servitude. You don't care about Daphne. You took advantage of my love for her. You used me. You've gotten everything you've ever wanted, you conniving *koprophage*, and I've lost the last good thing I had because of it."

I lunge at Jonathan, ready to strike, but Ethan jumps in the way. I take a swing at him. He grabs me by the shoulders and wrestles me to the ground. I feel a surge of electricity building in my chest. I'll blast his face off and then do the same to his treacherous father.

"You're being unreasonable," Ethan says, shoving me away. "It's the poison talking, not you."

I raise my fist, holding a crackling bolt of blue lighting. I don't care what excuses he has. *I don't care.* "Get out of my way so I can send your father back to the gates of the dead where he belongs. Where he should have stayed!"

Ethan raises his own bolt of lightning. "You're out of your mind, Haden. Look at your hands!"

I look at the hand that holds the lightning bolt. Every vein has gone black. My fingernails are dark and clouded, like each one has been smashed by a hammer. I am doing it again. Giving into the poison. Being unreasonable. I extinguish the bolt and Ethan lets me go. I roll onto my knees. "She's gone. They're both gone."

First I lost Dax, then I lost Daphne, and now I've lost Brim. I have absolutely nothing left to lose. I have nothing left to give.

"We'll figure out a new plan," Jonathan says, stepping closer. "I love Daphne as if she were my own child. By Apollo's Chariot, I promise you I will not rest until we find her. I didn't even let death stop me, need I remind you."

I nod, pretending to let him comfort me, but I know there's nothing more he can do.

But there is something left that I can do, I realize. There is one thing left I have to give. One last course of action I can take. The idea has been prodding at my brain since Jonathan told us about standing at the main gates of the Underrealm. No living thing can pass through those gates without it being unlocked with the

Key. No corporeal thing can get through. But the gate will open for the dead.

A dead soul could enter the Underrealm. A dead soul could find Daphne. A dead soul could help her escape from that Shade's cave. A dead soul could help her find the Key. A dead soul could help her escape the underworld and return her to her family.

"Do you want another dose?" Jonathan asks, searching his quiver. "Where's my last dart?"

"You gave it to me," I say. "You gave it to me and I vowed I wouldn't give up on finding Daphne. I vowed I wouldn't give into the nothingness again."

"Good," Jonathan says, clasping my shoulder. "We need you."

I nod again and let him help me to my feet.

"Do you want me to administer it to you now? I have my bow back, which means I can make more once we return to the mortal realm, but it will take time. Possibly too much time, though . . ."

"No," I say. "I'm fine for now."

I let Ethan and Jonathan lead me through the night back toward the hut where Terresa and Jessica wait with my father. When no one is watching, I pull the last emotion dart from my pocket. I wrap my fist around it. I will honor my vow to never give up on finding Daphne, but I was wrong about not giving in to the nothingness. I squeeze my hand, crushing the last dart into dust, and let it trail behind me as we leave Brim and the Black Hole behind.

There is one last thing I can do to find Daphne.

I need to die.

chapter thirty-one

TOBIN

"Why have you brought us here, boy?" one of the members of the Court says to Garrick as the royal guard escorts him and his companions down the spiraling stone staircase that leads into the Pits.

"You'll address us as your king," Garrick says with a glare that could melt ice. He stands next to what appears to be some sort of invisible barrier between us and the Keres. The shadow creatures keep throwing themselves against it, as if trying to take a swipe at me. I jump every time, even though it is evident that they can't get through. It reminds me of going to Sea World with my sister when we were young and the sharks would swim up to the aquarium wall. Abbie would dare me to touch the glass right in front of the sharks' bared mouths and then I'd scream and run away if one got too close. One even rammed the glass once, and Abbie had laughed so hard at my reaction, she almost peed her pants. What wouldn't I give to see her one last time? I'll most likely be dead by morning. Which is apparently in a few minutes.

Even if Daphne got my message, even if she has the Key, even if she chooses to come here to rescue me instead of escape on her own, I am still going to die. I heard Garrick talking to himself—or possibly to the Keres that is attached to him—and he made it very clear he plans on killing me whether or not Daphne comes.

I hope she doesn't, considering he also plans on killing her for her so-called betrayal.

"Why have you brought us here, *your majesty?*" the man says as he arrives at the bottom of the spiraling stairs. It is clear from the way he and the rest of the Court hold up the bottoms of their robes as if protecting them from grime, and avert their noses in the air against the smell of methane, that the Pits are not a place they visit often. If ever.

"We want you to witness our triumph, Lex," Garrick says. "At first light, we will have accomplished what King Ren was not able to, nor my two imbecilic brothers, nor any other Underlord since Hades's death. *We* will become immortal."

I gather from the way he says *we* that he is referring to himself and the Keres, not himself and the Court, but I doubt the Court realizes this.

"Immortal?" Lex responds. "You can't do that without—"

"The Key? Then it's a good thing we'll have it in a matter of minutes."

Lex scoffs and the other members of the Court follow his lead. "You expect us to believe that you've found it? I have it on good authority from my best men that all of your expeditions into the Wastelands have come back empty-handed. You promised us the Key, that is the only reason you've been allowed to survive." Lex turns to address his companions. "I grow tired of this charade, don't you? The boy has had his chance to play with the crown,

I think it's time we put it on the head of the real Lord."

Most of the Court call out in agreement, but one steps forward. "Alas, the Fates wanted him to have the crown. He is the one who brought us the Cypher—"

"And then he lost her," Lex says. "I say that means the Fates have turned their backs on him. Without the Cypher or the Key, he has no claim."

"Then it's a good thing we can deliver both right now," Garrick says, stepping forward.

"I'll see it when I believe it."

"Then believe it." Garrick points up the stairs, where a young woman in a tattered dress and a golden cloak has appeared in the middle of the stairway. I could have sworn she wasn't there only a second ago. The Court falls silent as she descends the stairs. She looks so strange to me in her fairy-tale clothes but with a modern, black fedora perched on top of her head. As she gets closer, I realize she isn't just any young woman. Panic thunders in my hollow chest.

"Daphne!" I shout. "Run away! It's a trap!"

Garrick grabs me and pulls a dagger to my throat.

"Do you have it?" he calls to her.

"I do," she says, continuing down the stairs instead of running away. Why doesn't she run? When she gets to the bottom of the stairway, the Court parts like the Red Sea. I don't know what it is about her, but she almost appears ethereal as she passes through their midst in her white dress. Despite the tattered dress and the smears of blood and dirt on her arms, it strikes me that she looks like a queen.

"Where is it?" Garrick says. "If you've come here empty-handed . . ." He presses the sharp blade of his knife against my throat as if to finish his sentence.

"It's here," she says, pulling a golden chain from her neck. On it is both a small red charm and what looks like an antique key.

"Don't try to fool us again," Garrick says.

"I'm not." Daphne gives me a quick glance and a small mournful smile, and then she detaches the key from the chain. She holds it to her lips and whispers something against the metal. With a burst of light, the tiny key transforms into a large two-pronged staff.

Garrick lets go of me and greedily grabs for the Key. Daphne lets him take it. As he cackles with pride, she holds her hand out to me, but I shrink back from her touch. I don't know why. I can't explain it. It's like how I'd feel if an angel had tried to embrace me.

Unworthy.

"Tobin, come on," she mouths the words. "We need to go."

I shake my head and shrink farther away. She still doesn't realize this is a trap. Garrick won't let us leave. His guards will never let us pass. We're both as good as dead because of me.

She shakes her hand at me more frantically. "I have a plan," she whispers. "I can get us out."

But she can't. I know she can't. I cower from her. She looks as though she wants to move closer but also like she doesn't want to move farther away from Garrick. Like she needs both of us within arm's reach. After a moment of hesitation, she juts forward, wrapping her hand around my shackled wrist. She yanks me toward her as she lunges for Garrick's arm. But she's a moment too late.

An inch too far away. He catches her movement out of the corner of his eye and swings away from her grasp. His other arm flies in a powerful arc and he backhands her against the face. Her grasp falls away from my wrist and she crumbles to the ground.

"You dare touch us!" Garrick shouts, standing over her. He looks as though he's about to stab her with the Key.

She doesn't respond. Only shakes her head and blinks as if the blow nearly knocked her unconscious.

"We'll show you who's in charge here," Garrick says. "We'll show you all!"

The Keres throw themselves against the invisible barrier, screeching as if cheering him on.

"What is going on here?" Lex says, stepping forward. "Give us the Key, boy. It belongs to the Court."

"It doesn't belong to the Court. It doesn't belong to any of you. It belongs to *us*. It belongs to the true heirs of the Underrealm. Hades's first creations. His first children. The Key is ours and so is this realm. And soon all the other realms will be ours as well."

"What is this insanity?" Lex says. "Seize him!" he shouts to the royal guard.

But the men don't move. They stand as if paralyzed by fear as a great shadow stretches up from behind Garrick. Looming over us all. Garrick sends a pulse of electricity through the Key. Lightning crackles and hisses around it, turning it into a fierce-looking weapon.

"You asked why we brought you here," Garrick says to Lex. "It's high time you meet the new royal family. *My* family."

"No!" Daphne shouts, struggling to get to her feet as Garrick thrusts the electrified Key into the barrier that separates us from the Keres.

"Do not do this, boy!" Lex commands.

"Why? Wasn't this your idea? Didn't you want to rip through the Pits in order to get out into the mortal realm? Didn't you plan on releasing the Keres yourself?"

"This is not what we wanted. The Keres were to be sent into the mortal and Sky realms. Not released here. We—"

But Lex doesn't get to finish whatever he had to say because Garrick twists the Key as if he were turning it in a giant invisible lock. Streams of electricity crackle along the barrier. "You thought you could use the Keres as your soldiers in a war against the Sky-realm. You thought you could use them as your attack dogs. But guess what? The Keres will be using you now. For food."

Garrick pulls the Key away from the crackling barrier. The lightning disappears. There is one full second of perfect, dead quiet before the Keres, with a screeching yelp, explode through the now nonexistent barrier.

chapter thirty-two

DAPHNE

I didn't expect Tobin to shrink from me. I didn't expect him to pull away. My plan had been contingent on my proximity to both Tobin and Garrick. The plan was to give Garrick the Key, but only for a moment—only long enough to distract him so I could take Tobin's hand. Then I was going to grab Garrick by the other hand and teleport us all as far away from the Pits as possible, taking the Key with us.

But it all went wrong. So very, very wrong. A moment's hesitation. One extra step needed, and the upper hand shifted to Garrick. Or the backhand, that is. I didn't expect him to be able to hit so hard. My eyes refuse to focus and my brain feels like it is rattling in my skull. I did not expect to have to fight against a concussion right now.

I didn't expect a lot of things, I think as the barrier falls and the Keres burst into the chamber. Great swirling shadows careen every which way until Garrick barks an order at them.

"Kill the Court first. The girl and boy are mine."

Horrible screams fill the chamber. Some men try to run for the stairs, but they don't make it. Through my blurry eyes, I watch a soldier try to fight off one of the shadow beasts with his sword.

His electrified blade passes through the monster, causing no harm. The Keres aren't solid. They can't be touched. I want to help somehow, but I also know I can't. The Pits are on the royal grounds. I cannot use my vocal powers here. I can't do anything to make the Keres solid so the soldiers can fight them.

Unprotected, a swarm of shadow encircles the Court. I watch in horror as giant boils form on the men's skin. They rupture and pus. The men scream and claw at the boils, taking chunks of their rotting skin from their own faces.

A wave of nausea hits me and I lean forward, putting my head between my knees. I will myself not to pass out. Whenever I think of the Keres, I think of them as being like the one that tried to kill my father by attempting to drain his life force. But I remember now that Haden had told me that there were different kinds of Keres. That they were all the evils that were said to be contained in Pandora's Box in the Greek myth, only the box wasn't a box, it was a prison. One that Garrick has just opened. The Keres that tried to kill Joe was a reaper, but the Keres attacking the Court must be bringers of plague.

Two members of the royal guard run to help the Court but are set upon by another Keres. In an instant, the two soldiers turn on each other with their swords. Instead of protecting the Court they are fighting each other with ferocious hacking swings. That Keres must be a harbinger of war or violence of some sort. Other Keres go after the rest of the men, and I am completely helpless to intervene as the chamber turns into a death trap.

The Underlords' screams and Keres' screeching is so overwhelming, ringing through my skull, that for the first time in my life, I wish I couldn't hear. Garrick advances toward me with the Key, holding it like a spear. Of course he wanted to kill me himself. He laughs, so proud of his accomplishments.

But then I hear it. Beyond the screeching and the screaming and the sickening laughter, I hear whispering voices. *Kill him. Kill the Lesser who thinks he can control us.* For a moment I think my damaged brain is playing tricks on me. That I'm hearing voices in my head. But then I realize that I can hear the Keres whispering to each other. It must be the work of the pomegranate Kronolithe. Shady had said that Persephone had been able to communicate with all of the creatures of the Underrealm. *Kill him. Kill Garrick. We no longer need the boy.*

I look up at Garrick just as he raises the bident to stab me. "They're going to kill you," I say.

He stops, holding the Key up. Ready to thrust. "I'm not afraid of them. They're my family."

"They're planning on killing you. They're whispering about it right now. Can't you hear them?" I make a swirling motion with my hand in the air. "You can understand them, can't you?"

Garrick stops. He holds his head as if he were straining to listen. I wonder how he learned their language, to interpret their speech beyond the screeching. The chamber boy had told me that Garrick is especially talented with languages. I wonder if that is a natural talent, or if it had something to do with the pomegranate necklace. Haden had told me the story of Garrick trying to steal it when he was a very young boy. He had eventually been compelled to give it back—and as punishment had been sentenced to work in the Pits with the Keres. But perhaps he'd kept part of the necklace for himself. I had noticed that a couple of the rubies were missing. I assumed it was because the necklace was so ancient, but perhaps Garrick had pried one off to keep. If he kept it with him in the Pits, perhaps that was how he had learned to communicate with the beasts. Why the necklace had deemed him worthy of its powers, I don't know. Perhaps he had been, long ago.

Garrick's face hardens and I know he's heard what the Keres are saying—that they should do away with him now that he's fulfilled his part. That they don't need him.

They don't want him.

"Some family," I say.

"Shut up," he says, but I am not sure if it is directed at me or the Keres that loom over us now. "Shut up. Shut up. Shut up."

He thrusts the bident at me, but instead of forking me in the chest, he goes for my neck. The two-pronged staff closes over my throat, the sharp ends of the Key grind into the stone floor at either side of neck. I am quite literally pinned to the ground.

I hold my hand out to Tobin again. This time he doesn't hesitate. He scrambles to me and wraps his fingers around mine so tightly. As if he's holding my hand at my deathbed, and he knows he's next.

"Come with us, Garrick," I say. "We can escape through Persephone's Gate. Get out of here before the Keres kill you. Right now."

Garrick shakes his head. "There's one thing you're forgetting. One thing you're *all* forgetting," he shouts as if directing it at the Keres. "I'm immortal now. You can't kill me."

Not if you don't have the Key, I think and wrap my hands around the two prongs of the staff that pin me to the ground.

A burst of electricity pulses from Garrick's free hand. He goes to wrap it around the hilt of the staff, meaning to electrocute me. "*Mikro!*" I shout.

The bident shrinks. With a pop it transforms into a tiny antique key and lands on my chest. Garrick looks from me to it and then to the Keres that circle above his head.

Kill him now, they say.

The Keres swarm Garrick. Wrapping him into a black cocoon. "You can't do this! I'm one of you!" he screams and screams.

I grab the key and make sure I have Tobin by the other hand and think of anywhere other than this place. The last thing I hear as Tobin and I vanish from the room is Garrick's terrible screams breaking off into utter silence.

chapter thirty-three

HADEN

"I think he's waking," Jessica says, greeting us outside the door to the hut at the outskirts of the Skyrealm. It takes me a moment to realize she means my father. "I wasn't sure what you'd want me to do." She holds up the small bottle of sleeping draught.

"I'll take care of it," I say, taking the bottle from her.

"Give him only a drop," Ethan says. "Too much could kill him, and I imagine Terresa wants her prize alive."

"Is she here yet?" I ask, dreading what needs to come next.

"She came by a little while ago," Jessica says. "She said she'll be back soon. She's growing impatient."

"I guess I'd better take care of my father then."

I go into the hut. The others stay outside. My father lies on his side, his back toward me. Jessica has rearranged his chains so his hands are bound over his chest as if he were a prisoner of war. Which I guess he is. The sounds of restless sleep fill the hut. He turns on his back. Jessica is right, he will be awake soon. I lean over him with a glass dropper from the potion bottle. I reach my fingers out to part his lips. His mouth opens in a sudden, teeth-baring grimace. I pull back slightly.

His eyes fly open and his large, bound hand shoots up, capturing my wrist. His eyes are not clouded with sleep, and I realize the sounds he'd been making were a ruse. He's been awake for a while. I brace myself for the lashing words that will come from his bared mouth. The berating he will try to cut me down with. He lost his crown because of me, so I can only imagine how hot his anger boils against me now.

"Are you really going to leave me here?" he asks, his voice gruff. "You're really trading me to the Skylord scum?"

His question is not what I expected, and from it, I gather that he must have overheard Jessica and Terresa talking at some point. "It was a necessary compromise in war." That was something we Underlords were taught from a very young age—necessary compromise. As in being willing to sacrifice yourself for the will of the king.

"Do you know what the Sky King does to his enemies?" Ren asks. There's no pleading in his deep voice, but I almost think I catch a flash of it in his eyes. I think of the bronze statues—the king's trophies—lining the walls of the throne room.

I nod.

"And you would leave your father to such a fate?"

"You've never been a father to me," I say, even though the thought of letting him become one of those gruesome statues gives me more than a pang of remorse. He had never been much of a father, but he had always been my king. I'd spent the first seventeen years of my life trying to win his favor.

"I may not have been a good father, but I am on your side, Haden."

I scoff and raise the dropper to his mouth again. I'll pry it open if I have to. He turns his head away from the potion.

Toward me. He looks me in the eyes for the first time I can remember. "We both want the same thing. We want to save the Underrealm. I've made all sorts of *necessary compromises* along the way. But if you'll let me, I will fight by your side. The Keres must be stopped. The realms must remain intact. That is all I have ever wanted."

His words surprise me. I expected him to blame me. To rail at me for causing him to lose his throne and be banished. I did not expect contrition. I wonder what he must have dreamed about while under the sleeping spell to cause such a change.

"*Elios*," he says, not looking away from me.

I avert my eyes. My father used to say the only thing weaker than invoking *Elios*—asking for mercy—was granting it.

But I know better than that now. No thanks to him.

I meet his gaze once more. I can see in his eyes that he's not merely asking for mercy, he's asking me to grant him my forgiveness. Something I never thought him capable of.

"*Elios*," I say with a nod. Saying the word makes me feel cleansed somehow. Redeemed. I pocket the sleeping draught and go for Jessica's keys instead.

If I am going to be gone, then the group will need more fire power. My father will take my place when I am dead. I can trust him to help destroy the Keres.

I unlock his hands and I am about to go for his feet when Terresa enters the hut. I gesture to my father to pretend to sleep. His loud grunting snores fill the hut once more.

"I've come for my prize," she says, her voice husky. "Both of my prizes."

She lays her fingers on my shoulder and I spin around into her arms. She stares at me with such desire, I am almost afraid she wants to devour me. I wrap one arm around her waist, pulling her against me. I clasp my other hand over her heart. "It's racing," I say, trying to make my voice sound husky and heady like hers.

"For you," she says. "I've been waiting so long for this kiss."

I lean into her. My lips almost touching hers. I stop as if taunting her. She groans in anticipation, her heart racing even faster under my fingertips.

"Let me have it," she says, clasping her fingers in my tunic.

I send a pulse of lighting from my palm into her ribcage. It's not enough to kill her. Merely to stop her heart momentarily. She crumples in my arms.

I lay her on the ground and whisper, "I'm sorry."

"I had no idea you were such a devastatingly good kisser," my father says as he stands, free of his chains now.

I stare at him. In all my years, I have never heard my father make a joke.

The others balk when Ren follows me out of the hut. They knew I was going to temporarily incapacitate Terresa, but the plan was to leave my father behind as a consolation prize to placate her temper when she wakes. "Change of plans."

The others follow me to the Skyrealm gate. "And we're flying all the way home," I say. I need to make it back to Olympus Hills as quickly as possible, and now that we don't have my unconscious father to deal with or Jonathan's bulk, there is no need for a car.

"Do you want me to carry you?" Jessica asks.

"I can fly on my own," I say, and step off into the clouds. I let myself fall for a moment, contemplating letting my death happen now, but no, I need to return to Olympus Hills first. If Brim ever escapes the Black Hole on her own, she will follow my scent all the way to the end of the line. I want that to lead her to Olympus Hills. To home. So she won't get lost in the wilderness somewhere. I send bursts of lightning out of my hands as I had watched Teresa do, slowing my fall. I tip myself forward so I am lying flat in the air like an owl. A few more bursts of lightning send me soaring through the sky back toward Olympus Hills. Normally, I would revel in the feeling—finally soaring like bird on my own as I had always dreamed. But I feel no freedom now, knowing I am sailing to my death.

chapter thirty-four

DAPHNE

I had intended on transporting Tobin and me directly to Persephone's Gate at the outskirts of the Underrealm, but my concussed brain is unable to focus. I lose the picture of the dock in my mind and Tobin and I end up reappearing midair over the pomegranate grove at the edge of the royal grounds. The branches of a pomegranate tree break our fall, and we topple head over heels to the ground. The impact doesn't help my head any.

"What was that?" Tobin gasps. "How did we get out?"

"Teleportation." I hold up my pendant. "I picked up a few new tricks recently."

"Nice," Tobin says, but he's shaking. Shivering uncontrollably. In the light of day, I can see that his face and arms are mottled with bruises and burns. He's still wearing the costume toga from the opera we had performed in just before entering the Underrealm. It's filthy, spotted with blood in some places, and hangs open, uncovering his hollow chest. A burn the shape of a handprint is melted into the skin just under his right pec. He's been tortured. No wonder he shrunk away from my touch.

Tobin crosses his hands over his chest, clasping his shoulders, and begins rocking back and forth. He barely looks like himself. "I'm sorry you came. I'm sorry I let them use me to send that message. I just needed the pain to stop. I'm sorry Garrick got the Key. I'm sorry the Keres got out . . ."

"You have nothing to be sorry for. Garrick opened the barrier, not you." I touch the top of my head, and to my surprise find that I'm still wearing Tobin's fedora. It's more than a little worse for wear but it should help keep him warm. I place the hat on Tobin's head at a rakish angle. "That's better," I say. "It's a bit tattered and stained but still intact. Just like you."

Tobin gives the slightest smile and then collapses against my shoulder. He sobs and I let him—and eventually join in. We hold each other and cry until I sense the sky darkening. I look up and see a pitch-black cloud forming over the palace.

No, that's not a cloud.

I tuck the Key into my bra for safekeeping and then grab Tobin's hand. "We have to go. The Keres are coming."

I concentrate once more on the image of the stone archway of Persephone's Gate. We have to get out of this realm with the Key before the Keres catch up with us. But once again, we don't make it. My mind clouds over, and we land in the water a few feet from the Elysium shore. The black cloud of Keres still follows.

"They're coming," Tobin says, shaking in my grasp.

I close my eyes once more and concentrate all my might on picturing Persephone's Gate, but I can't get a clear picture of it in my head. I'd been so frantic, searching for Haden, when we first passed through the gate, that I never really got a good look at it. Perhaps that's why my foggy brain is having trouble locking on to the image.

Instead, I think of the sandy beach by the dock near the gate where I last saw Shady. In the blink of an eye, we land in the sand.

"Kore, youuu returned," I hear Shady's familiar moaning voice say as I open my eyes. He approaches and even though he has no facial features, I can tell he's happy to see me.

"Shade!" Tobin shrieks, scuttling away. He pulls on my arm, trying to get me to follow him under the dock. "Daphne, get us out of here."

"It's okay," I say, loosening Tobin's death grip on my arm. "He's a friend."

"A friend?" Tobin backs away even more, as if he doesn't believe me.

"Kore, you're safe. Youuu saved your friend."

"Yes, and I got the Key as well. But we ran into a complication."

"Whoa. Wait. Are you talking to it?" Tobin says, and I realize all he would hear is Shady moaning instead of words. "Can you understand what it's saying?"

"I told you I picked up a few new tricks. And *it* is a *he*."

"Whattt complications?" Shady says.

"That dark cloud out on the horizon. Those are Keres. They're out of the Pits and looking for vengeance."

Shady goes rigid and it strikes me as particularly terrifying that even Shades are afraid of the Keres. "You muuust get out of here. You muuust get to the gate. They'll destroy you, Kore."

"Come with us," I say to Shady.

He shakes his head. "I am needed here. I will try to diiistract the Keres. Youuu must save your other friend sooo he can bring Persephone back."

I nod and much to my surprise, Shady gives me a hug, pressing my head against his leathery chest.

"I'm going to assume you're okay with this and not that he's trying absorb your soul or anything like that," Tobin says. "But also, we really gotta go."

Shady releases me and I grab Tobin. We leave Shady behind and head up the beach. "I can't picture the gate, so we'll have to go on foot." It's not far, but that black cloud is getting too close for comfort.

I wish I could break into a flat-out run, but my knee is still a mess and it's obvious that Tobin can barely keep up with my hobbling pace. His legs are so bruised, and he limps with every step. We leave the beach and enter the long ravine that leads to the gate. Once the stone archway comes into view, I grab onto Tobin and teleport us the rest of the way. I pull the Key from my bra and command it to enlarge.

"Hurry," Tobin says, pointing to the opening of the ravine. The sky above the beach has become black with shadow. I hope Shady is okay.

I stick the key into the air in the center of the archway, much like I had seen Terresa do when she unlocked the gate from the other side. I twist the key and feel a slight resistance, as if turning an old lock. A sphere of faint green light begins to pulse from the center of the archway. I pull the Key out and shrink it back down to an easy-to-carry size and slip it into the pocket of my cloak. We watch as the sphere of light pulses and grows, slowly filling the archway.

"Come on, come on," Tobin says besides me. His fingers twitch at his sides and he rocks on his toes like he's about to sprint through the gate as soon as it is ready.

Screeching cries echo through the ravine. The sky grows dark. The green light brightens to the shade of emeralds, and the symbols etched in the stone light up.

"I think that means it's fully active," I say.

"Good thing," Tobin says, looking back at the dark shadows filling the ravine.

I turn toward the gate. It's only wide enough for one person to enter at a time. Tobin insists I go in front. He stands closely behind me and I hold my hand behind my back, clinging to his. "Here goes nothing," I say, taking a deep breath. I know there's a possibility the gate won't allow me to enter. If Garrick is somehow miraculously still alive after being attacked by the Keres, I won't be allowed to leave. I tentatively stick one foot into the green light and sigh with relief when I'm not repelled back.

"Hurry," Tobin says. I can barely hear him over the screeching roar of the Keres. I step fully into the light, pulling Tobin with me. Only he doesn't come. As hard as I yank, he doesn't move.

"Tobin!" I look over my shoulder. My hand that holds Tobin's is still outside the green light. I try to pull it toward me, but it won't budge. Tobin stands outside the archway, a look of horror on his face. He tries to stick his other hand into the light, but it's as if he's hitting glass.

"I can't go!" he shouts, his voice sounding far away from me now like he's trapped underwater. "It won't let me in!"

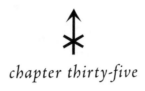

chapter thirty-five

TOBIN

Persephone's Gate won't let me enter. Daphne yanks and yanks on my hand until it feels like she might remove my fingers, but she isn't able to pull me through the archway.

"Did you eat anything?" Her voice sounds like she's at the end of a long tunnel.

"What?" I shout back.

"Did you eat or drink anything?"

I start to shake my head, but then I remember demanding water before I would deliver Garrick's message. I nod. "A guard gave me water."

Daphne's frantic expression turns to pure panic. I don't know what the problem is.

"You're bound," she says. "You must be bound to that guard."

I remember it then. A part from the play we performed about Orpheus's travels to the underworld. In it, he was warned not to eat or drink anything while in the underworld or he wouldn't be able to leave. I remember now Daphne warning me about this when we first entered the Underrealm—but I could barely remember my own name after being trapped in the Chair of Forgetfulness; it had completely slipped my mind. Even if I had remembered, I wouldn't have been able to help it. I was so thirsty. I hadn't had anything to drink in days.

"What do you mean?"

"I was bound to Garrick because he gave me the first thing I ate in the Underrealm. I think you must be bound to the guard who gave you water. I think unless you have his permission or he's dead, you can't leave."

A horrible dark feeling rolls over me and for a half a second, I will the Keres to find that horrible guard as quickly as possible. Then I shake myself, letting the terrible thought pass. This can't be happening!

Daphne tries again in vain to pull me into the gate. I realize now that the only reason she hasn't passed through into the mortal realm is because she's holding on to me. The ravine grows black as night around me. Daphne is shouting something, but I can't hear her over the Keres's wails that fill my ears. She needs to go. She needs to lock the gate from the other side.

"Find the others and come back for me!" I shout and pull my hand out of her grasp. She screams and tries to reach for me, but then she is gone. The empty gate glows green. I turn my back on it and step into the dark ravine.

chapter thirty-six

HADEN

I separate from the others when we make it back to Olympus Hills. I have no desire to return to Joe's mansion and have to face him or Daphne's mother empty-handed.

Jonathan tries to stop me. "I don't think you should be alone. The poison is spreading."

"I need some sleep. A few minutes at least. Then we can regroup."

He frowns.

"I'll dose myself beforehand," I say, patting my belt as if the emotion dart was still tucked in there. "What's this one do anyway?"

"It'll make you pontificate about love—you'll start spouting poetry."

"See, none of you will want to be around for that."

Jonathan gives a laughing sigh. "I'll set to work on making something new. It may take a day or longer."

"I'll be okay until then."

I head back to my empty house and walk up to my bedroom. There's a permanent impression in the blanket on my bed where

Brim always sleeps. This is the place I want her to come if she ever escapes.

And if she doesn't, if the minotaur bested her—then I will find her on the other side. Just as I will find Daphne.

I put my earbuds in and turn on a song from my iPhone playlist. It's one of my favorites. It features a mournful singer with a lone guitar, telling his lover not to fear death because when her soul embarks he'll be there with her to follow her into the dark. The song makes me think of Orpheus traveling in the underworld to save Eurydice. It makes me think of Daphne trying to come after me. Now it's my turn.

I made a vow to never give up on saving Daphne, and I intend to keep it, even if I have to do it over my own dead body. I will only be a soul, but that's good enough to find her, to help her locate the Key, and lead her back to Persephone's Gate, where she can pass through and go find her family. It is enough to save her from the Shades, and the Keres, and Garrick, and all the other monsters of my world. I will follow her into the dark and ensure she makes it back into the light.

She will have to leave me behind, but that is a sacrifice I am willing to make to ensure her safety.

There's a small voice inside my head that sounds so much like Dax. It reminds me of the voice I heard the first night I returned to an abandoned Olympus Hills. The one that tried to talk reason into my addled brain. It tries to tell me I *am* giving up. That I am taking the coward's way out.

But that is not the case. I am already dying. I will be dead in a day without the cure. Perhaps even hours. The last dart is gone, and I won't be alive before Jonathan can craft a new one. I am simply speeding up the natural order of things. I'm not giving up; I'm accepting my last resort. The last possible sacrifice I can make to save Daphne.

I've been leading to this option all along, I realize now. This is where I was destined to end up. Ethan should have let Lexie's car hit me. They should have let me go then. Or in the campground when I tried to blast myself. Perhaps I could have already found Daphne by now if they had. I've only been a coward by delaying the inevitable.

I will follow Daphne into the dark.

I lean against my pillow and pull the bottle of sleeping draught from my belt. Ethan had said to be careful with it. More than a drop could kill. I open the lid and pull out the glass dropper. *Stop,* says that voice inside my head. *You aren't thinking clearly. This isn't the answer . . .* I set the dropper aside and raise the bottle to my lips.

The taste is bitter, like asphodel blossoms—the flowers that grow in the Wastelands of the underworld—and this strikes me as oddly appropriate. *Stop!* The voice shouts. *Jonathan said the poison will drive you to hurt yourself. This idea isn't yours . . .* I let the liquid roll over my tongue and think of Daphne.

The poison is driving you to this . . .

And then I stop before I swallow. Dax's voice—the rational part of my brain, not tainted by the poison—shouts loudly in my head. Telling me I'm being a fool. That the Underrealm doesn't work that way—being dead doesn't mean I can run around the realm as a free soul looking for Daphne. No, I will be turned into a Shade, my memory wiped. I'd become the kind of monster I was trying to save her from. Even if I remembered, even if I found her, I would only be a danger to her.

Rational thinking returns to my mind, and I realize this isn't a reasonable plan—it was the black poison driving me to put an end to my suffering. Trying to trick me into thinking I am doing the brave thing.

I sit bolt upright, the potion pooled in my mouth. I lean over to spit it out, but before I can open my mouth, hands grab my head. One clasps over my mouth and nose, the other claws into my hair, wrenching my head backwards. I struggle against the hands, clawing at them, but their grip only gets stronger.

"What's the matter, little brother, you lose your nerve?"

My eyes focus on my attacker. Rowan. My brother bares his teeth in a malevolent smile. I can't breathe. He's suffocating me. He wrenches back on my hair, bending my head backward so hard I think he's trying to snap my neck. I gasp for air, not realizing the mistake, and the sleeping potion slips down my throat.

My eyes must show my panic because Rowan laughs and lets go with a forceful shove. My head slams into the wooden headboard, and I slump onto my pillow. Nothing happens at first and I hope to Hades that Ethan had been exaggerating about the potion. But then a heavy feeling falls over my shoulders and chest, and I cannot sit up no matter how hard I try.

"Why?" I ask, looking up at my brother.

"I am merely finishing what you weren't man enough to finish on your own," he says. "And because it's what Father would have wanted. Death to the traitor who sent him off to the Sky King with your Skylord scum friends."

"I didn't . . ." I try to say, but my tongue becomes so heavy I can't speak.

"I saw you," Rowan says. "I saw you take off to the Skyrealm with Father as your prisoner. I wasn't able to stop you, but I can certainly punish you."

I try to tell him that what he saw is not what came to pass. That I returned from the Skyrealm with Father. That I granted him his freedom. That the two of us had come to an understanding. A reconciliation. Alas, my mouth no longer follows the commands of my brain.

He smiles. "Not that I need any more reason. I've always wanted you dead. Ever since Mother decided she like you best."

It becomes almost impossible to keep my eyes open.

"You've ruined everything. There never should have been any question. You're the Lesser brother, not me. I should have been the heir apparent. I should be sitting on the immortal throne right now with the Key in my hands and your precious Cypher at my side . . ."

He goes on but I can no longer make out the words. I close my eyes and it feels like I am sinking in thick water, falling limp. I can't feel my fingers, then my arms and my legs. My chest feels too heavy to breathe. I am tired. So very, very tired. And I don't want to fight the dark nothingness anymore. As I let it settle into my brain, I think I hear someone calling my name. The voice sounds like Dax's again.

A bright light engulfs me. I am standing in some sort of forest or corridor lined with trees. A black gate stands at the end of it. I hear Dax calling me again. Perhaps he is on the other side.

Waiting for me. The gate creaks open a few inches as I approach. I hear my name once more. I look back behind my shoulder. The trees and the corridor are gone. There's only darkness behind me. The light from beyond the gate beckons me.

I push the gate open wider and step through.

chapter thirty-seven

DAPHNE

I find myself lying in the grove in Olympus Hills. Or at least I assume it's the same grove, even though it looks so different. The ground is scorched and littered with upturned earth and broken tree branches from burned trees. There must have been a battle here. I look up at the sky and shield my eyes from the noonday sun. It's so much brighter here than the ethereal daylight of the Underrealm.

The Underrealm. Tobin!

I push myself up and hobble to the two arched trees that cloak Persephone's Gate in the mortal world. It pulses with green light. Tobin is on the other side with the Keres. I know it even though I cannot see him. My first thought is to jump back through and try to save him, but then I remember what he shouted when he let go of my hand. He wanted me to get the others and come back for him. And he was right. Even though I can use my vocal powers to make the Keres solid, there's nothing I can do to stop them without someone who can throw lightning.

I need Haden.

But as much as I hate the idea of locking Tobin out, the first thing I need to do is lock the gate. I can't risk any Keres slipping through. One had done enough damage on its own—an entire swarm would decimate Olympus Hills in no time. And if what Haden had told me was true, if the Keres get strong enough from feeding on the life forces of people, they could multiply exponentially—and destroy the world.

I dig into my pocket to pull out the Key, but it isn't there. The talisman and Joe's coin remain, but instead of the Key, I only find a small hole in the lining of the pocket, just big enough for the Key to slip through.

I let out a string of swear words and shake my cloak and my skirts. I search the ground, looking for anything metallic in the burned grass. I try singing to the Key, beckoning it to come like when I removed it from the tree where it had been hidden for millennia. When that doesn't work, I swear some more. The Key is gone. Once again it's lost. Either in this realm, the other, or possibly somewhere in between. Only this time, the gate is unlocked.

I pick up my skirts and run, dashing wildly, adrenaline driving me to ignore the throbbing pain in my knee, out of the grove and onto the jogging paths that will take me away from the lake. I don't know where to go—back to Joe's perhaps?—to find Haden and the others. What if they're still in the Skyrealm?

I remember the communication talisman. I pull it from my pocket, and without slowing my pace, I try to make a call. My talisman glows with a green light but no one picks up on the other end. I try once more and then shove it back in my pocket, when I come to a crossroads—a fork in the path. One direction will take me back toward Joe's, and the other will take me to the other side of the lake, where Haden's house is. I stop for a moment to catch my breath. Logic tells me to head toward Joe's because that's the most likely place they would use to rendezvous, but my heart tells me to turn to Haden's.

I get an idea and grab the pomegranate charm between my fingers. I close my eyes and envision Haden's living room where he and I sat at the coffee table eating the French toast we'd made. I remember wanting to kiss him so badly but not wanting to allow myself to do so. How could I have been so dumb? I get a clear picture of that coffee table in my mind, but when I open my eyes I find myself still standing on the lake path. A few more choice words come out of my mouth. Apparently I can only teleport in the Underrealm.

I take off in a limping run once more. Not stopping for anything until I make it to Haden's doorstep. The door has been left wide open. I enter the house. The smell tells me that no one has been living here for days, but I don't let that stop me. I run up the stairs, feeling as though some invisible thread is pulling me there.

I hear voices and follow them all the way to Haden's bedroom. A group of people stand around Haden's bed. I recognize Ethan, Joe, and Lexie. They're joined by a few other people but I don't take the time to notice who they are because of what I see on the bed. Haden, lying as still as death on his back.

"Haden?" I say from the doorway. Someone gasps. I don't know who. I can't take my eyes off of Haden. He looks like some sort of ghastly marbled statue, the way his veins have gone black and hard under his too-pale skin. "What happened?"

"It's too late," someone says. "Haden is dead."

I am reeling. Spinning. The whole world feels like it's spinning off its axis.

"No," I say. "It can't be. I thought I had time. I thought I could make it back."

Had I wasted too much time trying to save Tobin, only to have to leave him behind? Did I make the wrong choice?

Did I cause this?

"Sleeping potion," someone says, but I don't know who. I don't care. I can't focus on anyone but Haden. "Someone helped him down the whole bottle."

"Someone?" Haden was murdered? It wasn't even the black poison.

"I only finished what he started," someone else says.

Started? Haden would do this to himself?

I remember Jonathan saying the black poison would drive its victim into madness. Make him the greatest danger to himself.

"Sleeping potion?" My mind finally focuses on that fact. The other thing it focuses on is all the worried and melancholy tones bombarding my ears. The sounds of sorrow coming from Haden's companions are so overwhelming that I almost don't catch the other noise. It's a small sound, like a distant chime of a small bell coming from the direction of Haden's chest. I don't think anyone else can hear it—which means . . .

"Everyone get out!" I say.

"Daphne . . . What . . . ?" I think it is Joe who says this but I don't know.

"Get out!" I demand, waving them away. "I need to listen."

The other people and their overpowering tones shuffle out of the room. I hear someone whisper that I might be out of my mind, but I don't really care. When the room empties, I rush to Haden's side and listen closely, placing my ear over his chest. The tone, so faint, is coming from inside his ribcage. Having worked for the only florist in a small town, I had seen my fair share of dead bodies when delivering wreaths and bouquets to the local funeral home. Something that had struck me as interesting ever since I was a young child was that even though other organic things like rocks and rain have inner songs, the bodies of dead people and animals do not give off any sound.

"He has no pulse," someone says from the doorway. The voice strikes me as familiar but different somehow. Deeper. More commanding. "We tried resuscitation. He's as good as gone—"

"No," I say. He may not have a pulse but he does have a song, a tiny chime, coming from his heart. "I don't think he's dead. Not yet. I think he's in a deep sleep."

"Perhaps not," that voice says. "You're his true love. You're bonded. There's still the kiss."

True love's kiss. The thing that fairy tales were made of. Only, according to Jonathan, he's the one who invented the concept. I had administered the true love arrow to Haden, but I had not sealed the cure with true love's kiss. The only thing that could release him from the black poison's grip.

I practically throw myself on top of Haden's body. I grip his blackened hand. "Come back to me." I press my lips to his marbled mouth. They're as cold and unyielding as stone. I press harder, trying to give him all of my warmth. "Haden, I love you. You have to come back to me."

chapter thirty-eight

HADEN

I find myself standing on what appears to be an old boat dock on a riverbank. I don't know how I got here. I don't remember why I came. I feel as though I should be looking for something—or possibly a someone—but I don't remember what.

A woman dressed in veils appears beside me. Is she who I am looking for?

"Haden," she says from behind a veil that hides her face. Her voice strikes me as familiar, but I cannot place it. "I was sent to greet you."

"Where am I?" I ask.

"In Elysium."

"Elysium?" I had dreamed of this place. It is where heroes go when they die with honor. "But I don't belong here. I had my honor taken from me years ago."

I should be a Shade.

"True honor cannot be taken," the woman says. "But it can be given. And there are many who honor you. As a friend. A leader. A loved one."

I shake my head but then remember Dax telling me after I decided to take up the fight to find the Key and destroy the Keres that I was honorable to him. "Alas, I have failed. I am not a hero."

"A hero is one who would sacrifice all to save his friends." She steps closer and her veils float around her as if blown by an invisible wind. "But I have been sent with a message for you. A choice."

A large black boat approaches the dock. A crooked old man with a long oar steers the ship.

"Your life thread has not been fully severed. Not quite yet. So you have a choice. You can get on this boat and it will take you to the Temple of Judgment. You will drink from the water of Lethe and forget your former life, and then return here to live with the Oracle as I do. She has chosen you to be one of her companions. You will rest and your quest will be considered over. You can be at peace with your honor." She points toward the gate with a long, glittering finger. "Or, you can choose to go back the way you came—back through the gate—before it closes. And return to the fight. Darkness is coming but the light is gathering in order to beat it back. Your friends still need you. Your world still needs you, Haden. But it is your choice. Your destiny is in your hands."

I look at my hands. They're no longer black, and the pain is gone.

The woman holds one of her arms out as if to escort me to the boat. "You've fought so hard already. No one will blame you if you choose to rest. Choose to forget all that you have lost . . ." Then she holds out her other arm, gesturing back toward the gate. "Or you can choose to live and return to the fight."

I remember the feeling of being so very tired before giving in to the poison in my system. That feeling still clings to me now. It's so heavy that I don't know if I can even make it all the way back to the gate, let alone go on fighting. It would be so much easier to take the few steps needed to get on the boat. To sit. To rest. To be done.

I think of everything I have lost. Images of Dax and Daphne and Brimstone flash through my mind. Each comes with a sharp stab to the heart. I have lost so much . . . It would be nice to forget . . .

No. I don't want to forget Daphne. She is who I am supposed to remember, I think just as I hear a voice calling my name again. This time it isn't Dax's voice. It sounds like Daphne's, calling to me from somewhere beyond the gate. But that can't be. Daphne is gone. Trapped. Possibly dead.

As am I.

"Is he coming or what?" the old man calls from the boat. "I haven't got all century."

I stare at the boat and then look at the gate. I hear Daphne call my name once again. *Come back to me.* Those were the words she spoke that saved my life six months ago. Am I hearing her now, or is it a trick my dying brain is playing on me? Recalling old memories? Telling me what I want to hear?

Haden, I love you. You have to come back to me.

A feeling of warmth radiates through my body. I turn toward the gate. I try to run but my legs feel like lead. Every step weighs me down, but I don't stop moving. I finally make it back to the gate. It stands open only a crack. It will close soon but I look back at the dock, wondering if I am making the right choice. The boat is pulling away. The woman lowers her veil, revealing her young face, and gives me a nod of approval.

Mother, I think as she vanishes into thin air.

With all the strength I have left, I push the gate open and stumble into the dark.

chapter thirty-nine

DAPHNE

Haden's lips become soft. Pulsing with warmth, with life. The black veins that mar his otherwise perfect face recede and disappear. He opens his eyes. It takes a moment for them to focus. "Daphne?" he says sleepily. "You're here."

"I know," I say.

"I was coming to rescue you."

"I know."

"I was going to save you."

"I know."

"But you saved yourself."

"I know."

"And now you've saved me."

"I know," I say, clasping my fingers behind his head and drawing his lips closer to mine. "I love you." I kiss him once more. He melts against me, his body and mouth showing me his gratitude.

When we finally pull apart, looking for air, he caresses my jawline with his fingers. "You have no idea how nice it is to be fully cognizant while hearing those words." He kisses my cheek, soft and lingering. "I love you, too."

"I know," I say.

Haden shivers. Electricity prickles my lips as he closes them over mine again. "Is there anything you don't know?" he says after a moment. His lips, so close to mine, quirk into a smile. There's nothing better in this world than Haden smiling. It strikes me that there are all sorts of things I *don't* know, and would like to discover with him . . ."Ahem," comes the sound of someone clearing his voice from behind us, followed by a gentle knock on the door.

I pull away from Haden, suddenly remembering all the people out in the hallway. Heat rushes into my face.

"Hey guys," Haden says to the crowd in the hall, waving his hand and smiling sheepishly as if in a dreamy daze.

"As the newly restored god of love, I have my qualms about breaking up this little reunion—however, before you get too carried away, there are more of us who would like to say welcome back to both of you. In a less amorous way, I imagine."

I look over my shoulder to see that the speaker is quite possibly the most beautiful man I have ever seen—if you have a thing for older men with Greek god–like good looks and *wings*, that is. At first I think he is a stranger, and I am even more embarrassed by my public display of affection, but then I recognize the crinkles around his eyes and the jovial smile. "Hello, Daphne," he says as he enters the room.

"Jonathan?" I say, throwing my arms around him. He might be half his former size, but he still manages to envelope me in one of his bear hugs. "What happened to you?"

"Got my bow back." He lets go of me and pulls a golden bow

from where it was slung over his shoulder. He shows it off to me with great pride. "Got my wings back too," he says, giving them a little flap when I reach out to touch the silky feathers. "And my wife. This is Psyche," he says, introducing me to the woman who follows him into the room.

"*The* Psyche? As in the *soul* part of heart and soul?"

"The one and only," she says, giving Jonathan the most loving look.

"The strangest thing," I say to Jonathan. "I thought for a moment that I saw you in the Underrealm."

"That's a story for another day." Jonathan exchanges a look with Ethan, who enters behind his mother.

"Daphne!" Joe says, bounding into the room and pulling me into a hug. "I thought I'd never see you again."

"Me too," I say, hugging him back. Tears fill my eyes and it's hard to see who else is in the group that filters into the room behind him. That's why I'm surprised when a woman grabs me next. She smells of flowers and sunshine.

"Mom?" *My mom is here?*

"You came back just in time," Joe says. "Your mother was just about to murder me for selling your soul—*before I knew you even existed*, I might remind her."

"I may murder him yet," she says, throwing him a bloodcurdling glare, but she squeezes me tighter.

"You know?" I ask.

"Yes, your *father* filled me in." From the way she says father, I can only imagine how that discussion went down, and I realize Joe is lucky to still have all of his pieces. "And now you and I are going to have a good long talk about this running off with somebody into this so-called Underrealm without telling your mother."

I am hit with a wave of guilt, remembering the vow I had made to my mother before moving to Olympus Hills. *Cross my heart, hope to die, I will not go running off with some guy.* "Though technically I didn't run off *with* Haden to the Underrealm, I went running in *after* him," I say sheepishly.

Mom turns that murderous—though somewhat softer—glare on me. "Do not think you are getting out of the grounding of your lifetime—as in your whole lifetime—with semantics."

"I am sure this is a discussion that can be revisited later," someone else says. "There're more hugs to go around."

"Dax?!" It's Haden who says it. He's sitting up in his bed, rubbing his tired eyes in disbelief. I take it Dax has been missing for quite some time. Dax gives me a quick hug and then bounds over to Haden. The two exchange one of those man-hug-slap-you-on-the-back-at-the-same-time deals. "How?" Haden says in disbelief. "Where have you been? What happened to you?"

"Terresa set me up the night of the school play. She used Abbie to lure me out to the old mill but had an army waiting for me. I've been in a Skylord prison ever since."

"Nice of Terresa to mention she had my best friend locked up in her prison," Haden says.

"Well you never did ask her," Ethan says.

"Good point," Haden says.

"I thought we were going to be trapped in there forever until Brim found us," Dax says.

"Brimstone?" Haden says. "Yours must have been the scent she picked up on." Haden looks around, expectantly searching for his tiny cat. "Where is she? Where's Brim?"

Dax lowers his head. "She didn't make it out. I'm so sorry, Haden. The minotaur was on our trail. She created a diversion so we could escape. She saved us but got lost in the maze in the process."

A mournful tone spirals off of Haden, but there are still faint notes of hope underneath. "She'll find a way out," he says softly. "She always finds me." He looks up at Dax. "Who's *us?*"

That's when I see who is standing in the doorway now.

"CeCe!?" I take in her red curls, beaming smile, and friendly, syncopated tone. She looks and sounds just like she did back in Ellis Fields when we worked in the flower shop together, I forget momentarily that she had been living under an assumed identity while on the run from her Skylord father. "I mean Abbie."

"You can call me whichever you like," she says, taking my mother's place and giving me a hug. I take it all in for a moment, basking in it. I have never felt so loved in all my life. Maybe I should get trapped in the Underrealm more often.

Abbie pulls away. "My brother?" she asks.

"Yeah," Lexie says from where she lingers in the hallway. "Where's Tobin?"

Tobin!

Haden's peril, and then the reunion with my friends and family, had momentarily distracted me from the reason I'd run here. In an instant all my happiness is set aside. "Tobin is trapped. He can't leave the Underrealm. He sent me to get help. The Keres are free and the gate is stuck open. And Garrick lied. You know how he said there were only a couple of dozen Keres? Yeah, try more like a couple thousand." The others straighten up, paying closer attention when I say this. Ethan tries to hide his shock and fear behind a stoic mask, but I can hear it eking off of him. "And they're coming this way."

"So are the Skylords," Dax says, indicating the darkening sky out the window. There's a roll of thunder in the distance. "We came here to warn you. I walked into your room just as you were losing consciousness. I thought I was too late to save you . . . But at least I'm not too late to help you fight."

"My half-sister, Terresa, she's convinced our father to let her lead a Skylord troop this way," Abbie says. "We heard her say that she won't rest until you and all of your friends are dead."

"Hell hath no fury like a woman scorned," Ethan says, giving Haden a knowing look. He nods, and I assume there's another story there that will need to wait for another day.

"What do you want us to do?" A deep, completely unfamiliar voice says from the corner of the room. I realize there are two more people here—and they're the last two people I expect to see. Rowan is tied up in the corner, and his father, Ren, former king of the Underealm, steps forward. I can't help shivering. One of our greatest enemies is standing before us.

"What is your command, *Lord* Haden?" Ren says with a slight bow to his head.

Okaaay . . . I think, blinking at Ren's unexpected behavior, *I've definitely missed a lot.*

G

chapter forty

HADEN

The Keres are free. The gate is open. The Skylords are coming. And my father is deferring to me for guidance.

I hold my hand out to Daphne and see that my skin has returned to normal. No more black veins. No more poison. She has cured me with her kiss. Daphne clasps my hand and stands next to me. I don't want to ever let go of her again.

I take in the group in front of us. Dax—returned to me in the nick of time; Jonathan with his godhood newly restored; Ethan, son of Cupid and grandson of the Sky King; Psyche, the former Skyrealm princess who has lived as a servant in her own home; Abbie, a half-human, half-Skylord who has been in hiding for six years; my father; and Daphne's parents. Excluding Rowan who is restrained in the corner, they all look at me with the same expression on their faces. They want me to lead.

"What should we do about the Skylords?" Dax asks when I don't respond to my father.

I stand, finding my legs working once again. "Let them come. We'll need all the firepower we can get."

"You mean to lead them into the Underrealm?" Dax asks.

"Exactly. A messenger from the Oracle of Elysium appeared to me." I almost tell them that the messenger was my mother, however I feel strange sharing that in front of Rowan and my father. As if it were something intimate for only me to know. "The messenger told me that darkness is coming. I assume she was referring to the Keres. But she also said the light is gathering in order to beat back the dark. That is us. We are the light. I do not think it is a coincidence that we've all gathered in this place now. The Fates have brought us back together. If we had not gone into the Skyrealm, we would not have gotten Jonathan's bow back, and we would not have found Psyche. Brimstone would not have found Dax and Abbie, and my father would not have agreed to join the fight. Our mission to find Persephone may have been a failure, but it is what brought us all together."

"Failure?" Daphne asks. "You didn't find Persephone?"

"No," I say. "She wasn't in the prison."

A surprising look of remorse crosses her face.

"What's wrong?"

"I promised someone . . . Never mind . . . This is more pressing. Go back to fate bringing us together and all that."

I squeeze her hand, worried about the look of concern on her face. "Not just fate. Destiny. Even Terresa's wrath and the Skylord army headed this way. It'll take an army to beat back the Keres, and now we'll have one."

"You trust them?" Dax asks. "You were so against letting the Skylords help us before, and those were Ethan's trusted men. Why would you allow Terresa's army inside without a compelling reason to believe they'll help us?"

"Rejecting Ethan's help was a mistake. *My* mistake. I should have listened to Ethan and accepted his help. I thought we had to do this on our own and now I realize we need all the help we can get. Before we were working under the assumption that the Keres were still locked away in the Pits and the Skylords would go after our people instead of them, but I believe the Keres being free will be a compelling reason enough for the Skylords to help us. We want the same thing—to keep the Keres from entering the other realms. This is the same reason I believe the Court will help us as well."

"The Court is gone," Daphne says. "The Court, the royal guard, Garrick. Those were the first things the Keres destroyed." Daphne quickly relates what happened when Garrick opened the barrier and released the Keres. It does not surprise me that they turned on him. What is surprising is Daphne's account of being able to . . . What was the word she used to describe the way she transported herself through the Underrealm? . . . Teleport? That could be very useful to our cause. Another gift from the Fates.

"Our first priority needs to be keeping the Keres from crossing through the gate," I say. "Our second is getting Daphne to the palace so we can defend the people against the Keres."

"We'll have to evacuate the palace and get everyone out of the royal grounds," Daphne says. "My vocal powers don't work anywhere on the royal grounds. I learned that the hard way."

My confidence falters for a moment, but then I realize that this is also a gift from the Fates, in a way. If we had accepted Ethan's help the first time around and gone into the Pits to make a preemptive strike against the Keres, we would have failed. We most likely would have died. The Pits are on royal ground and we would have had no idea that Daphne's powers would not work. We would have opened the barrier and been completely defenseless.

"That complicates things," I say. "But it is a complication we can work around. Ethan, are your men still willing to fight with us? I want trusted guards surrounding Daphne at all times."

"I've already sent Jessica to collect them. Daphne will be in good hands."

"Wait," Daphne's mother says. "What are you talking about? I'm not sending Daphne back into the Underrealm."

"Mom, I have to go," Daphne says.

"No, you don't. You're not a warrior and this isn't your fight. I just got you back, I'm not letting you return just to help these . . . these . . . Underlords who wanted to kidnap you. You'll have no part in this."

"I am afraid Daphne plays the most important role in this," I say. "The Keres are creatures of shadow. Daphne's voice is the only thing that can make them solid enough to be killed. Without her, no one stands a fighting chance against them."

"I don't care," Demi says. Daphne had once told me that her mother was like a force of nature, and I can see that now. She stands tall and commanding—unmoving. "They can find a different way without you. I forbid you to go, Daphne. You're coming back to Ellis Fields with me. Where you'll be safe."

Daphne's head cocks ever so slightly to the side. "Did you know?" she asks.

Her mother's eyes narrow slightly. "Did I know what?"

"Did you know who I am? That I am a descendant of Orpheus and the Amazons? That my voice has special powers? That I was

259

the Cypher? That I needed to be protected? Did you know that Ellis Fields is a safe haven for our people? Is that why you never wanted to let me leave?" Daphne's voice catches. "Have you been lying to me all my life?"

Demi's hardened stance wavers ever so slightly. "No," she says, reaching her hands out toward Daphne. "No, my little sprout. I mean, there were stories. Family legends, you know. Mostly a joke about how we must be descendants of the Amazons because we're so tall, and how our family had been living in Ellis since before the town was even a town, and how no one in my family ever wanted to leave. But I have never known why—it was always just this driving feeling. A need to keep you safe inside Ellis—as in the very idea of leaving Ellis Fields brought on panic attacks. But I never knew why. Not until now. I always knew you were special to me— priceless—but I swear I never knew anything beyond that. I didn't know how special you were to this Underrealm . . ."

Daphne finally takes her mother's outstretched hands. "And that is why I need to go, Mom. There are women and children in the palace. They're completely defenseless without me. I have to go." It's not a question. She's not asking for permission. She says it with authority, informing her mother that she will be going and nothing will stop her.

Daphne's determination and compassion are two of the things I love the most about her. She was only their queen for a few days, and already she feels responsible for the people of the Underrealm.

Demi lowers her head, as if resigned to the idea that Daphne's fate is no longer in her control. "I just don't want to lose you."

"I don't want to lose you, either," Daphne says. "That's one of the reasons I agreed to join this fight. If the Keres get free in this world, I will lose everything and everyone I care about. Including you."

Daphne embraces her mother. Demi doesn't let go until Daphne tells her it's time for her to go. She returns to my side and takes my hand again.

"What about you?" Daphne asks me quietly. "Are you okay to go with us? I mean, you basically just died and all. Maybe you need to rest."

"No," I say. "I've slept enough for this lifetime. I actually feel strong. Stronger than ever, now that you're back."

I hold her hand tightly in mine. I understand her mother's plight. I wish nothing more than to keep Daphne out of harm's way, but I know that is not where she belongs. The Fates have reunited us for a reason. It's something I've known since she very first took my hand back in Ellis Fields and insisted that she help me find the Key—that if we are going to succeed, we can only do so together. Our destinies are intertwined.

chapter forty-one

DAPHNE

The sky grows darker and darker with storm clouds, and the air is thick with the smell of rain. We all know what that means—the Skylords are upon us.

"We need to get to the grove," Haden says. "We need to drive the Skylords away from town and into the gate."

As much as I wish I could just revel in the presence of my loved ones for a few more minutes, I know he's right. There isn't even time for planning.

Haden approaches Rowan, who is tied up in the corner of the room. There wasn't much opportunity for storytelling, but I've gathered that Rowan had something to do with Haden's near-death. I can hear the angry tones rolling off of Haden. Rowan flinches away from Haden's touch and at first I think Haden is going to wring his brother's neck, but instead he pulls the bindings from Rowan's hands. Haden's tone changes suddenly from angry notes to a tight, restrained tune. As if he were willing himself to remain calm and collected. "I should hate you, Rowan. I should want to punish you for what you did to me. For what you've always done to me. Alas, what is happening today is bigger than you and me and we need all the help we can get, so instead I will offer you a second chance. Will you fight with us?" he asks Rowan. I can tell from his inner tone now that Haden has had to humble himself quite a bit to offer this olive branch to his horrible brother. It makes me love Haden even more. "For the sake of the Underrealm?"

Rowan stands, rubbing his wrists. He looks from Haden to their father, who stands behind him. His lip curls in disdain. "I'm done with this," he says. "I'm not going to risk my life to clean up your mess. Find someone else to watch your back." There's a dark tone wafting off of Rowan that makes me shiver, but there's not time to analyze what it means now.

"Then you are free to leave," Haden says, showing him the door. "But I never want to see you in this town again."

"As if *you* will ever see it again? Have a nice death, little brother." Rowan throws Ren and Haden one last glare and then marches from the room. I watch out the window until he's down the driveway and on his motorcycle that's parked a few houses down. He drives out of sight.

Good riddance.

"As soon as we go I need you to get my mother out of here," I say to Joe. "Drive her as far away as you can get."

Joe shakes his head. "I can't drive your mother. I'm coming with *you.*"

"Joe, you can't."

"I can, Daphne. And I will. I was supposed to be there last time. I was supposed to help you. Maybe none of this would have happened if I had been."

"It's okay, Joe, I don't blame you . . ." Joe had been under so much stress and he was an addict after all, I should have realized he wouldn't be strong enough to resist the temptation to drink. . .

"Yes, but *I* blame myself. Even if I was drugged—"

"You were drugged?" I ask, sticking my hand in the pocket of my cloak and clutching the sobriety coin. So he hadn't given in? "*That's* why you didn't come."

"Yes, someone drugged my water bottle. We think it must have been Garrick trying to manipulate the situation. But I should have pulled myself through it. I should have been there for you no matter what. There's nothing you can say to stop me from going now." Notes of absolute determination pound off of him, and I know there is no way to deter him. He wants to be redeemed, not only for not being there the last time the gate was open but also for all the mistakes he made in the past. That was the reason he had wanted to go last time. I can't deny him the opportunity now.

I nod, conceding, and he gives me a cheeky smile. I think for a moment that I always want to remember him with that expression on his face.

"Do you know how to wield one of these?" Dax says, offering a large sword to Joe. "We had to incapacitate a few guards on our way out of the Skyrealm. Thought a few of their weapons would come in handy."

Joe takes the sword. "I've never handled a sword, but I have wielded a few guitars in my day," he says, playfully swinging the sword as if it were a guitar he was about to smash against an opponent's head.

"I guess that will do," Haden says, but I can sense the worry in his voice.

"I can help," Lexie says.

We all look at her as if she's growing a second head all of a sudden.

"What I mean is that I'll make sure Daphne's mother and I get as far away as possible. Maybe an outlet mall near Vegas? That'll be fun."

My mother raises an eyebrow at this but doesn't protest being taken away from this mess.

"Phew, Lexie," Haden says. "For a second there, I was almost worried you were going to insist on coming with us, too."

"Whatever, I know my strengths and my limitations," Lexie says. "I'll let all of you with the superpowers take on the monsters. I'll provide the hot chocolate and muffins when you get back." She sounds flippant, but to my surprise the hidden tone behind her words makes it sound as if she actually does care.

"Thank you for watching out for my mother," I say to her.

"Please, make sure Tobin comes home, okay?" she says, her tone softer and sincere.

"Okay," I say, but I don't know if it's a promise I can keep. I try not to think about the likelihood that Tobin is even still alive after facing the swarm of Keres that pursued us to the gate. Instead, I give her a reassuring smile.

Haden takes my hand again. He holds it like he never wants to let go. I wish he never will. Ethan, Jonathan, Dax, Abbie, Psyche, and Joe follow us out of the house. There's a car parked askew in the driveway, and a woman in a rumpled red dress-suit jumps out when she sees us. She looks so frazzled, with frizzy, disheveled hair and sleepless eyes, it takes me a minute to recognize her.

"Mayor Winters, what are you doing here?" I say to Tobin's mother.

"My son, where is he?" she asks, tones of desperation clinging to her words. "He hasn't come home in days."

"You know where he is," comes a voice from behind me. Abbie steps forward. "The same place you tried to send me in order to get seed money for your company."

"Abbie?" Mayor Winters looks even more crazy-eyed than before. "How? Where? What about Tobin?"

"Nice to see you too, Mother," Abbie says. I realize it's been at least six years since they've stood face to face. "But I don't have time for this not-so-pleasant reunion. I need to save Tobin from the Underrealm."

Mayor Winters's mouth drops open. She stammers until Haden puts his hand on her shoulder. "I need you to evacuate the town again. Get everyone as far away from here as possible. Things are about to get far more stormy than last time."

She nods, still in shock, and we leave her behind. Haden leads us out into the street.

"Shouldn't we drive?" I ask. "There's no time to waste."

"We're going to fly," Haden says.

"Fly?" I ask, thinking maybe he isn't feeling quite well after his near-death experience.

He smiles and hooks my arms around his neck. "Hold on," he whispers, his breath caressing my ear, and a second later we're rocketing into the air.

"What the—?" I cling to his neck, looking down at the ground below us. We're actually flying. Haden laughs and I stare into his jade-green eyes, forgetting for a moment that we are heading off into battle. "Well, I definitely picked a winner. What's better than a boyfriend who can fly?"

"Boyfriend?" he asks.

"Do you have a problem with that title?" I say, punching him playfully.

"Not at all," he says. "I was just thinking that the word seems inadequate to me."

"It does, doesn't it?" I light a kiss on his cheek. I can't believe we're together after all this time, I can't believe I'm in his arms, and we're flying no less. I look at the town below us and notice a toddler pulling on her father's pant leg, trying to get him to look up from his iPhone to see the "big birds" above them. I laugh and then close my eyes.

"Are you okay?" Haden asks.

"Yes . . . It's just that . . . I know I shouldn't feel this happy when the world is coming apart at its seams."

"I know what you mean."

Jonathan flies up beside us, flapping his great wings, with a less-than-enthused-looking Joe wrapped in his arms. Ethan, carrying Ren, and Psyche and Abbie hefting Dax are not too far behind. "Look," Jonathan says, nodding toward the grove island in the middle of the lake. A thick, black cloud swirls up from the center of the island. It almost looks like smoke. "Skylords?"

I swallow hard. "Keres," I say. "They're coming through the gate."

chapter forty-two

HADEN

Once I see that the Keres have breached the gate, it is as if I cannot fly fast enough. It feels as though we are stuck in slow motion even though we are soaring through the air. I was hoping we would have time to regroup and plan once we got to the grove, but that is not an option now. We must go headfirst into the fray.

I set Daphne down on the ground in the grove, only a few yards off from the spiraling cloud of Keres. Their screeching fills the grove. We are followed by Jonathan and Joe, then Ethan and Ren, and finally Psyche, Abbie, and Dax land as well.

A moment later, Jessica descends into the grove with two men who look like twins. They have golden skin and white-blond hair. One carries a battle-ax and the other a spear.

"Aris and Crux," Ethan says, saluting his men. He turns to Jessica and reaches a hand toward her. She doesn't take it but I can tell she wants to. "Is this all?"

Jessica nods. "Most of the brigade went into hiding after the last battle with the Skylords. They've all got bounties on their heads. This is all I could find, short notice."

"Don't worry," the man with the battle-ax says, "My brother and I fight like six men. Each."

"That you do, Aris," Ethan says, clapping him on the shoulder, but I can tell from the look in his eyes that he was hoping for more men. Our troop may fill the grove, but it feels small compared to the thousands of Keres that Daphne reported escaped from the Pits.

I can only hope the Fates will deliver the Skylord army soon.

I signal to the others. Jonathan, Ethan, Dax, Ren, Abbie, Psyche, Aris, Crux, Jessica, Joe, and I create a wall around Daphne with our bodies. Jonathan draws his golden bow and knocks it with a graphite arrow from the sporting goods store. There wasn't time for him to make more arrows from his Kronolithe, but I don't doubt he can be just as deadly with mortal-made weapons. Joe tentatively raises his stolen Skylord sword in front of them. Aris and Crux electrify their weapons, and Dax, Ren, Psyche, Abbie, and I create lightning bolts in our hands.

I can tell Abbie is relatively new to using her powers and that Psyche probably hasn't used hers in years. It takes her a couple of tries to get a bolt to spark. Psyche catches me giving her the side-eye. "Don't worry about me. I might be rusty, and I might be a former princess, but I was trained by my father's personal guard. It'll come back quickly."

I nod, not questioning her assertion. We will all need to adapt quickly. There are at least two dozen Keres in the spiraling cloud above the gate, and more coming. I thank Hades that the gate is so narrow, slowing the Keres's progress into this world. However, we will face the same obstacle, trying to get our forces inside.

Once flanked, Daphne doesn't hesitate. She plants her feet on the ground and opens her mouth. I expect her to let out a magical scream, as she did the last time she and I fought a Keres together, but instead she sings. Not words, but a high pitched scale of notes. It reminds me of one of the songs I downloaded when I bought an entire music store's inventory. It's a song from something called *The Phantom of the Opera*. Daphne keeps singing the notes, scaling higher and higher until she hits the same frequency and tone of the Keres's bloodcurdling screeching. It sounds like she's singing a scream.

The noise makes me want to throw my hands over my ears, but I keep them at the ready because the Keres are even more irritated by the sound—because it causes them to take a solid form. The misty cloud of shadows transforms into a knot of winged creatures. They look like a fearsome crossbreed of black birds of prey and the statues of things mortals refer to as angels. Their forms are distinctly female, as if they were women with large black wings and horrible talons. They clack and screech and point their claws at Daphne. She's made them angry, and they've chosen their first target. They shift position, creating a "V" formation as if they were a flock of birds. At the center of the "V" is the largest of the Keres. It bares its fanglike teeth at Daphne.

"Now?" Dax asks, holding his lightning bolt.

I shake my head. I don't want to spook the Keres too soon—cause them to scatter and disappear into Olympus Hills, where we'll have to hunt them down. There's no time for that.

The Keres dive, swooping down at us with their talons extended.

"*Now?*" Dax says.

I wait one more second, until I can see the falcon-like pupils of the lead Keres's blood-red eyes. "Now!" I shout and fling my bolt of lightning. My comrades follow my instruction, and lightning flies toward the swooping monsters. My bolt hits the leader, blowing it back into one of the other Keres. Dax hits it with a second strike. With a third strike from me, the Keres explodes. It shatters into thousands of pieces, as if someone has taken a mace to an alabaster statue. Bits of stone rain down on our heads. In the meantime, Ethan, Abbie, and Psyche take out two more of the beasts. Jonathan slings two arrows into the chest of a fourth Keres, skewering it to the ground before it explodes. Aris waits until a Keres is almost on top of him and then slams his electrified ax into its chest. Crux does the same with his spear. Joe hacks wildly at the air with his sword, keeping any creature from coming close. Ren grabs a low-flying Keres by its wings and climbs on top of it. The beast sends a primal shout echoing through the grove before Ren throttles it, sending bolts of lightning from his hands into its throat.

Five Keres break off from the group, trying to flee the grove. "Don't let any escape!" I shout. Ethan goes after one, and Jonathan shoots down the second. Dax and Ren are on the tail of the third, and Aris and Crux run after the fourth and fifth.

I generate another bolt and fling it at a monster who has taken up the lead of the flock of Keres. They have circled the grove and are coming back for a second dive at Daphne, who is now only protected by me, Abbie, Joe, and Psyche. Right as the bolt is about to strike it in the abdomen, the beast flickers from solid to shadow. My bolt passes right through it, striking a tree. The four of us duck down to the ground, barely escaping the swooping shadow. I realize Daphne has stopped singing. She is gasping for breath. How she maintained the song for so long, I don't know. She holds her hand up, telling me she is fine but needs a moment.

The mass of shadows swoops around, coming for a third diving pass. Daphne takes another breath and picks up her song again, and the Keres take their solid, gruesome form once again. I turn back to the fray right as a Keres swoops down on top of me. The Keres grabs me by the shoulder, ripping its talons into my flesh, and flings me away from Daphne and the group. I fly through the air and smack into the tree that has been set aflame by my stray bolt of lightning. Two Keres land on top of me, pinning me against the ground. One of them claws at my chest, going for my heart. Daphne's song continues—my only way of knowing she's okay.

A roll of thunder shutters through the grove, sending the trees quaking. A bolt of lightning hits one of the Keres that sits on top of me. The beast explodes. Another bolt sends the second Keres toppling away from me. I look up, expecting to see Dax or Ethan, but instead, Terresa stands over me with a ball of lightning in her hand.

"Back off, harpies," she says to the Keres. "If anyone is going to kill this lying piece of *kopros*, it's going to be me."

"Terresa, wait!" I shout, but she flings the bolt of lightning at my head. I roll out of the way, the lightning only singeing my right ear. "I'm sorry. I'm sorry you didn't get your kiss. You, um, can get it now if you want."

"Ugh, as if I'd kiss Underlord scum." She sneers and generates a second bolt. "I don't care about the kiss. I care that you made me

272

feel like I loved you," she says with such disdain that I realize the love spell must have worn off. "And then you just . . . just . . . left me behind!" She raises her hand over her head, her bolt aimed at my face. It might be a trick of the light from the lightning crashing around us, but I swear it looks as though she is about to start crying. "You made me love you and then you hurt me."

I am hit with a sudden pang of guilt so powerful I don't think to defend myself as she tries to stab me with her bolt of lightning. Fortunately, before she can land the blow, a Keres launches itself on top of her.

Thunder claps above us, shaking the ground. I look up and see at least a hundred Skylords descending from the clouds above. Daphne is doing her best to keep the song going, and my comrades are locked in battle around us. We've managed to take down a handful of Keres, but it is as if for every one we fell, another two escape from the gate. The Keres wraps its wings around Terresa. She screams as I watch terrible boils burst forth on her face. The thing not only is draining the life from her body but is also making her sick. I launch myself at the creature. As much as she wants to blow my face off, I need her in this battle. I grab the Keres by the head, clasping it at its temples with both hands. Searing sores cover my hands but I don't let go. I send a pulse of lightning into the creature's temples. The thing writhes and screams and then its head combusts between my hands, shattering into pieces of stone that slip through my fingers.

Terresa blinks up at me. The sores on her face slowly recede. "I don't need your help, you filthy mongrel. My men will tear you and your precious Daphne apart."

So much for a thank you.

Terresa continues ranting. I grab her by the shoulders. "Hate me all you want, but I am not the threat here. Look around you, Terresa! The Keres have escaped." Terresa looks around her. Her eyes go wide as if really taking in the scene for the first time without revenge in her eyes.

"I need you to order your men to help us fight them back! We need to get through Persephone's Gate and stop them at their source before they destroy my world."

"I'm not going to help protect Underrealm filth!"

"Then do it for your world. Where do you think they'll go once they've torn mine and the mortal realms apart?" I let go of her shoulders. "You can go back to hating me as soon as this is over. Please, we need your help."

She brushes her shoulders as if my touch has somehow made her dirty. I take out a Keres that charges at her from behind. She jumps as the thing explodes, sending shards of stone around us. "Fine," she says. "What do you need?"

"I need to get Daphne to the gate. I need to get her and as many soldiers through the gate as possible. We need to destroy the Keres before any more escape. But you know the drill, anyone who isn't from the Underrealm has to go through the gate willingly. They have to want it with every fiber of their soul or they'll burn up rather than pass through."

Skylords begin to land in the grove, both male and female. They seem more than surprised by the monsters swirling around us. Some don't hesitate and join the fight right away, while others wait for Terresa's command.

"Listen up, soldiers!" she shouts. "We need to get that ugly girl over there," she points at Daphne who continues to sing as Abbie and Psyche defend her, "into that gate." She points to the two arched trees that cloak Persephone's Gate. The bright green light that shines in the middle of the archway is almost completely blocked out by the black shadowy forms that billow through it like smoke. As soon as the newly arriving shadow creatures hear Daphne's music, they solidify into black angel-birds. More than one Skylord soldier takes a step back at the sight. "But if you don't have the ovaries to fight your way through the gate, then you had better stay here. Only the brave and willing are needed in this fight."

Terresa continues giving instructions to her troops and I run back to Daphne, giving Abbie, Joe, and Psyche some backup from the swooping monsters. "Hey, did you see?" Joe calls, pointing at a pile of stone shards at his feet. "I killed one!"

I nod in approval and take on a defensive stance. My other comrades are busy keeping any Keres from escaping the grove. Daphne tries to give me a reassuring smile while she sings, but I don't know how much longer she can keep it up. And we haven't even seen the worst of it yet. Once we get through that gate, I don't know what we'll find, but it definitely won't be any easier than this.

"Ready!" Terresa yells.

I blast a Keres and call back the rest of my comrades to make a knot around Daphne. Terresa's soldiers—considerably fewer than before—take their shields and spears and swarm around those of us who do not have physical weapons. The Skylords create a phalanx position, locking their shields together around us, creating a wall. The first three rows of soldiers project their electrified spears out over the wall of shields, creating a hedge of sharp, crackling points. We advance slowly, moving as one large mass toward the gate. Any Keres attacking from the front are beaten back and destroyed by the spears, and any monsters that try to fly away have their wings clipped by Jonathan and another archer from the Skylord ranks. Daphne keeps up her song, breathing only when absolutely necessary.

Getting to the gate is agonizingly slow but effective. It's passing through the gate that will be difficult. It will need to be done one by one in single file, breaking the phalanx position that protects us.

I hear more than one soldier scream as they reluctantly step into the gate, burning up on impact. The ones who make it through will be greeted on the other side by Keres who can't be killed—at least not until Daphne crosses through the gate.

I position myself in front of her, but cling to her hand from behind. I want to go first so I am ready to protect her. Before stepping through the gate I look back over my shoulder. "Are you sure you want to do this?"

"With all my heart," she says.

I step through the gate with a bolt at the ready and pull her in behind me. And then suddenly I remember something and worry that I have made a grave mistake. What if the gate won't allow her to pass through after me because of the unbreakable vow I made? The vow that I would never bring Daphne to my father in the Underrealm? I hadn't even thought of that until this very moment . . . but the gate lets us pass. I can only assume it is because my father is no longer the king of the Underrealm, or because he is still in the grove behind us. Or possibly my dying earlier today has released me from any vows I made in my former life. Whatever the case, I am grateful the gate does not repel us.

Grateful, that is, until I see the scene in front of me as I enter the Underrealm. The sky above the ravine is almost completely black, swirling with shadow beasts. Thousands and thousands of Keres. They've become strong enough to multiply. The floor of the ravine is littered with bodies. Not only of the Skylord soldiers who passed through the gate before me, but also of Underlords. Men who either tried to pursue the Keres here, or who were trying to flee to the gate. Either way, they failed.

They're all dead.

chapter forty-three

DAPHNE

As soon as I cross through the gate I am so overwhelmed by the scene in front of me that my voice fails me. I am rendered speechless, or songless, by shock—and by trying not to wretch from the carnage at my feet. The ravine is filled with shadows, but through the darkness, I can still make out the dead bodies. Some are covered in flesh-eating sores, others look as though the soldiers turned on each other, like what I witnessed when the Keres were first released. But they're all the same, lifelessly strewn on the ground around us.

My gaze searches for Tobin amongst the dead, but I can't really make out the features of any of them—especially the ones who look as though part of their faces have melted away. Then I scan the ground for the Key, but see no sign of that either. If only there were a way to shut the gate and keep more Keres from escaping into the mortal realm.

Only a few of the Skylord soldiers who proceeded through the gate before us remain standing. One soldier, only a few feet from me, is wrapped in a black cocoon of a Keres, who is feeding on his life force. Another soldier tries to strike the Keres with his spear, but the weapon passes through the shadow creature and impales his comrade in the shoulder.

The man screams, and another three Keres swarm the two soldiers. Haden grabs my arm and tries to push me back through the gate. "It's too late. Too dangerous. We have to go back," he says frantically. His words finally shake me out of my shocked state and I don't let him deter me. I step around him.

"These people need my help."

Haden protests, but a swarm of Keres descends on us. I sing a scream, louder than ever before, causing the Keres around us to take solid form. Haden flings two blasts, freeing the two men I'd seen in the Keres' embrace.

The few soldiers who survived regroup into their rectangular formation, creating a wall in front of the gate with their shields and spears, allowing for the rest of our group to pass through the gate, one by one, into the Underrealm. When Joe enters, brandishing his sword, his eyes go wide with shock. For a moment I think he is about to turn back, but instead he joins the soldiers' huddle. Dax and Abbie are the last to enter. They hold hands just like Haden and I did. All of our friends made it through, but only about twenty-five of the Skylord soldiers remain, including Terresa and Ethan's friend Jessica.

I keep singing, trying to keep the Keres solid and killable, but my voice is growing hoarse. Matching the high-pitched shrill of the Keres is murder on my vocal cords. It kills me that I'm not able to physically fight like the others, but I know my part in this is the most important. Without my voice, the others would be defenseless, even with all their special powers.

"What should we do?" Ethan asks. "Go back or press forward?"

Haden shakes his head as if he doesn't know the right answer. I grab his sleeve and point out of the ravine. "Palace!" I have to sing the word in my screeching tone because if I let the song drop, the Keres will lose their solid form. "The women and children."

Haden shakes his head again, remorse filling his eyes. "We'll never make it there!" he shouts to be heard over the screeching. "Not even with the protection of the phalanx. It would take days. Based on the Keres's numbers, the odds that there are any survivors are slim at best."

I tap my pomegranate necklace. "I can teleport." I feel more than silly singing the words, but I have no other choice. "We can't just leave them there. I can go to the palace and check it out. Bring any survivors back here."

Haden lobs a lightning bolt over the wall of shields, taking out a Keres that was attempting to fly off with Crux in its clutches. The Skylord drops to the ground with a sickening crunch. He moans and rolls over, clutching his leg. Aris and Jessica break away from the formation in order to drag him back to safety.

"You're the only one that necklace works for?" Haden asks.

I nod. As Persephone's heir, I am the only who can control her Kronolithe—at least, according to Shady. My mind wanders for a moment, wondering what has become of my unlikely friend . . .

"That's no good," Haden says. "You're the only one who can teleport to the palace, and you're the only one who can keep the song going here. If you leave, the gate will be unprotected. All of these soldiers will die and the Keres will escape into your world.

280

Our first priority has to be protecting the gate." He tries to squeeze my hand but I pull it away.

I shake my head, refusing to believe it even though I know he's right.

Haden swallows hard. "Believe me, Daphne, if there was a way to do both, I would will it for the Fates to make it so. I don't want to let my people die, but even you can't be in more than one place at once."

Tears well in my eyes as I think of the Lesser boy who shared my breakfast and the woman who brought my clothing. I think of all the other innocent people who will die because I can't make it to them. My voice begins to falter from emotion but I choke back my cries. I can't lose control or I won't be able to sing.

"She can't be in more than one place, but I can," Jonathan says. He shoots a Keres with an arrow and then crouches beside us. I notice he only has three more arrows in his quiver.

Haden nods but I just stare at him, not sure what he means.

"Music is from the metaphysical realm," Jonathan says. "Now that I am a god of the Metarealm once again, that means I can manipulate it. I can take Daphne's voice and spread it through the Underrealm. I can keep it here while she goes to the palace."

I clap my hands together. I have no idea how Jonathan's plan will actually work, but I grab on to the idea with all my heart. We have to at least try.

"You're forgetting one thing, Daphne. You said your vocal powers do not work on the royal grounds. Even if Jonathan can spread your music throughout the realm, if you go to the palace *you* will be unprotected."

"I don't care," I sing. I can't let innocent people continue to die because I wasn't willing to try to save them. I told Tobin not to blame himself for Garrick freeing the Keres—that that choice was on Garrick alone—but I cannot rid myself of the guilt I feel over being the one who put the Key in Garrick's grasp. That was my choice.

I hold my hands out to Jonathan, telling him I am ready.

Haden tries to protest, wanting to protect me, but Jonathan clasps his hands over mine. He closes his eyes, and a moment later he disintegrates into a golden mist. My eyes go wide and I wonder if they're playing a trick on me. The golden mist swirls around my face as I sing and then dives into my mouth and down my throat. It feels as though I am choking until the mist sails out between my lips. It pulses and glitters, and slowly the misty particles form into the shapes of tiny musical notes. Then the strangest thing happens—I hear my voice outside of my head. It sounds like a recording. Distant and higher-pitched than normal. The mist sails away, circling through the ravine. It splits in several directions, taking my voice with it.

The Keres, still solid but no longer focused on attacking just me, break apart and follow the different paths that my voice takes. I can only hope they can't harm Jonathan in his metaphysical state.

"Dax, Joe, Ethan, Crux, Psyche, and Abbie, stay and protect the gate," Haden commands. "Jessica, Terresa, and Aris, take small bands of soldiers and follow the Keres. Attack and kill as many as you can while they're broken off from the flock." He turns to me. "You can transport me with you?" he says, pointing at my pomegranate.

Yes—I try to say the word but no sound comes out. My hands fly to my throat. Jonathan hasn't just copied my voice, he's removed it from me. It feels like being stripped of my heart and soul. I take a deep breath and hold my hand out to Haden. Now is not the time for panicking. I mouth the words, "Yes, I can take you with me but I don't want to put you in more danger." No music in the palace won't just mean I will be unprotected, it means he will be as well.

Haden shakes his head, and at first I think he doesn't understand what I was trying to convey. But then he holds his hand out to me and says, "We do this together or we don't do it at all. That's the way it's supposed to be."

I take Haden's hand, knowing he is right.

"Let's go save your people then, my queen," he says.

I close my eyes and imagine the one place in the palace I can picture best. A moment later, Haden and I land on the bed in my queenly cell.

chapter forty-four

HADEN

I am completely astonished when in the blink of an eye, we go from the ravine swarming with Keres to a room that looks like one of the bedchambers in the palace. Our impact is soft, and I realize we've landed in a bed. I can't help it—seeing Daphne lying next to me, tangled in the sheets—I lean over and kiss her softly on the lips. I want to take solace in her if only for a moment. She tries to say something but no sound comes out. I gather from the look on her face that she is trying to scold me. But she kisses me once more before pushing me away. I stand and hold my hand out to her. I want to search the palace as quickly as possible and get out of this place.

Every moment we are here is a moment I cannot protect Daphne.

We head for the door that will lead us out of this room, but I am stopped by the sound of a chair crashing to the floor. I whirl around and catch a glimpse of a small foot being pulled under the cloth that drapes over the table in the corner of the room.

Daphne dashes to the table and pulls up the cloth. A scrawny Lesser boy cowers underneath. He flinches and cries, "Please don't hurt me!"

Daphne tries to say something but no sound comes out. I can tell the loss of her voice is deeply disturbing to her. She taps the boy's leg, trying to get his attention.

He cracks his eyes open and gasps when he sees her. "You're alive?!" he says. "I knew you'd make it." The boy speaks ancient Greek but Daphne seems to have no trouble understanding him. She nods with a smile and holds her hand out to him, not seeming to care how filthy he is.

"No, we have to hide," the boy says, gesturing for her to join him under the table. "There are monsters out there. Keres. They'll kill you if they find you."

"We know," Daphne mouths the words. "We came to find you."

"What?" the boy says, shaking his head. "What is wrong? Why can't she speak?" he asks me.

"She lost her voice," I say, switching to Greek so the boy can understand. "What she's trying to say is that we've come to rescue you."

Daphne holds her hand out to the boy again, gesturing for him to come.

"We need to hurry," I say.

The boy crawls out from under the table and takes her hand.

"Any others?" Daphne asks.

The boy shakes his head in confusion.

"Do you know if there are any other survivors?" I ask for her.

"The mothers," the boy says. "They escaped the harem and took the nurslings to the healing chambers. Some of the Lessers were headed there as well. The hallway was filled with Keres. I couldn't make it so I hid in here."

Daphne looks toward the doorway. I can see the thought in her head—*is the hallway still filled with Keres?* A screeching cry echoes from somewhere nearby. If not in the hallway, they are somewhere close. "Nurslings?" she mouths to me and I am thankful I studied lipreading while in the mortal realm. "As in *babies?*"

I hesitate for a moment then say, "Infants, yes. And children."

Daphne takes in a deep breath, staring at the door, and I know I've just told her the one thing that will send her running into the hallway.

"What about your pomegranate?" I ask. "Can you transport us there with that?"

She shakes her head, pointing from the pomegranate to her head.

"You have to be able to picture it in your mind in order to go there?" I ask.

She nods remorsefully, and I gather that she has never seen the healing chambers.

"What about the stables?" the boy says. "The search party left from the stables. Do you remember what they look like? Can you can get us there?"

I give the boy an approving look. He catches on fast. "If you can get us to the stables," I say, " you can see a tower that connects to the corridor that will take us to the healing chambers."

Daphne takes both me and the boy by the elbows. She doesn't hesitate. One moment we are in the bedchamber and the next we are in the stables beside an overturned chariot. Daphne's grip on my arm tightens and she lets out a loud breath—which I realize would have been a cry if she had a voice.

The stable is littered with weapons, broken fragments of chariots, and the bodies of horses and soldiers. Alas, not merely adult soldiers but also the apprentices. Boys as young as six, dressed in armor that is several sizes too big. In the Underrealm boys are expected to become men in their sixth year. Expected to learn to fight and run into battle with their adult counterparts.

These boys never made it out of the stables.

Daphne cries silently beside me, her grasp shaking against my skin. "We're too late," she mouths. "Too late."

I brush my hand against her cheek, wiping away tears. "Focus," I say in a calming voice. "We can still save the others. There's still hope." The windows of the stables begin to darken. The sound outside heralds an approaching group of Keres. "Look out that window. Look before it's too late. See that tower? Take us there."

Daphne opens her tear-filled eyes and looks out the window. The tower is almost completely obscured in shadow. She seems to focus on an open window at the very top of the tower—the owl roost where I spent so many hours as a child, hiding from my father's wrath.

Daphne closes her eyes and we vanish from the stables. However, either she couldn't get a good enough look or something shakes her concentration, because when we reappear we're in midair. Floating a few feet above the window. Floating until we're falling. I swing my arm out, grasping at the stone walls of the tower. I almost grab the windowsill, almost stop our fall, but the weight of Daphne and the boy are too much. My fingers slip off the stone and we tumbling toward the ground. I try to summon a bolt of lightning to propel us upward, but my power fails me. A silent scream echoes from Daphne's mouth. She clenches her eyes shut as I prepare to meet the ground—and we vanish.

We reappear inside the owl roost. Sitting in pile of straw. The owls startle and burst from their roosts. Sending feathers floating all around us.

Daphne sighs—it almost sounds like she's in disbelief. "Got a look in the window," she mouths.

I almost laugh in relief but there's no time. The cooing call of the owls that flew out the window shifts into a horrible noise. I glance out the window to see the owls captured in mid-flight, swathed in black shadowy cocoons. Even the animals aren't safe.

"Come on," I say, pulling Daphne and the boy from the roost out into the spiraling staircase that will bring us to the corridor that leads to the healing chambers.

Once the Keres are finished with the owls, they will come for us next.

chapter forty-five

DAPHNE

I am shaking. Not only from the near bone-crushing fall and the horrible things I've seen, but also because I have no outlet for finding relief. I cannot speak, I cannot scream, my cries have no sound. My voice has always been my greatest strength, the thing that made me who I am—my heart and soul. Without it, I feel naked and vulnerable. Weak.

But there's no time for weakness. I run down the spiraling staircase with Haden at my side and the Lesser boy trailing behind us. Screeching echoes from the owl roost we have only just left behind. The twist of the staircase makes me dizzy and my injured knee throbs from the constant downward movement—and I find myself wishing I'd taken the time in the mortal world to find a replacement for the makeshift brace Shady had made for me. I am shocked when I realize that was only a couple of days ago. At the moment it feels like a lifetime.

Haden leads me out of the tower into a long corridor. The air feels heavy here and I realize we must be underground. We run until we come to a dead end. The corridor ends at a pair of golden doors that look like they have been carved into rock wall. As if the doors lead inside an underground cavern. An intricate pattern depicting some sort of ritual is carved into the doors, but they have no handles, no knobs. No way of opening them that I can see. At the side of each large door is a small hole, only large enough to fit a balled fist.

Haden holds up his hand. His fingers are laced with crackling strands of blue electricity, and he clenches it into a fist. "Are you able?" he asks the boy.

The child nods and holds his hand open. He scrunches his eyes as if concentrating, and a moment later a few sparks of blue light dance up from his palms. When I first met the boy I had assumed he was older because he was already a servant, but looking at him now I realize that he can't be much older than five. Maybe six.

"Come on, come on," Haden whispers in encouragement. "You can do it."

The boy takes a deep breath, and when he exhales the sparks grow into thin wisps of electricity. The boy lets out a little cheer. Haden shoves his lightning-engulfed fist into the hole on one side of the doorway and instructs me to lift the boy so he can do the same on the other side. I gather they are initiating some sort of unlocking mechanism when blue light begins to spread through the carved pattern in the doors. When the light reaches the center where the two doors connect, I hear a thunking noise followed by a loud click. The doors crack open.

Haden throws the doors open and pushes the boy inside. I follow, looking back over my shoulder to see a swarm of shadows rolling through the corridor. Haden enters the chamber and pulls the doors shut. There's another loud thunk, and the doors lock behind us.

"We need to cover the crack in the bottom," Haden says, ripping the golden cloak off my shoulder. He wedges it under the door, closing off the sliver of light that shines through the crack. At first I don't know what good that will do, but then I realize—how else would shadow enter a room, if not through the nooks and crannies? I don't know how long it will hold off the beasts, but I hope it will be long enough.

The cavern is dark. No torches or overhead lights, but as my eyes adjust, I can see that the chamber is dripping with crystals. They hang from the ceilings and protrude up from the floors like stalactites and stalagmites. The air tastes salty but as I breathe it in, the strangest sensation tingles through my body. I feel as if I am getting stronger. The pain in my knee eases ever so slightly. No wonder they call this place the healing chambers.

I look around, trying to get my bearings in the dark. At first I think we are alone, that there is no one else hiding in here after all, but then a sound echoes through the chamber that makes my heart race.

A baby's cry.

Followed by the shush of a mother and a gasp of another.

"Hello?" I try to call but no sound follows.

"Come out," Haden says, calling to the people who must be hiding behind the outcroppings of crystals. "There's no time for hiding."

Someone coughs and someone else cries, but no one moves.

"We're here to help," the Lesser boy calls into the chamber.

"Link?" someone calls from within the cavern. "Link, is that you?"

"Mama?" the boy calls back. A pang of guilt catches me by

surprise—I had never bothered to ask the boy his name. Almost as if by being a Lesser, I didn't think he had one. "Mama!"

A woman appears from behind a crystal wall. Her dress is made of fine silk and dripping with jewels, and she holds a baby on her hip, but she's so thin and frail, I don't know how she can bear the child's weight. Link runs to her and she wraps her arm around him as he clings to her side. Haden and I step forward and the woman suddenly pushes Link back—as if embracing her child were forbidden. Her eyes lock on Haden, assessing him like a gazelle would look at a lion.

"It's all right," Haden says, slowly stepping closer.

She takes a step back.

"He's not like the others," Link says. "He's here to help us. The new queen, too. They can get us out of here."

The woman gives Haden another once-over. "You're the disgraced prince?" she says. "The one they banished?"

Her words make me want to jump to Haden's defense—tell her there's nothing disgraceful about him, but I literally have no words.

"Yes," Haden says. I wish I could read his tone right now—know exactly how he feels about answering to that title.

"And you came back for us?" she asks.

Haden nods.

"Follow me, then," she says, taking Link's hand. She leads us deeper into the chamber, past rows of what look like bed-shaped stones that I imagine they lay the sick on top of. I remember Haden telling me about when his mother was dying, how he begged his father to bring her here. I wonder if he's thinking of that now.

We pass the last row of stone beds and then follow the woman around a crystal-encrusted outcropping. What we find on the other side makes me wish I could cry out in joy.

People. Dozens and dozens of people. Women and children mostly. So many children. Babies and toddlers and older boys. Some dressed in armor, others in rags. A few old men, and even a few soldiers, most looking like they are healing from various injuries. I even recognize the woman who had brought me my clothes—the former queen.

"Moira," Haden says, nodding to her.

She looks up at him, and her expression makes her seem dumbfounded. As if he were the last person she ever expected to see again. She doesn't ask about her husband, King Ren.

"They left us," Link's mother says. "The Lords said we were the weak ones and left us behind. The other Boons and I gathered the remaining children and came here. The soldiers took the chariots and rode for the gate. "

"They didn't make it," Haden says. These are the words I would have spoken if I could. "You may be the only survivors of this world."

"Then the children must be saved," one of the old men says. "They're the future of this realm."

Haden looks at me and I nod, knowing what he's saying with his eyes.

"We'll get you all out," Haden says. "I promise."

Link's mother places her hand on Haden's arm. "I was there the day of your Choosing Ceremony. I was serving the Court. I heard what the Oracle said when she chose you. She said you were the one who could save us."

The woman leaves us and starts to gather the children. A strange faraway look settles on Haden's face. I tug on his sleeve, as if asking if he's okay.

"I'm fine," he says, caressing his fingers over mine. "I'm good. I only now realized something. Only a thought . . . When the Oracle chose me to come find you all those months ago, she said that you were the one who could restore what had been taken from my realm long ago. She said I was the one who could save my people. I thought all along she was talking about you being the Cypher and finding the Key—but maybe that's not what she meant. Maybe this is what she foresaw. That I would be the one to bring you here to save the last of my people right now."

I nod. I don't know if he's right, but I like the idea. It gives me hope that we can get all of these people out. Get them to safety.

But another thought pulls at me—if not the Key, then what is it that the Oracle foresaw that I would restore to this realm?

I don't dwell on the thought because Link's mother has gathered the children in front of me. There are so many people here—so many more than I had hoped we could save. I know I can't carry all of them with the Kronolithe at once. But I also don't want to leave anyone behind.

chapter forty-six

HADEN

Daphne takes ten people at a time. Five clinging to each of her arms. I know she wants to try to carry more but I don't want her to risk it. I doubt she can get far carrying that many people at once, and I am not sure where it is that she deposits them since she's unable to speak. I wish I had something for her to write on—or better yet, that I could read her mind.

Every time Daphne leaves, I feel as though my heart stops beating until she returns. I guess it is a good thing each trip takes her only a few seconds.

The Keres grow impatient outside the door. This chamber is protected by powerful magic set in place by Hades himself, but the way the door rattles and shakes, I worry it won't hold much longer.

It takes ten trips—there are a little less than a hundred of us—and I can tell Daphne is fatigued when she returns for the last group. "Take a minute to rest, " I say, even though I keep a wary ear out for the Keres.

She shakes her head. "No time," she mouths.

This makes me worry what I'll find on the other side.

Daphne scoops up a nursling and then grabs on to Link and his mother. An elderly lord takes her other hand. We're the last of the survivors. I wrap my arm around Daphne's waist. She lets out an inaudible sigh and we disappear.

Where we land is one of the many docks along the River of Woe. This one is only a couple of miles from the border of the royal grounds. I assume this is as far as Daphne could get with so many people, but it will have to be good enough for now. I can hear her song here, floating through the air as if it were carried on the wind. If the Keres come, at least they will be killable.

The refugees from the palace are huddled under the dock. Link and his mother help the elderly Lord join them. Daphne takes a step to follow and then collapses. Her legs give out and fold under her. I catch her up in my arms and hold her to my chest.

"Are you all right?" I ask, kissing her forehead. Her brow is damp and her skin is pale.

She nods, but I know she's lying. Her right nostril crinkles when she lies. She points off toward the horizon, and I know she's trying to indicate that we need to get back to Persephone's Gate, but that's not happening now. What we need to do is find better cover so she can rest. Trying to get all these people to the gate now would only serve to kill her from exhaustion.

I circle around, holding her in my arms, scanning our surroundings. I know there are caves nearby but those might take us back onto royal land. I search for a better form of shelter than the dock or a hiding space, but come up empty. This place is nothing but rolling dunes of dust and sand.

"Look! Look!" Link calls out, grabbing my attention. I follow his frantic gesture and see a large black *V* in the sky, heading our way. No, not only one *V*. That one is only the first. Several others follow. A legion of Keres. A legion of Keres coming here.

They may be killable, but there is no way I can defend all of these people against thousands of monsters. Have we saved my people from the palace only to bring them to their deaths? I run under the dock and lay Daphne down next to Link's mother.

"What are those creatures?" she asks.

"Keres. That is their true form. The music has made them corporeal, which means they can be killed—but I can't take them all on my own."

"I can fight," one of the injured soldiers calls out. He has a badly mangled foot, as if it had been caught in a chariot wheel, but I won't refuse help.

"Us also," another soldier says, indicating himself and his five other comrades.

I nod, grateful to have seven men on my side. Alas, that number is so small compared to how many Keres are headed this way.

"Me too," Link says, coming to stand beside me. He holds a tiny wisp of lightning in his small hand. The boy can't be more than five years old—still considered merely a child in the underworld.

"Link, no," his mother shouts.

"I always wanted to be a soldier, Mama," he says. "This might be my only chance."

What he means is *last* chance. I hate this idea, but I also know it will be all of our last chances if we can't fight off the Keres.

The black flocks of monsters draw closer. More of the older children gather around me, volunteering their help. Some are apprentices dressed in armor and others are Lessers like Link.

I decide I hate that word. There is no one Lesser here. They are all brave to me.

Five of the soldiers climb up on top of the dock. The Keres have the high ground, so defending those under the dock is our objective—if we can hold the creatures off until Daphne regains some strength, she may at least be able to get some of the women and younger children out of here.

When the first V dives for the dock, I know immediately my little band of soldiers isn't enough. We fell three Keres but they pick off two of our guards from the top of the dock. The Keres rip them apart and toss them into the river. A second V dives right after the first. I lose one of the boy soldiers. My bolt misses the beast and it flies off with its prey. The third flock dives and I give it all I've got—but my bolts are not enough. As many as I pick off, they keep coming. They break through my thin line of small soldiers and go after the women and children.

"My brother!" Link shouts, and I see one of the Keres snatch up a nursling in its talons. I recognize the child as the one Link's mother had been carrying. The beast has snatched it right out of her arms. She shrieks as the birdlike monster flaps its black wings and takes off with the child. Link chases after it, throwing his small bolts of lightning. I leave the safety of the dock and chase after them. I form a sphere of blue lightning in my hand and fling it at the beast. It hits the Keres square in the back between its wings. The blow causes the Keres to drop the child.

Link dives, catches his brother, and tucks and rolls away from the exploding beast.

I am amazed. Absolutely amazed. I cannot imagine either of my brothers—Rowan or Garrick—ever doing such a thing for me.

But it's not enough. None of it is enough. We don't have enough manpower. A fourth flock of Keres comes, swooping low to the ground. I hear more screaming from the dock and watch two Keres fighting over one of the women, threatening to tear her in two. I run to help her, preparing a new bolt, when I see another Keres swoop low to grab Link and his brother.

I cannot save them all.

A great moaning wail echoes over the riverbank. A dark gray figure jumps out from behind a boulder and launches itself on top of the low-flying Keres that has its sights on Link. It grabs the beast by the throat with two large hands and . . . rips the Keres's head clean off. The Keres explodes, and a strange sound fills the air—the mixture of screeching and moaning. I blast the Keres that fight over the woman and look out over the horizon and see a horde of other gray figures running down the hillside toward the riverbank.

Shades.

A horde of Shades is coming this way.

I start to run for the dock, wanting to tell the people to dive out into the water. They will be out in the open for the Keres, but at least the Shades cannot swim. But then I see it—the strangest sight in all of my days in both the Underrealm and the mortal world. I see a very large Shade riding on the back of a giant three-headed hellrat, and behind the Shade sits a short boy in a fedora with a purplish ribbon.

"Tobin?!"

Yes, Tobin, along with the abnormally large Shade, appear to be leading the charge. The Shade shoves his fist in the air and gives a great moaning shout. Tobin waves his hat in the air. "You heard the boss," he shouts. "Attack the Keres!"

I would have never believed it in a million centuries—a cavalry of Shades is coming to our rescue.

chapter forty-seven

DAPHNE

I can't believe my eyes. Not only is Tobin alive, he's brought reinforcements. And not just any reinforcements, but an unstoppable horde of hungry Shades. There are thousands of them. They just keep coming over the hill and go straight for the Keres. At first the winged beasts try to go on the offensive and pick off the Shades with their dive-bombing tactic, but whenever a Keres gets less than ten feet from the ground, the Shades spring into the air. They jump on the creatures' backs, tearing their wings and heads from their bodies. The flocks of Keres fly higher, trying to stay away from the Shades' reach. The distance gives Haden and the remaining soldiers the relief they need to strike with their lightning bolts. It rains stone chunks of Keres from the sky as if were a monsoon. The Shades feast on the fallen black angels.

I gather a group of children around me under the dock, protecting them from the falling carnage. The children cover their ears—the sounds of moaning and screeching almost drown out my song that circles through the air. Finally, the Keres do more than pull back. They retreat. They flap away from the river back toward the palace, where they can't hurt anyone, at least for now.

The children let out great whooping cheers as we watch the beasts retreat. I wish I could join them. Instead, I throw my hands up in the air.

That is until I realize we are now surrounded by thousands of Shades.

The Shade sitting on the hellrat shouts a command. "Fooollow the Keres!"

The others take off, running after the Keres toward the royal grounds. I stand, gathering the children behind me as the gray, faceless Shade swings off the hellrat's back and approaches me on foot. He's larger than the others, almost twice the size, and I realize when his gaping mouth twists into a grin-like expression that I know him.

"Shady!" I shout even though I have no voice.

Shady and Tobin brought the Shades to save us.

"Kore, youuu safe," he says, holding out his arms.

I run to him and throw my arms around his chest. He grips me tight in his leathery gray arms.

Haden starts to yell out a warning, but then stops. "Um . . . Are my eyes playing tricks on me or is Daphne hugging a Shade?" he says.

"I had the same reaction earlier today," Tobin says.

"Tobin!" I let go of Shady and practically tackle Tobin to the ground.

He laughs and pretends to push me off of him. "You trying to make Haden jealous?"

I laugh too. I can't help it. It's a strange sensation—considering my laughter makes no sound. I am so relieved to see him.

"What happened to your voice?" Tobin asks.

I point to the sky, indicating the song that flutters through the air.

"Okaaay?" Tobin says.

"Long story," Haden says.

"How?" I ask, mouthing my words. I point to Tobin and throw out my arms and slash my hands about as if I were a Keres clawing at him. Something I noticed from tackling him is that his skin is unmarked. All the burns, and bruises, and even the melted hand-print on his chest, are gone. Faded away without leaving any scars behind. I had expected to see more marks on him after his getting left to fend for himself with the Keres, not . . . none.

"What now?" Tobin smirks at my terrible attempt at communicating via charades.

"I think she's asking how you survived the Keres after you two were separated at Persephone's Gate. Granted, we're grateful you're not, but honestly we all thought you'd be dead."

"Me too," Tobin says, placing his hat back on his head. He digs into the pocket of his toga. "Turns out you dropped something," he says, holding up a glittering antique key in front of me. "Did you know this thing can make you immortal? The Keres couldn't hurt me—though they certainly tried. I had five Keres cocooned around me at one point. Your friend here, Shady, he came to my rescue."

I beam up at Shady. "How?" I mouth, pantomiming pushing through a swarm of Keres.

"How did he get through the Keres to rescue me?" Tobin asks, trying to interpret my gestures.

I nod.

"Keres suck life force." Shady shrugs. "Shady already dead."

The Shades—they were the ultimate weapon against the Keres. They can't die because they're already dead. It's a good thing they're on our side.

But *why* are they on our side?

"Shady got me out of there, thinking I was about to die. It wasn't until later that I realized I had the Key. It must have fallen from your pocket into my shoe or something, because that's where I found it. Shady was the one who gathered the Shades. He's like a Shade whisperer or something. He told them what he wanted and they went from being all, 'Let me eat your face' to 'Sure thing, Boss' almost instantly. We figured we'd fight our way back to the gate and lock it to keep the Keres from getting out. We were headed there now when we saw your group in trouble."

"Thank goodness you did!" I shout, grabbing both Shady and Tobin into a group hug. "Thank you, Shady, for saving my friend. Thank you for saving us."

"Daphne," Haden says, approaching. I wave to him to join our group hug. He refrains. "Daphne, if you haven't noticed yet, you're speaking to a Shade."

"I know, we can understand each other."

"I gathered that . . . But the point is, *you* can speak."

"Of course I can speak . . ." I let go of Shady and Tobin. "Oh! I can speak!"

My voice has returned—the others can hear me! I let out a little trill of notes, testing it out. I have never been so grateful to hear the sound of my own voice inside my head. It's something I'll never take for granted again.

"What do you think it means?" Haden says, pointing up at the sky.

I listen, and realize the song has stopped. My voice no longer echoes along the beach.

"Jonathan?" I say. "Do you think something happened to him?"

Haden shakes his head. "I don't know. Maybe he stopped because the Keres retreated. Maybe they've retreated from the gate also?"

"Or maybe he's hurt."

"Either way, if you're feeling well enough, we should get these people to the gate as quickly and possible and find out what's going on."

Before I turn away, Shady places his gangly hand over my shoulder. "Persephone?" he asks. "Was youuur friend able to find Persephone? Has she been returned tooo this realm?"

I lower my eyes and shake my head. "Not yet."

It takes only seven trips to get everyone to the docks near Persephone's Gate, instead of the ten it took to transport everyone out of the palace. That's how many men, women, and children we lost during the Keres attack. All the back and forth takes less than a minute, but I am so exhausted by the time I bring the last group—me, Shady, Tobin, and Haden—that I let Haden scoop me up in his arms again and carry me up the riverbank. The sky is clear here, no dark clouds, no flocks of Keres in the air, but I hum my song as Haden carries me, just in case.

The sandy beach is strewn with evidence of battle. I am glad I do not have to pick my way through the remnants of Keres and the bodies of both our allies and the fallen Underlords. I bury my face into Haden's shoulder when I see the body of a man lying face down in the sand with a familiar battle-ax clutched in his blood caked hand. Aris, one of Ethan's men.

We enter the ravine, our band of Underrealm refugees trailing behind us. The air is smoky from small, smoldering fires that must have been set by lightning, so it takes a moment before I can see our friends. I hold my breath all the while. They're gathered at the far end of the ravine, still protecting the glowing green gate. I recognize Jessica, Dax, and Abbie right away, as well as Ren, with a few of the Skylord soldiers, but I don't see Jonathan, Ethan, Psyche . . . or Joe.

Abbie comes running from the group when she sees us, her arms stretched out and her red curls bouncing around her head. "Tobin!" she shouts.

"Abbie?" Tobin breaks into a run, meeting his sister halfway through the ravine. They hug like two siblings who haven't seen each other in years—which is exactly what they are.

"You've gotten so tall!" Abbie says, which is funny because she's at least three inches taller than he is. He must have been pretty darn short six years ago.

Dax follows Abbie. He's got a terrible gash on one of his arms. He gives us a welcoming wave with his other one but there's a deep look of concern in his eyes.

"What happened here?" I ask as Haden sets me down. "Is everyone okay?"

"Things got pretty hairy. Terresa and many of her Skylords bailed on us and retreated back through the gate. Joe was injured . . .

"Joe?" Panic rises in my voice. "What's wrong? Where is he?"

"Don't worry, Daphne. He'll live and that's what matters . . . I sent him back into the mortal world. Crux is making sure he gets to the hospital. Like I said, things got pretty hairy and our numbers were dwindling. Just when I thought all hope was lost, the strangest thing happened. Hundreds of Shades came and started attacking the Keres. With their help, we were able to kill most of them. The rest retreated and the Shades chased after them."

"Your doing?" I ask, turning to Shady, who stands a few feet behind us.

He nods.

"Whoa," Dax says, taking a step back. "That's the biggest Shade I've ever seen."

"Don't worry, he's a friend," I say. "He's the one who sent the others to help you."

"Then thank you, friend," Dax says, nodding to Shady. "We were able to keep the gate secure, but we're glad you're back, Daphne. The Keres may return now that the song has stopped. Jonathan . . ." Dax's voice trails off and he and Abbie exchange a mournful look before Dax glances back over his shoulder. "Jonathan is . . ."

"What?" I ask. "Is Jonathan okay? Is he hurt?"

I don't wait for Dax's answer and push past him to where I see Ethan standing behind the wall of shields. Jessica stands beside him. Both their heads are bowed. Dax and Haden follow me. The soldiers break rank in order to let us through their defensive formation. Jonathan sits on the ground, his back to us. His head slumps over his chest.

"It isn't Jonathan, it's Psyche," Dax says.

I realize then that Jonathan is holding Psyche cradled in his arms. He rocks slightly, clutching her to his chest. Her arm hangs limply out from her side. It takes me a moment to realize she isn't sleeping—she has passed away.

"She saved me," Ethan says in a reverent whisper. "I would have died if she hadn't intervened."

"Then perhaps she can still be saved," Haden says to Jonathan. "Surely her soul went to Elysium. Perhaps you can call her back—with true love's kiss—as she did with you."

Jonathan shakes his head. "I already tried. It's no use. I heard the Oracle's voice. She said Psyche's journey is over. Her thread has been cut. It's time for her to rest . . ." His voice falters into a sob. I kneel by his side, and wrap my arms around his shoulder.

He leans his head against mine, and I hold a god while he cries.

C

chapter forty-eight

HADEN

Daphne holds Jonathan while he sobs. His pain is almost palpable. I know the agony of being torn from a loved one. Daphne and I had only been separated for a few days and it almost killed me—yet, I still can't fully fathom how Jonathan feels, having been kept from Psyche for centuries only to be reunited and then lose her again in one day's time.

After a while, Ethan takes Daphne's place holding his father, and she and I remove ourselves from their small huddle around Psyche, giving them time to mourn in relative privacy. I call the rest of our comrades together. We need to regroup. The Keres have retreated for now, but they will surely return.

"Do you still have the Key?" I ask Tobin.

He holds it up. "Nifty little thing. Saved my life. Think I might hang on to it for a while."

"What I do not understand," I say, "is *why* the Key protected you. I am happy it did, but I was under the impression that a Kronolithe will only work in the hands of a proper heir."

"What do you mean?" Tobin asks.

"Because of the vow Ren made saying that the heir to the

Underrealm would be whoever brought the Cypher to him, that made Garrick the rightful heir. But he's dead," I say. "And there was no successor in place, so the authority would have fallen to the queen, I suppose."

"As in me?" Daphne says. "Did I become the new heir?"

"Possibly," Dax says.

"But then I dropped it—essentially handing it off to Tobin," Daphne says. "So perhaps that's why it worked for him. I'd passed on the mantle, so to speak. Or maybe it just sees something in Tobin. Shady told me the pomegranate Kronolithe only works for me because it recognizes me as a suitable replacement for Persephone— so if the Key saved Tobin's life, does that mean he's the new—" Daphne exchanges a look with me. I know what she's thinking. We both look at Tobin. He doesn't seem particularly godly with his rumpled fedora and torn toga—but there does seem to be a strange glow about him. And all of his wounds have been healed . . .

"Wait, why are you staring at me like that?" Tobin asks.

"All of your bruises and burns are gone," Daphne says.

"Yeah, so?"

"I think what Daphne is saying," I interject, "is that the Key has chosen you to be the new ruler of the Underrealm."

"Wait, what?" Tobin says, staring at the Key. "Ruler? No way."

"Not just a ruler . . . The new Hades."

Tobin gapes at us.

"Look at you, little bro," Abbie says, clapping him on the back. "New god of the Underrealm."

"No, seriously, what?" Tobin holds the small Key out in front of him as if it were something distasteful to touch. "I don't think I want this anymore. I mean, my goal for this year was to get a lead in the school play and have a date for prom. I did not sign up for godhood. Who's going to take this thing from me?"

The group falls silent, looking from one to another.

"Seriously, guys," Tobin says, his voice growing high-pitched with panic. "I am not qualified to run an entire realm. Somebody take this thing from me."

After a moment, Ren steps forward from the soldiers' phalanx. "You wish to pass on the mantle of Hades?" he asks.

"Um, yeah. Like with all my heart," Tobin says.

"Then as the former king of the Underrealm, I think it is my duty." Ren takes the Key from Tobin, who does not protest, and I find myself holding my breath. For several months I have worried what would happen if my father ever got his hands on the Key. What he would be like with the power of immortality. I didn't imagine I would stand motionless at the time, allowing him to take it in his hand.

Ren holds the small Key on the flat of his palm, almost as if trying to judge its weight. He looks up at me with a small smile on his lips. It is such an unfamiliar expression for his face that it catches me completely off-guard. "It is my duty and my honor to hand this to you, Haden," he says. He falls to one knee and holds the Key out to me. He bows his head and shoves his other fist against the ground—the ultimate sign of respect in my realm. "My son. My king. My god."

I feel the breath I had been holding rush out of my lungs. I stare at my bowing father and the Key he holds out in his hand. This moment, this thing he offers, it's everything I always wanted from him—and more. The honor alone, not to mention the trust he is putting in me. I merely dreamed of being his heir, the crown prince. His son. Now he is offering me so much more—godhood. Immortality. An entire realm at my command . . .

Daphne places her hand on my back. Her touch reminds me to breathe again. Reminds me of what I truly want . . .

"I cannot take it," I say.

"Yes, you can," Ren says. "You deserve it. Much more than I ever could. You saved the last of our people. They will forever be loyal to you. You are the one who can lead them into a new era . . . Besides, it is high time I accept my forced retirement. The Key is yours."

"I thank you for the honor, Father," I say. "Alas, I do not want it, and I cannot accept it."

I do not want to be immortal. I do not want to be a ruler. I want to be human—or at least embrace my human half. When the battle is over, I want to return to the mortal realm. I want to be with Daphne.

I look at her. She stands beside me, but her focus is set on the edge of the ravine, where her Shade friend stands like a sentinel. I can hear the screeching cry of the Keres in the distance. They are returning.

"Then to whom shall I bestow it?" Ren says. "This realm may be in shambles, but that is exactly why we need a leader. Someone who can bring us out of the dark."

Daphne steps forward. "Give it to me," she says, outstretching her hand.

chapter forty-nine

DAPHNE

Since I was a young girl, I've known exactly what I wanted out of life. To be a singer. To use my music to become a star and have an impact on the world around me. But it isn't until this very moment, as I take the Key in my hand, that I truly realize what my life has been destined for.

I see it now—that every step in my life has brought me to this place at this very moment. If I had not inherited Orpheus's voice, making me the Cypher. If Joe hadn't brought me to Olympus Hills. If Haden himself had not been chosen to find me. If we hadn't joined forces to find the Key. If I had not fallen in love with him and followed him into the Underrealm after he was kidnapped by Rowan. If I had not traded myself for Haden and bound myself to Garrick, receiving his gift of Persephone's pomegranate necklace. If I had not escaped. If Shady hadn't saved me and I discovered that he and I could communicate. If I hadn't experienced the plight of the people here firsthand and found compassion for the dead, and realized how badly the original rulers of this realm are sorely needed. If Shady hadn't become my friend and brought the Shades to save us. If Haden had not told me the Oracle's prophesy that I would restore something that had been lost from the Under-realm centuries ago. If all of that hadn't happened, then I would not know what I am supposed to do—what I am *destined* to do with the Key now.

I take the small key and whisper the word *megalo* to it. It elongates into a two-pronged bident in my hand. Hades's golden staff. I leave Haden and the others behind—I know they don't understand what I need to do, but there isn't time to explain. I walk to the end of the ravine where Shady waits, preparing for the Keres's return.

"They'rrre coming," Shady moans.

"I know," I say. "I can hear them, and they're angry. They cry for retribution. For blood."

"Can youuu stop them, Kore?" Shady asks, turning his feature-less face toward me. He takes in a quick breath when he sees the Key. He steps back with a bowed head as if showing it reverence.

I think about how large he is—at least twice the size of any other Shade I've ever seen. He's more cognizant, too. Smart and full of feeling. I think of his devotion to Persephone even in death—as if he were bound to her somehow. I think of the way the other Shades followed his lead. The way he could command them.

"No. I can't stop the Keres, but I think you can." I hold the Key out to him. "I think this belongs to you."

Shady shakes his head and takes another step back in protest. "I cannnnot touch such a thing. I am merely a Shade. I ammm not worthy . . ."

The screeching wail of the Keres cuts off his protest. Black shadowy clouds—masses of the remaining Keres—have infiltrated the beach, and they're headed this way. They'll overtake the ravine in seconds.

"Daphne, sing!" Haden shouts from the barricade, but I know that's not what is needed from me now.

"I know you don't remember your former life. I know you don't know who you are—but I do." I reach out and grab one of Shady's leathery hands and step close to him so he can't escape. I press the staff against his palm and wrap his gangly fingers around it. "Take your Kronolithe, Hades. Let me restore you to your realm."

I let go of his hand and take a step back, leaving him standing in front of me with the staff clutched in his hand. He starts to say something, but then his whole body seizes. He shakes and trembles as a bright, ethereal light bursts out from the Key like it did when I first uncovered it in the grove. The light encircles his body, blinding him from my sight.

I lift my hand, shielding my eyes from the brightness. That's why I don't see the Keres that swoops down on top of me. Blackness wraps around me, encasing me in shadow. My body convulses, and I can feel the Keres trying to drain my life out of chest. I hear my friends screaming. I hear them shouting for me to sing so they can destroy the beast. But there is nothing I can do. I am paralyzed in its cocoon.

"ENOUGH!" A booming voice echoes through the ravine, and the Keres releases me.

I look up to see a large man towering over me. He must be at least seven feet tall. His long black hair flaps in the wind behind him and his face is lined with a black beard. He's cloaked in an ebony robe and golden armor—and holds the Key of Hades in his large hand. It glows with a green light, pulsing with power.

He holds it aloft in his mighty grasp, pointing it at the swarming Keres. "Enough!" his voice booms once more. The Keres stop, pulling back into a large cloud-like mass. "Return to the Pits from whence you came," he commands, sounding like a parent who has truly had enough from his petulant children. He slams the end of the staff against the ground—the sound of which echoes like a cannon blast through the ravine. Bright green rays of light shoot off the prongs of the bident, chasing the retreating Keres from the beach.

When the beasts are gone, the ravine falls completely silent. It's so still that I almost jump when the man leans down and offers me his hand. I take it and he pulls me to my feet. Then he turns toward the ravine where the last remaining people of the Underrealm wait. They fall to their knees, Haden, Dax, and Ren included, paying homage to their god.

chapter fifty

HADEN

I fall to my knees, my fist shoved into the ground. I cannot believe my eyes.

"Uh . . . who's that guy?" Tobin asks from where he stands behind me. "And why is everyone bowing?"

Tobin is one of the few people in the ravine still on his feet. The other citizens of my realm kneel before our god.

"Hades," I say with reverence.

"For real?" Tobin says.

"For real."

Tobin looks around and then awkwardly bows like he's not sure if he's supposed to or not.

I did not understand what Daphne was doing when she took the Key. For a moment, I thought she had decided to choose a path different than what she always wanted. Different from what I chose when I refused to take the Key for myself.

Hades approaches, leading Daphne by the hand.

"You have all fought bravely," Hades says, addressing his people. His voice echoes ethereally around him. "You were all willing to sacrifice yourselves to save this realm even though I have been forced to watch from afar the atrocities the Underlords have put you through since I was taken from your presence. For your courage, I grant you all release from this realm. You are welcome to leave and live out normal mortal lives, or if you choose to stay and help me rebuild this world, you may live in my palace with me as equals. The choice is yours. Your destinies are in all of your own hands." A murmur filters through the women and the servants in the group. Hades turns to Daphne, who stands at his side. "That offer stands for you as well, Kore. This realm needs someone like you. Someone who embodies compassion and determination. I need someone who can help me care for the dead."

Daphne looks up at Hades. She clasps her fingers around the pomegranate pendant that sits above her heart. She truly would make a prefect queen of the dead. I hold my breath waiting for her answer. Perhaps she still will choose a different path than the one I chose for myself.

A different destiny than me.

"You do need someone," Daphne says. "But that someone isn't me. You need the real Kore. The real Persephone." She pulls the pomegranate necklace from around her neck and places it in Hades's hand that he holds out to her. "You need her the way I need someone else. I've fulfilled my destiny by restoring you—and as you said, the rest of our futures are in our own hands, and I know where mine belongs."

She leaves Hades and stands beside me. She holds out her hand and smiles in a way that makes me unable to breathe for a whole different reason. I stand and take her outstretched hand, entwining my fingers with hers.

"Are you certain?" Hades asks. There's a loneliness that clings to his words. "You can be my queen without being my bride. We are . . . friends . . . And Persephone is lost . . ."

"I promised you we would find her and return her to you. I believe she is still out there, somewhere, and I intend to keep looking for her until I keep that promise." Daphne looks up at me with a question in her eyes. I nod, confirming that I will help her in her search. "But for now, I just want to go home."

"Very well," Hades says, pocketing the pomegranate necklace. He looks over his shoulder out of the ravine. "I must go," he says. "The Keres must be locked away, and there is much work to be done."

I am about to question him as to why he wants to lock away the Keres again rather than destroy them, but then I realize the audacity of questioning my god's decisions. I suppose since the Keres were his first creation, his first children, he would not take the idea of destroying them lightly.

Hades looks out over the refugees. "If you are choosing to stay, then follow me now and I will transport you to the palace."

More people than I expect stand and follow him. Even Link's mother with her two boys. She must see the question on my face because she says, "This is my boys' world. This is where we belong." Link hugs both Daphne and me around the knees at the same time. "Do you think I'll get to be a real Underlord now?" he asks.

I nod. "I think so. But will you look after the owls for me? They'll need a lot of care to rebuild their nests."

Link smiles and runs off to join his mother and the others who follow Hades. My father clasps my shoulder and then joins the group as well. He fought so bravely, with no regard for his own personal safety, and then humbled himself by offering me the Key. I know now that even though he made mistakes and was a terrible father, deep down he has always wanted the best for the Underrealm. I believe he can become a good man under Hades's guidance. He will be useful in rebuilding this realm.

Jonathan approaches Daphne. Ethan walks at his side. "I am staying as well," he says. "Psyche's soul is here. I can't bear leaving her behind again. I'm going to follow her to Elysium."

"Jonathan?" Daphne asks, tears prickling in her eyes. "You can't."

"I can," he says. "I've lived a long life. Longer than most. It's time to pass my mantle to someone else."

Jonathan holds his bow out to Ethan.

"Father?"

"Do well with it," Jonathan says. "The realms have been without Eros for far too long. They could use a lot more love."

Ethan hugs his father and then accepts the bow. A golden light swirls around him and then a moment later, Ethan sprouts wings.

"That's an nice look on you, Ethan Bowman," Jessica says a little too enthusiastically, and then catches herself. "I mean, Captain Bowman."

Ethan gives her a quick smile and flaps his new wings.

"I will leave the gate open," Hades calls from the edge of the ravine. "You and the others are free to come and go as you please. I intend to hold you to your word, Daphne of Olympus Hills."

Daphne nods, and then Hades and his followers vanish from the ravine.

Only a dozen women and a couple of children remain with us—preparing to enter the mortal realm through Persephone's Gate—but they are still more than I know what to do with.

"What are we going to do with them?" I ask Daphne.

She shakes her head.

"I have an idea," Tobin says. "Don't worry, I'll take care of it."

Daphne squeezes my hand. "Let's go home."

"Yes," I say. "Home."

chapter fifty-one

TOBIN

My mother is more than surprised when I show up at our doorstep with a dozen Underrealm refugees.

The rest of town has been evacuated, but I find her sitting on our porch. Her clothes are rumpled and her hair is a mess, and she looks like she hasn't slept in days.

"Tobin?" she says, blinking at me in disbelief. "Tobin, what happened to you?"

"A lot of things. First I was in a boat wreck, then I was a prisoner, and then I was bait, then I very briefly became immortal . . . It's kind of a long story."

She stands. "And Abbie is back too?" she says, taking in the sight of her daughter behind me where she stands with Dax.

"Don't worry," Abbie says. "I won't be moving back in."

"Wha . . . Where will you go?"

"With my fiancé," Abbie says.

"With Ethan?" I ask, remembering the two are betrothed.

"No," Abbie says. "With Dax. We had a lot of time to talk in the Skylord prison, and we decided we're both still quite fond of each other. We're getting married as soon as possible."

"*Kalash!*" Haden says and claps a beaming Dax on the shoulder.

I narrow my eyes at Dax and hold my fists up like I want to punch him. "I just got my sister back and you're already taking her away from me?"

Dax's smile falters. "I'm sorry, I didn't think of it that way . . . And we're not leaving town . . . I mean Haden still needs a guide to this world and the school needs its Mr. Drol . . . I swear I'm not stealing her from you . . ."

"Relax," Abbie says. "Tobin's messing with you. His ears get all hot when he's trying to pull a fast one."

"They do not," I say, rubbing my burning ear.

"Who are all of these people?" Mom asks, speaking as if in some sort of daze as she takes in the sights of the Underrealm women and children.

"They're the ones who will be moving in," Abbie says.

"Or at least into town," I add. "They're refugees from the Underrealm, and you're going to find places for them to stay until you can help them get back on their feet or reconnect with their families. I imagine there are some empty dorms at the school, and I am sure you have enough political pull to get them jobs. It's the least you can do after being complicit in handing over some of them to the Underrealm."

Mom takes a step back. "You know?"

"Yes, I know. I've known for three months."

"You have to know, Tobin. I did this for you," she says frantically. "For you and your brother, Sage . . ."

My ears burn hot again but not because I'm lying, I'm angry. "No you didn't, Mom. You did what you did for you. Don't you dare try to make me feel guilty or responsible for your actions. The blame is yours and yours alone."

It feels so good to finally say all this. I'd had to hide my knowledge of her involvement in the Underrealm's plot to steal away young women for so long it had practically made me crazy with anger. Having to sit in the house and share a table with her and pretend to be none the wiser of her evil ways had been nearly impossible. Letting her make me feel like she made all of her choices because of me and my brother made me feel sick. Well, I wasn't having any of that anymore.

"You're taking these people in, and you're going to make things right with them, with me, and with Abbie. If you ever want to see me again, that is." I look back at Dax and Abbie. My sister smiles at me with pride. "Um, can I live with you guys in the meantime?" I feel like the biggest cock-blocker in the world asking to live with a soon-to-be-married couple, but the idea of sharing the same roof with my mother is one I can't even fathom at the moment.

The couple nod their heads and then I turn back to my mother. "So what's it going to be?" I ask.

"Yes," she stammers. "I'll do it."

We leave my mother to sort out arrangements for the refugees and then go with Daphne to the hospital to check on Joe. We're all anxious to see how he's doing. The doctors say we can't go in yet because Joe is still in surgery. We join Crux in the waiting room. He looks so strange, a big hulking man dressed in bronze armor, sitting in a too-small chair with a tiny cup of coffee.

"My brother?" he asks, standing when he sees us.

Daphne shakes her head. "Aris died in the battle," she says.

Crux bows his head. "He died with honor then. That is what matters."

After a while Crux, Ethan, and Jessica take their leave in order to go smooth things over in the Skyrealm. I wonder how the Sky King will take the news about Hades's return. Daphne begins to pace the room, and her anxiety over Joe is infectious. I start bouncing my knee and playing with the brim of my fedora. I can't believe this thing has traveled to hell and back and is still mostly intact. I can't believe the same about myself.

"Tobin?" says a gasping voice from the doorway. A thrill runs up my spine and my cheeks blush hot. I'd know that voice anywhere. I place my hat back on my head and look up as Lexie practically flies in my direction. I am barely standing when she throws herself into my arms. At first I am so shocked, I am not sure how to respond. Then I remember what a hero is supposed to do—I dip Lexie in my arms and kiss her.

And she kisses me back.

"Way to go, little bro," Dax says and then whistles. "Snagging the most popular girl in school!"

The others clap and cheer until I'm sufficiently embarrassed. I pull away from Lexie. She almost looks a little sheepish—which is a super weird expression on Lexie Simmons—and then she pecks my cheek with her lips. "Welcome home," she whispers.

"I can't believe you're back," Daphne's mother says from the doorway. Daphne stops pacing and runs to her.

Demi embraces Daphne. "I am so glad you're okay, little sprout. We turned back as soon as the hospital called. How's Joe?"

Daphne shakes her head that is still buried in her mother's shoulder. "I don't know. He was still in surgery when we got here."

A small knock sounds on the open door to the waiting room. Daphne looks up. A nurse with a clipboard asks her to come with her. Daphne holds her hand out to Haden and the two leave us behind, holding our collective breath.

chapter fifty-two

DAPHNE

The nurse leads us to a small recovery room. "You can have a few minutes with your father now," she says, pushing the door open. "I must warn you, he's been through quite the ordeal and he's still pretty groggy. He keeps going on about fighting angels of death in the underworld or something like that."

"Huh, weird," I say and feign a shrug.

She leaves, and I find myself standing outside the door until Haden squeezes my hand. "I'll wait out here and give you some time alone with him," he says. I nod and finally enter the room.

I find Joe lying in a hospital bed. His head is bandaged and his face is black and blue, but he still manages to smile at me.

"'Ello, Daphne. Is it morning already?" he says, reminding me of the first day we'd spent together after I'd come to live with him. Though he hadn't been so enthused then to be woken up. His British accent is especially thick in his groggy state.

"It's afternoon already," I say, echoing what I said then. My voice catches and tears fill my eyes. "You have no idea how happy I am to see you in one piece!"

"Well, not exactly one piece," he says, lifting his bandaged arm and I realize the doctor had been dead serious when he said he didn't think they would be able to save his hand. "Say 'ello to Stumpy!" Joe says far too cheerily as he holds out his handless arm as if he wants me to shake it.

"Hello, Stumpy," I say, but refrain from touching his bandage. The tears only come harder now. "That's your strumming hand," I say, thinking of how my father the great musician will never be able to play guitar again. Or the grand piano in his studio. Or any of the instruments that he prides himself on.

"Don't fret," he says. "Heheh. Get it? Fret. Like a guitar fret?"

I playfully roll my tear-filled eyes. Even *the* Joe Vince isn't immune to dad jokes—but it does make me crack a small smile.

"Maybe they'll give me a hook and I can get an eye patch and change up my whole act. Arrg, the band'll be Joe Vince and the Pirates!" he says in a terrible pirate accent.

I give a little laugh. This seems to make him happy.

"Seeing you here, smiling, means the sacrifice was worth it," he says.

"I love you," I say and rest my head on his chest.

He strokes my hair with his good—I mean, *only*—hand. "I love you too, Daph." After a minute he yawns and his eyes grow sleepy. "Now what are you doing hanging around here for? You should be out celebrating your victory!" He sits up a little bit. "Wait, we won, right?"

"Yes, we won."

"Then get out of here," he insists. "Go party. Go celebrate. Let this old pirate rest and come see me tomorrow. You can give me the play-by-play then."

"Okay," I say. I give him a kiss on the cheek and rejoin Haden in the hallway.

"Are you okay?" Haden asks, giving me a mournful smile. I nod and then fold myself into his outstretched arms and let him hold me. We survived. Joe is going to be okay. And the world is safe. I let the shock of it all wash through me until I can smile again.

"I love you," Haden whispers against my hair, sending tingling electricity through my body.

"So, what should we do now?" Tobin says as we leave the hospital. He walks hand in hand with Lexie down a wooded path that leads to the road. Dax and Abbie are with us also. Much to my surprise, Mom had said she was going to stay and sit with Joe for awhile. I think she wanted to give us kids a chance to celebrate without her hanging around, but I also hope she doesn't plan on smothering Joe with a pillow when the nurses aren't looking.

"There's that promise to find Persephone," I say, "but for now I really need something to eat. I think it's been days since I had anything other than flower blossoms."

"Tell me about it," Tobin says, rubbing his stomach. "Shady— I mean, Hades—was all about those gray flowers, but man, they tasted like bitter black licorice."

"I promised everyone hot chocolate and muffins," Lexie says. "I know a good place the next town over, since Olympus Brew is probably closed with the evacuation and everything."

"Sounds good to me," Tobin says.

"Us too," Dax says. He's got his arm around Abbie. It makes my heart swell to see the two of them reunited. I had worried what

Ethan's reaction would be to Abbie's announcement about being engaged to Dax, but seeing the way he looks at his lieutenant, Jessica, when he thinks no one is watching makes me think he'll get over it.

"Congrats, by the way," I say to Dax and Abbie, realizing that in my worry over Joe, I hadn't said it before.

"I'm still not okay with this marriage business," Tobin says, letting go of Lexie and giving his sister a playful shove. She grabs his hat from his head.

"You are, too! Your ears are completely burning!"

Tobin chases his sister up the path. Dax and Lexie jog after them, laughing.

I pull on Haden's arm, slowing him down so we have a little distance from the others.

"Have you thought about what you're going to do now?" I ask him.

"What do you mean? I thought I'd stay here, go to school, maybe join a band or something. I read on the Internet that girls like that sort of thing. I thought I'd give being human a try . . . with you." He looks deep into my eyes as if searching for something. Then he glances away. "Unless that's not what you want. I assumed when you said you wanted to go home, you meant Olympus Hills. But I guess you might want to go back to Ellis Fields with your mom . . . And leave all of this behind . . ."

"Don't be addled . . ." I say, using a term he would. "Of course I'm staying here with you. What I meant is that you need to give some thought to where you're going to live now. I doubt you're going to want to share a place with a honeymooning Dax and Abbie and with Tobin hanging around."

"Oh, yes. I suppose you're right."

"You know, Joe has an entire empty wing at his mansion. I bet he's going to need an extra hand around the house—pun not intended. I could ask him if we could have an indefinite house guest? You know, if you don't mind living under the same roof as me . . ."

Haden pulls me tight against him. "I would like that very much," he says in a voice so low and soft it makes my heart beat faster. "You know, for a minute there in the Underrealm, I thought I'd lost you. That you had decided to choose a different destiny than one with me . . ."

I shake my head, hating the idea that I made him worry. "I wouldn't do that. Our destinies are intertwined, you know?"

"I know." He leans in and kisses me. Electricity crackles between us, warming my lips and sending a tingling sensation down my spine. I kiss him back, running my fingers into his hair and then down his neck and chest. When we part in order to breathe, Haden pants against my cheek, "So what does our destiny hold now, Daphne Raines?"

"Apparently muffins and hot chocolate," I say with a little laugh against his skin. "And froyo. I could really go for some froyo right now."

Haden leans in to kiss me once more . . . but a burst of lightning explodes above our heads. I reel around to find Rowan standing in the trees next to the path. He holds a pulsing ball of lightning in his hand.

"I told you to watch your back, little brother!" he snarls, and pulls his arm back, ready to strike. Before he can release the sphere, a large gray paw sails out from behind a tree, swiping his feet out from under him. Rowan slams into the ground. A large, three-headed panther springs out from behind the bushes.

"Brimstone, you're back!" I sing, matching her growling tone.

With a little pop, the panther shrinks back down to the size of a kitten. Brim jumps up onto Haden's shoulder. She purrs as he scratches her ears. "I knew you'd find me," he says. "You always do." She nuzzles his cheek.

Rowan moans and then collapses against the grass in a faint. Brim hisses down at him.

"Yeah, I know," I say to her. "I've always hated that guy, too."

"Go home," Haden says to Rowan. "You'll find it very different there now, what with Hades's return."

"What?" he blinks up at us, I imagine both dazed from the blow and astonished by the news.

Haden pulls my hand to lead me away.

"That's it?" I ask. "Shouldn't we restrain him or . . . ?"

"He's not important anymore," Haden says. We leave Rowan behind and continue down the path toward our friends. "So this froyo you speak of," Haden says tentatively, "what exactly is it?"

"Frozen yogurt." I smile at him. "I forget you still have so much to learn about being human."

"Is it like ice cream?"

"Yes, it's like ice cream. And you get to mix in whatever toppings you want. Like fruit or candy or marshmallows or whatever."

Haden squeezes my hand. "Then froyo is definitely part of our destiny," he says.

ACKNOWLEDGMENTS

Many of you may not know that the fate of this book was uncertain for several months in 2015. I was well into the manuscript when I found out that my then publisher, Egmont USA, had decided to close their doors, and that the contract for *The Immortal Throne* had been cancelled. After hearing the news, I was heartbroken for my editor and the staff of Egmont who had been my publishing family since 2008, and devastated by the idea that Haden and Daphne's story may not get the ending that it deserved. For the sake of my readers and my love of the characters, I decided not to give up on the story. I looked into other avenues for publishing, and just when I was feeling daunted by the idea of doing it on my own, I got a call from my agent, telling me that Carolrhoda Lab (an imprint of Lerner Publishing) had decided not only to pick up and continue publishing all of my backlisted books, but that they also wanted to publish *The Immortal Throne*.

This book may have taken a little longer to find its way into reader's hands than they may have expected, but it's here (finally) because of the many wonderful people who worked on it behind the scenes:

My editor from Egmont, Jordan Hamessley, and the rest of the Egmont USA crew; my agent, Ted Malawer; my new editor at Carolrhoda Lab, Anna Cavallo, who did a wonderful job of picking up the reins and helping me finish this almost-abandoned story; Alix Reid, who oversaw the edit as the Associate Publisher of Carolrhoda Lab; the designer who made this book beautiful inside and out, Emily Harris; along with Kayla Pawek and Erica Johnson, who also worked on the book.

I would also like to thank my friends who have supported and encouraged me through the highs and lows of this publishing journey, especially J.R. Johansson, Michelle Argyle, Natalie Whipple, Kasie West, Renee Collins, Michelle Sallay, Sara Raasch, Kim Webb Reid, Jenilyn Collings, Rachel Headrick, Colleen Houck, Shani Despain, and a special shout out to Egmont's Last List (a group of fellow authors who were left without a publisher when Egmont closed), who helped each other through the stormy waters of Egmont's closure.

Much gratitude and hugs and kisses to my amazing family: my parents, Tai and Nancy; my siblings, Noreen, Tai, Brooke, and Quinn; my in-laws; and the plethora of nieces, nephews, and siblings-in-law. And I most especially want to thank my husband, Brick, and our two boys—I love you all right up to the moon and back again!